"What if I had told you I was pregnant?" Sarah demanded. "What then, Logan?

"Can you tell me you'd have been happy? That you'd have changed your life to be the kind of father she deserved?"

"And so you chose Will." The bitterness in Logan's accusation scalded her.

"Yes," she declared defiantly. "I chose Will—a man who wanted the same things I did. A home. A family. A man driven by his love for his family, not by some twisted need to prove himself!"

"Is that what you thought?" he whispered. "I would have married you."

"I know. I knew you would have done the right thing. Out of honor. Out of duty."

"Out of love," he said so softly she almost didn't hear....

ABOUT THE AUTHOR

Laura Gordon is a western Colorado author with a penchant for romantic suspense. She is the author of eleven novels. Her greatest joy comes in creating characters who face extraordinary challenges and discover that the magic of their once-in-a-lifetime love is worth the risk.

Spencer's Secret is the latest installment in the popular THE SPENCER BROTHERS series, and follows two previous books, *Spencer's Shadow* and *Spencer's Bride*.

When not tied to her desk by deadlines, Laura likes nothing better than hiking the high-country trails of the magnificent mountains near her home. Readers may write Laura Gordon at P.O. Box 55192, Grand Junction, CO 81505.

Books by Laura Gordon

HARLEQUIN INTRIGUE
220—DOUBLE BLACK DIAMOND
255—SCARLET SEASON
282—DOMINOES
316—FULL MOON RISING
345—LETHAL LOVER
387—SPENCER'S SHADOW*
396—SPENCER'S BRIDE*

* The Spencer Brothers series

Spencer's Secret
Laura Gordon

TORONTO • NEW YORK • LONDON
AMSTERDAM • PARIS • SYDNEY • HAMBURG
STOCKHOLM • ATHENS • TOKYO • MILAN • MADRID
PRAGUE • WARSAW • BUDAPEST • AUCKLAND

To my Loveknot sisters
for all the love, laughter
and prayers

ISBN 0-373-22491-5

SPENCER'S SECRET

Copyright © 1998 by Laura Lee DeVries

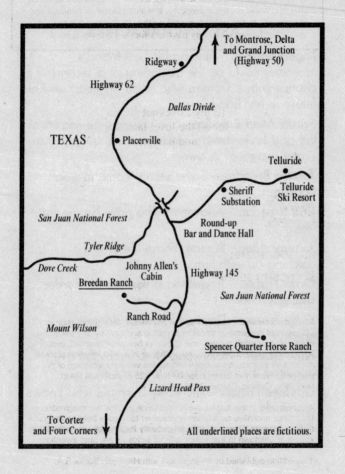

To Montrose, Delta
and Grand Junction
(Highway 50)

Ridgway •

Highway 62

Dallas Divide

TEXAS

• Placerville

Telluride •

• Sheriff
Substation

Telluride
Ski Resort

San Juan National Forest

Round-up
Bar and Dance Hall

Tyler Ridge

Dove Creek

Johnny Allen's
Cabin

Highway 145

Breedan Ranch

San Juan National Forest

Ranch Road

Mount Wilson

Spencer Quarter Horse Ranch

Lizard Head Pass

To Cortez
and Four Corners

All underlined places are fictitious.

CAST OF CHARACTERS

Logan Spencer—Finding his best friend's murderer could be the beginning of a second chance with a woman who holds his heart and his future in her hands.

Sarah Allen Breedan—She believes the secrets of the past have determined her future, but love has a few secrets of its own.

Jessica Breedan—Some secrets come in small packages.

Will Breedan—A lawman who gave his life for love.

Johnny Allen—A man whose life of lies is catching up with him.

Orrin Fraizer—Respected statesman or murder suspect?

Early Fraizer—Devoted friend or dangerous enemy?

Nick Gallus—Hollywood Nick seems to have acquired the Midas touch, or has he?

Gaylene Fraizer—The savvy barmaid who knows too much.

Bess Spencer—Peach pie and homespun wisdom are her specialties.

Prologue

Will Breedan had been a cop long enough to know when he was being followed, and he'd ridden this trail for enough years to know the difference between natural and man-made sounds. The difference between the wind and the crunch and snap of dried pine needles and twigs beneath the weight of a stalker.

And he knew what it felt like to be observed by a pair of unseen eyes. This late summer morning, with the sun just breaking the horizon, he felt those eyes on his back.

Pulling his horse to the side of the trail, he peered into the forest, trying to spot whoever was in there. With his senses fine-tuned, he waited. Somewhere amid the dappled shadows of looming blue spruce and leafy aspen someone watched. But was that someone the mysterious Daisy Allen? Or could it be the anonymous tipster who'd left the cryptic message taped to his windshield yesterday afternoon? The message that replayed in Will's mind as his eyes searched the shadows and his heart drummed against his breastbone.

I know where to find Daisy Allen. Meet me tomorrow. Tyler Ridge at dawn.
Come alone.

Or maybe someone else. Someone whose feathers he'd ruffled during the investigation. Was the message real? Could the answer to his quest really be as close as Tyler Ridge? After all this time, had it finally come down to this, a message on the back of a plain white envelope and a faded photograph?

Would he finally meet the woman herself? Or was this merely an elaborate hoax, another false lead?

In the end it had been the picture that had convinced him that this time the tip was real. At least the picture was real, of that much he was certain. He knew, because it was identical to the photograph framed in silver that he looked at every morning on his wife's dresser.

The picture of the woman with the uncanny resemblance to Sarah seemed, at times, to mock him. For the past three years he'd found himself staring harder and harder at the woman in the picture, always looking for the same thing. Differences.

And there *were* differences, he reminded himself. Subtle dissimilarities between Daisy Allen and her daughter: Daisy's slightly larger mouth, the way she wore her hair, the hardness around her eyes.

And although he would never admit it, noting those differences always assured him. Just as the startling physical similarities would always disturb him, make him wonder what other traits Sarah had inherited from her mother.

When Daisy Allen left her home and family twenty years ago, some said she'd run off with a lover. Others said she'd joined a cult. Some said she was dead. Others said she ought to be.

Sarah herself had admitted that her mother and father had endured a loveless marriage, that even as a child she'd sensed her mother's restless spirit.

And what about Sarah? he wondered. How much of her

mother's legacy had she inherited? Was that faraway look he glimpsed too often in her eyes a portent of some dark chapter waiting to be written in her own life? Would the bonds of their marriage of convenience be strong enough to keep her from following the longings of her own restless spirit if and when the time came? Would she someday go running back to the only man who'd possessed her heart? A man Will called friend?

For all those questions, and for his pathetic need to be needed, Will hadn't told Sarah about the photograph or the message that had brought him to the ridge this morning.

He told himself he'd kept it from her because he didn't want to get her hopes up. After all, hadn't she already suffered too many disappointments? The false lead that had taken them to Los Angeles two years ago had been especially crushing. The tip had seemed so real, the sighting so reliable. When they'd returned after that trip with no more information than when they'd started, Will put his foot down, insisting Sarah give up her search.

If Daisy Allen was still alive, Will vowed to find her, but without Sarah's knowledge. His investigation would go on, but in the meantime his wife had to be protected.

Protecting her was his job. His responsibility. The unspoken terms upon which their marriage was grounded.

In three and a half years, Will had never kidded himself into believing she could love him—really love him. But she'd needed him once, and he wanted her to need him now. And forever.

Last night when he'd told her he planned to spend the day fishing, she'd applauded his decision to take what she'd called a well-deserved day off. They both knew there was hay to be baled, horses to be shod and fences to be mended. But if Sarah had thought about those things, she'd never mentioned them.

Always the kind and considerate wife, Will thought, careful to place his needs above her own. Sarah's selflessness should have made him grateful, but too often it had quite the opposite effect. At times her solicitous nature angered and frustrated him, reminding him of the unhealthy state of their union.

He didn't want her gratitude. He wanted her heart. But they both knew she could never promise him what she'd already given away.

A movement in the brush jerked Will's attention to the top of the ridge. He tensed, but when he spotted a doe and her fawn picking their way down the hillside, he released the breath he'd been holding.

He looked at his watch. Four-forty-nine. Sarah would still be sleeping. In another hour she'd be up and about preparing Jessica's breakfast.

Thinking about Sarah nestled in slumber, her blond hair splayed across her pillow, her skin as soft as warm silk, made him wonder what kind of fool would leave such a woman to engage in what might well turn out to be just another wild-goose chase.

He was no fool, he told himself, but a determined man. A lawman. A husband who wanted more than anything to win his wife's adoration, or at least her genuine affection and respect.

When a branch snapped to his right, his horse's ears pricked up, and Will twisted in the saddle and swept the forest with keen eyes. The horse, sensing his rider's edginess, tossed his head, and Will's heart pounded. Suddenly a man moved in the shadows.

In the murky light of predawn, Will couldn't make out anything but an outline. Whoever it was, he was tall and broad-shouldered.

The hair on the back of Will's neck rose and sweat

dampened his palms. Sliding his hand slowly beneath his split-leather vest, he touched the reassuring butt of his revolver.

"Come on out!" he yelled, and slid the gun from its holster, careful to keep it concealed beneath his vest. Experience told him informants could be spooked too easily into silence, and Will hadn't waited this long and come this far to go away empty-handed. Again.

"I'm waiting," he said.

But still the man in the shadows didn't move.

"Stop playing games. I did what you asked. I'm here. Alone."

Suddenly and completely without warning, the edgy silence was shattered by a loud crack. Metal whizzed past Will's head, so close it made his ears ring. A branch exploded overhead. Pine needles and bark rained down on him, and his horse pranced, barely in control.

Will dug his heels in his mount's sides and tried to wheel him around toward the trail, but the animal seemed crazed. He reared, and Will had to forsake his hold on his gun just to stay in the saddle.

The first shot had come from the right. This one from behind. Damn it! He'd been set up! He ground his heels into his horse's quivering sides, but the terrified animal still balked. Another shot, and Will decided to take his chances on foot. To stay with the horse would get him nothing but killed.

He dove from the saddle, cursing all the way to the ground, as he heard footsteps rushing toward him through undergrowth.

Another shot, and the wild-eyed horse reared again. Will grabbed for the reins dangling mere inches from his face, but before he could grasp them, one thrashing hoof crashed into his head with the force of a hammer blow. The world spun out of control as a galaxy of pain exploded behind his eyes.

He heard someone move up beside him and, clinging to the edge of consciousness, he heard, "This is going to be easier than we thought."

He struggled to get to his gun, to clamber to his feet, to fight, to run, but a second blow immobilized him, sending paralyzing fingers of pain down his spine.

"Let's get on with it." The voice above him seemed vaguely familiar, but Will's scrambled senses wouldn't clear long enough for him to identify its owner.

"Get his gun," he heard someone say—a lawman's worst fear, and yet Will was helpless to stop them from disarming him.

Rage flared inside him as he felt himself being dragged through the brush to the edge of the ridge. Of all the stupid mistakes, his mind screamed, allowing himself to be ambushed. The greenest rookie would have known better!

His mind swirled black with regret, and then, out of nowhere, a vivid picture of Sarah and Jessica formed in his mind and he felt his heart break, knowing he would never see them again.

Chapter One

Logan Spencer pushed open the rickety wooden gate and found himself immediately and enthusiastically greeted by two blue-eyed dogs, one a blue heeler, the other of dubious parentage. Vying for his attention, the dogs pushed and mouthed each other and bumped against his legs as he made his way up the walk, past a pink tricycle and an aluminum washtub bursting with bright red geraniums.

A jar of sun tea sat steeping on the windowsill, and a pair of mud-caked work boots had been left outside the front door to dry. Logan wondered if the boots belonged to Sarah. If they did, she was working too hard, and by the looks of things, losing ground. In the battle to maintain the five-hundred-acre Breedan ranch, it appeared no one was winning.

Around the windows, bare wood showed through where the white paint had worn away, paint he himself had helped Will apply the summer of his junior year.

The big red barn opposite the house was in a similar state of neglect. The roof sagged, and the lightning rod at its peak drooped at half-mast. Weeds grew unchecked around the split-rail corrals. On his way in, over the four miles of rutted dirt road from the highway, he'd noticed a number of fence posts leaning precariously close to the ground.

In fact, the only aspect of the Breedan ranch that didn't seem hopelessly neglected were its animals. The horses grazing in the pastures were sleek and fat, and these dogs certainly seemed healthy enough, definitely well fed and well loved.

As he walked up the steps and crossed the front porch, he paused a moment to gaze out over seemingly endless acres of green. Against a cloudless blue sky, the craggy peaks of the San Juans loomed in the distance. The snow-caps seemed to beckon him, reminding him how long it had been since he'd breathed in pine-scented air or spent a day on horseback exploring a high-country trail. Too long since he'd cast a line into a crystalline stream or dipped his hands into water so cold it took his breath away.

Longer still, since any place had felt as much like home.

One of the dogs nudged his hand and drew him out of his reverie. As he stooped to stroke the animal's glossy coat, the sound of laughter—Sarah's, mingled with the bubbling giggles of a child—drifted out of the house through the screen door.

When he rapped on it, the door rattled against its wobbly frame, and the laughter subsided. He hadn't told her he was coming, and he didn't expect anything more than a chilly reception. Despite all that, he couldn't remember ever wanting to see anyone more than he wanted, at this moment, to set eyes on Sarah.

When she appeared on the other side of the screen, the dogs yipped and wagged their tails and lunged against the door.

"Get back, Shep. Ozzie, be good," she scolded. "Sit! Both of you!"

The dogs obeyed reluctantly and dropped down to wriggle on their haunches at Logan's feet. They whined and gazed up at her adoringly.

"Hello, Sarah," he said. "Nice dogs."

She didn't return his smile, but only blinked as some of the color drained from her face.

"Logan," she said coolly.

The child's laughter erupted again from somewhere inside the house. "Your daughter?" he asked, looking past her.

Only someone who'd known her as well as he once had would have detected the subtle change in her demeanor—the slightly defensive tilt of her chin. "Yes."

"She sounds happy."

"She is," Sarah said blandly.

Despite the tension that stretched between them, Logan couldn't help staring. Her eyes were even bluer than he remembered, her delicate features and soft smooth skin even lovelier. "May I come in?" he asked.

She hesitated, and although she was reacting exactly as he'd expected, her reluctance still stung.

"I need to talk to you, Sarah. It's important."

"All right," she said without enthusiasm, and ran one hand idly through the blond mass of hair that fell loosely past her shoulders. The familiar gesture caused his heart to convulse. She had always done that when she was nervous.

"You two stay out," she told the dogs as she pushed the door open.

Logan stepped inside and followed her through the narrow entryway and into the living room. As he did, he couldn't help thinking that if all women looked as good as Sarah Breedan in faded blue jeans, high-fashion designers would soon go out of business.

"You've done a lot with the place," he said, purposefully directing his attention to safer objects.

In contrast to the exterior of the house, the interior of Sarah's home reflected her loving attention. The wood floors gleamed, the walls were freshly painted, and the furnishings, while not grand, reflected her subtle good taste.

"It suits us," she said simply. When she took up a position beside the fireplace on the opposite side of the room, her body language told him the distance between them was still not enough for her comfort.

A child dressed in blue denim overalls and a bright yellow top looked up from a jigsaw puzzle. "What's your name?" she asked brightly.

He gazed down into a pair of wide blue eyes so similar to Sarah's he almost forgot to answer. "Logan," he said finally and extended his hand. "What's yours?"

She smiled and placed her small dimpled fingers in his. "I'm Jessica Lynn Breedan," she said. "And I'm four years old going on—" she withdrew her hand from his grasp and held up the appropriate number of fingers "—five."

The sun streaming through the window behind her danced across dark brown curls. Her eyes were definitely Sarah's—the same arresting shade of cornflower blue—but the lustrous head of dark hair must have sprung from Will's side of the gene pool.

"You got any kids?" she asked, but before he could answer, Sarah intervened.

"I think I hear Terri taking the cookies out of the oven. Why don't you go into the kitchen, Jess, and ask her to give you a couple with a glass of milk?"

Logan wondered if the faceless Terri had been the individual to whom he'd spoken earlier, the same young woman who'd been making Sarah's excuses for the past year.

Jessica Lynn Breedan raced out of the room. "Cookies!

Yeah! Chocolate-chip!'' As quickly as she'd left, the child reappeared to retrieve the stuffed animal she'd left on the floor. ''Come on, Pansy!'' she demanded, snagging one floppy ear. ''Cookies!''

A smile illuminated Sarah's face as she looked after her child. ''Don't forget to wash your hands,'' she admonished.

''She looks like you,'' Logan said when they were alone.

As her attention slid back to him, her smile disappeared. ''What are doing here, Logan?''

So much for small talk. ''Like I said before, I need to talk to you. That's why I've been calling.''

She took a deep breath and clasped her hands in front of her. He wondered if it was meant to keep them from shaking.

''All right,'' she said. ''What is it? What do you want?''

This wasn't going to be easy. ''What makes you think I *want* anything?''

Her gaze was steady, but her mouth was set in a tight line. ''Because I know you.''

She did know him, probably better than anyone, he conceded. Or at least she *had* known him once. ''How are you, Sarah?''

''I'm fine.''

Oh, you're better than fine, he thought. Even in blue jeans, a simple white T-shirt and worn sneakers, she managed to look sexy as hell. ''I'm sorry about Will,'' he said. ''He was a good man. A good friend.''

She acknowledged his condolences stiffly with a nod.

Despite their past, he knew she would have expected him to attend Will's funeral. He could have told her the truth, that he'd been out of the country and hadn't learned of Will's death until three months after the fact. He could have told her, but he didn't, knowing his explanation would ring hollow even to his own ears. The excuse of work had worn thin years ago, for both of them.

"I left messages for you." Dozens. None of which she'd returned.

"I've been busy." But he knew what she was thinking. He knew because he was thinking the same thing: *You didn't come when he needed your help. Why would I call you now?*

Her resentment was almost a palpable presence between them, as tough an obstacle as his own guilt. "I'm sure you've had your hands full," he allowed.

She didn't elaborate on the opening he'd given her, and as her measuring stare continued, he was struck by a renewed sense of loss. There had been a time when she'd greeted him with open arms and an open and generous heart. A time when her pretty face had brightened at the mere sight of him walking through the front door. What a fool he'd been.

"I came here because I want to help," he said. "This is a big ranch, and I know it can't have been easy trying to run it alone this past year."

With a look that said, "Too little too late," she brushed past him to the hallway. "Thank you for the offer, but I'm afraid you wasted your time coming here."

He caught up with her at the front door.

"I don't need your help, Logan," she restated. "I'm getting along just fine."

From his shirt pocket he withdrew the clipping he'd taken from the local paper. "Not according to this. 'Wanted: Full-time ranch hand. Experience a must. Room, board and small salary. Mountain setting, good working conditions. References required.'"

A frown pulled the sides of her perfect mouth down.

"This is your phone number."

"So?"

"So I'm applying for the job."

Her eyes opened wide as the shock registered on her face. "You're what?"

"I'm no longer with the force."

Her expression reflected her shock. "But I thought..." Her voice faded.

"That being a top homicide detective with Denver PD was my full-time obsession? That making chief before I turned forty was all I ever cared about?" *That proving to my old man that one good cop was worth a dozen Harvard law degrees was more important than you?* he finished to himself.

Obviously taken aback by his frank admission, she stood staring hard into his eyes. "Well, yes. Now that you mention it, that's exactly what I thought."

He shrugged off her comment. "Things change." But now was hardly the time to try to explain just how much.

"Not that much." She took a deep breath. "So. You're out of work. You've left law enforcement?"

He had never been able to lie to her, and he didn't want to try now. "No."

She nodded knowingly, and for a second he thought she looked almost disappointed. "I see. Well, I'm sorry Logan. I need full-time help, and I know you too well to believe you'd walk away from a ten-year career to become someone's hired hand."

"Not just anyone's," he reminded her. "I want the job, Sarah. I'm offering you the summer." He was prepared to offer her a whole lot more, and he would have, here and now, if he thought for one minute she'd accept.

"You know I'm experienced, and your terms sound more than fair." He didn't need the salary, but he knew her well enough to know she'd insist on paying him something. "I'm your man, Sarah."

When she winced, he cursed himself for not choosing his words with more care. "I want the job," he said simply.

She shook her head. "Thanks for stopping by, Logan, but I'm afraid now you're wasting both our time." She pushed the screen door open and stood waiting for him to pass.

He didn't move, except to drop the clipping on the small telephone table beside the door. "I spotted five colts in the pasture when I drove in. If you haven't started working with them yet, they'll be impossible to handle by the end of the summer."

Again with a defensive tilt of her chin, she said, "I can take care of my horses."

"And what about your fences?"

"What about them?"

"There were three steers out on the road when I drove in. I herded them back into your pasture and shored up the downed posts as best I could. It's dangerous to have your cattle wandering onto the highway."

Worry moved over her face like a shadow, and guilt nipped him. On the other hand, if he had to frighten her into seeing things sensibly, he would. "Even from a distance, I can tell that your barn roof won't last another winter, and I'll bet there's hay in at least one field ready to be baled. You need that hay for winter feed, and selling the surplus will more than pay your expenses until spring."

Worry turned to anger and it radiated off her in waves. "Are you finished?"

"Just getting started." He thought back to the muddy boots on the porch. "I know you irrigate your hay. If your system is working one hundred percent, no clogged ditches or broken pipes, then you're the only rancher in the valley living a charmed life.''

Her hands clenched at her sides. ''You're out of line, Logan.''

''Maybe.'' But he didn't intend to stop now that he had her attention. ''You can't afford to let things get ahead of you on a place this size, Sarah, not if you intend to make a go of it—you *are* planning to stay?''

''Of course I'm staying.''

That came as no surprise. This was the life she'd always dreamed of living, as different from their life together in the city as night was from day. ''Then you know what you have to do, and this ad tells me you know you need help doing it.''

''I have help,'' she informed him. ''Nick Gallus harvests the hay in exchange for a split in the yield.''

As the image of his former high-school classmate sprang to mind, Logan frowned. With his pretty-boy looks and world-class ego, Nick Gallus had once been considered a lady-killer. Although never friends, Nick and Logan had competed at jackpot rodeos in the area. Calf roping had been their specialty, and one or the other had taken the purse at every event.

Despite their shared interests, an undercurrent of tension had always existed between them. One memorable Saturday night, behind the chutes at the county fairground, their differences came to blows when Nick made the mistake of bragging about his next intended conquest.

Logan suppressed a smile when he recalled the satisfying crunch of Nick's nose beneath his knuckles. When he looked up and realized Sarah was watching him, he couldn't help wondering if she remembered the first time he'd defended her honor.

"So how is the golden boy?" he asked. "Last I heard he was playing cowboy again."

"I wouldn't know about that," she said with a look of open disdain. "But he is ranching now. Herefords, mostly. He came back to the valley after Margie divorced him. He bought a couple of hundred acres just this side of Ridgway."

It was a good location, but even in that lush country, two hundred acres wouldn't support a large herd.

"He's leasing another thousand acres from Earl Fraizer with an option to buy," she added.

For as far back as Logan could remember, Earl Fraizer had been the owner-operator of the Round-up, the area's most popular country-western bar. In addition to running the bar, Earl had become one of the valley's most influential citizens, due in large part to the achievements of his only son, Orrin.

Always the apple of his old man's eye, Orrin had been given every privilege. Fresh out of an Eastern law school, he'd become active in state politics, and after serving a couple of terms as county commissioner, Orrin moved on to the state capital as a congressman. Over the years, he'd successfully cultivated a blended image of youthful vigor and down-home charm, and now, if one could believe the polls, Earl's pride and joy seemed destined for the governor's office—not bad for a kid virtually raised in the back of a bar, Logan mused.

"I didn't know Earl owned land," he said.

"From what my dad says, Earl's been parlaying profits from the Round-up into land deals for years. He bought out Stan Bailey last spring. Four thousand acres of the best grassland in the county. Nick's thousand is part of that parcel."

With a powerful landlord personally invested in his operation and Breedan hay to get his herd through the winter, it seemed to Logan that Nick Gallus had all the ingredients in place for a successful cattle operation.

"It's hard for me to imagine you doing business with Nick," he said.

"People grow up," she informed him pointedly.

Did she know firsthand that Nick had changed? Logan wondered. Or was she taking the smooth-talking Nick's own word for it? "Whose idea was it that Gallus take over your hay production?"

"Nick hasn't taken *over!*" she said defensively. "He merely harvests it. And, not that it makes any difference, but it was Earl who suggested the arrangement." She put her hands on her hips and eyed Logan assessingly. "Look, I really don't know why I'm going into any of this with you. I've got work to do, and I'm sure you have someplace you need to be."

Her meaning wasn't lost on him. During their time together, it seemed he'd always had something or someone else making demands on his time. "So you're turning me down."

"That's the long and short of it," she said, pushing the door open wider.

"Even though you know darn well I'm the perfect choice for the job."

She let the screen door slap closed and turned to face him squarely, her arms folded. "Oh? And just how would I know that?"

"In the first place you know how well I know this ranch—hell, I grew up not a full mile from this very spot. As a kid I was over here as much as I was home. I know how this place operates almost as well as I know the workings of the Spencer spread." His late father might have said even better. "And secondly—and even more importantly—I know you."

Her expression said that was anything but a plus.

"And I don't think you'd be comfortable allowing a stranger to move in here with you and your daughter."

"He wouldn't be *moving in*," she informed him tersely. "There's a trailer out back. Will's mom lived there until she passed away last fall."

"Sounds good. I'm sure I'll be very comfortable."

She threw up her hands. "You haven't changed one iota, have you, Logan? You're still impossible!"

He fought a smile as color rose to her cheeks in that way it always did when she was excited or angry. "And you're still the most beautiful woman I've ever known."

She blew out an exasperated breath. "I don't know why I'm even talking to you!"

He did smile then. "Do you want me to guess?"

The blush of color on her cheeks deepened. "You're reprehensible!"

"All right, Sarah. Let's get serious. You need help and I'm offering it, so why not just climb down off your high horse and start acting like the smart woman you are. Admit I'm right, or if your pride won't allow you that, think about your child. Think about what's best for her."

This time she pushed the door open with a determined shove that rattled the hinges, and when she stormed out onto the porch, he followed her. Watching the sunlight turn her hair to strands of white gold, he wanted nothing more than to touch it, to bury his hand in its lustrous silk.

"How dare you mention my child? You don't know what you're talking about!" she informed him. "You know nothing about me, and you have no right to presume you know what's best for my...family." She whirled around to glare at him. "What are you up to, Logan? And this time,

spare me all the double-talk about fences and irrigation systems.'' She stood, hands planted on her slim hips, chal-
lenging him for an answer.

''I already told you. I want to help out an old friend.''

Her eyes narrowed. ''Not good enough, Logan. What do
you really want?''

You, he longed to tell her, but knew he didn't dare. If
he'd learned anything as a cop, it was that timing was everything, and this was definitely not the time. ''Will was
my best friend,'' he said simply.

''And he was my husband. What's your point?''

Her directness had always earned her his admiration, and
this afternoon was no exception. The lady was no pushover,
and in this instance, she seemed determined to make things
as difficult as possible. He knew her. And he also knew
that if he didn't put an end to their bantering soon, they'd
end up saying things they'd both regret—just as they had
the last time push came to shove between them.

Five years and a hundred regrets ago, he'd allowed his
pride and hers to ruin any chance for their future. This time
it would be different. This time he held the trump card, and
as much as he disliked having to beat her this way, he
decided now was the time to play it.

Chapter Two

"I hadn't intended to tell you this way," Logan said. "I didn't come here just to apply for the job. I came here to talk about Will."

Her chin rose another notch. "What about him?"

"I have reason to believe his death might not have been an accident."

All the color drained from her face. "What are you talking about? Of course it was an accident."

With a hand to her elbow, he ushered her across the porch and down the steps. "Let's walk." He wanted to get her away from the house. Explaining would be hard enough without the intrusion of an inquisitive four-year-old.

But even as the thought occurred to him, Jessica charged out onto the porch, breathless and giggling. A teenager carrying a pink plastic cup hurried after her.

"Jessica! I told you your mother was busy. Now come back here and finish your milk!"

Logan guessed the exasperated girl was the cookie baker, Terri. The young woman's small face was round and devoid of makeup. Her short brown hair was a cap of loose curls. Dressed as she was in baggy denim jeans and a man's wrinkled flannel shirt, she looked like any other kid at the mall. Except that this young woman was very obviously pregnant.

Jessica ran over to her mother, still giggling, with the teenager hot on her heels.

"Terri Rhodes, this is Mr. Spencer," Sarah said.

"Logan," Jessica corrected.

"Nice to meet you, Terri."

The young woman nodded. "Yeah. You, too." When she turned to Sarah, she frowned. "I'm sorry, Sarah, but you did promise her she could ride this afternoon, and she's getting antsy."

Sarah turned to her daughter. "Jess, Mr. Spencer and I have some business to discuss, and I need you to go with Terri and do as she says until I'm finished."

Jessica's pout drew the corners of her small mouth down. "But you said—"

"I know what I said," her mother reminded her in a no-nonsense tone. "And as soon as I've finished my business with Mr. Spencer, we'll saddle your pony and take a nice long ride. Maybe we'll see those baby foxes we glimpsed last week down by the draw."

Listening to Sarah deal with her child, Logan felt his respect for his former lover redouble. Though she was obviously a stern parent, Sarah's commands held just the right touch of gentleness.

The child's face brightened. "Promise?"

"Absolutely. Finish your milk and then, if Terri doesn't mind, maybe she'll go with you to the barn and help you brush Sugarfoot and get him all ready to saddle."

"Would you, Terri? Please?"

The teenager and Sarah exchanged a smile.

"Sure," Terri said, and handed the child her milk, which was dispensed with in one quick noisy gulp.

"Good girl," Sarah said, brushing the milky mustache

from her daughter's upper lip. "Now please go with Terri, and I'll catch up with you in a few minutes."

Jessica smiled. "Bye, Mom. Bye, Logan."

Logan couldn't help smiling. Sarah's child was spirited and full of life, and obviously very loved.

"Bye, Jessica," he said. "It was nice meeting you. Maybe I'll see you later."

"Okay, Jess," Terri said. "Let's go see Sugarfoot."

Terri reached for the child's hand, but Jessica was too fast for her and bolted out of the yard at a dead run as Terri waddled to catch up.

"Jessica, slow down and wait for Terri," Sarah shouted after them. "Terri, please keep a close eye on her around the horses."

Terri waved her reply.

"The child is absolutely fearless," Sarah told him when they were alone again. "She thinks horses are just big dogs." There was a mix of pride and concern in her voice, and Logan bit back the urge to point out the similarities between mother and daughter.

"We can talk over here," she said.

He moved with her to the redwood picnic table situated beneath a large cottonwood tree at the edge of the yard.

He sat down on one of the wooden benches, and when he suggested Sarah do the same, she walked around the table to sit opposite him, communicating without words the subtle message that she intended to keep barriers between them.

Focusing her full attention on his face, she said, "What's this all about, Logan? What do you know about Will's accident?"

"Not much at this point," he admitted. "But three days ago I received a call from someone who says he has information about what happened the day Will died."

She looked relieved. ''But that's no mystery. The details of the accident are a matter of public record.''

''I know what the record says. I spoke to Will's deputy.''

''Glenn?''

''Yes. This morning.'' Will's deputy, Glenn Driscoll, had been justifiably reluctant to believe Will and Logan had been close friends. He hadn't hesitated to point out that he hadn't noticed Logan among the mourners at Will's funeral.

''All right, you're familiar with the official record,'' Sarah said. ''What else *is* there?''

''I'm not sure.''

''Are you saying you don't believe the sheriff's report?''

He shook his head. ''I wouldn't go that far. Not yet. Though, I admit, when I heard what happened, I found it hard to believe. I grew up with Will, and I know how he handled himself in the saddle.''

She sighed. ''I know. It wasn't easy for any of us to accept.''

''Will would never have taken a green horse up to Tyler Ridge.''

''He didn't. He was riding Jax, as levelheaded as any horse on the place. In fact, Jax came home on his own. I have to tell you when I saw that horse come running in still saddled but without Will, I panicked. I knew then and there something was wrong.''

Dead wrong, Logan thought grimly.

''Look, Logan, you and I both know even the most trust-worthy horse can spook. It happens.''

According to the coroner, Jax had spooked that day, and Will's injuries had been the result of the horse kicking him after he'd been thrown from the saddle. Dazed and severely injured, Will had somehow managed to stagger to his feet, only to stumble and fall over the edge of Tyler Ridge, his body not discovered until late the next day, partially sub-merged in the icy waters of Dove Creek.

"It was an accident," Sarah said. "A terrible freak ac-cident, everyone agreed. I can't imagine what additional information someone might have now almost a year later. Who was it, Logan? Who called you? What did he say?"

"I don't know."

"What?"

"He wouldn't identify himself, and when I tried to force the issue, he threatened to hang up." He studied her face for a moment, wishing there was an easier way to tell her the worst. "He just kept insisting Will's death was no ac-cident." Logan watched the implications of what he'd said taking agonizing shape in her mind. "He said he has proof."

Obviously shaken, she had to fight, he knew, to keep her voice from trembling. "What proof? I don't understand. Are you saying Will was…murdered?" The word came out in a strangled whisper. "But why would anyone say such a thing?"

"I don't know. That's what I came here to find out."

She turned to stare at the peaks in the distance, and Lo-gan waited. What he'd said was shocking and she needed time to regain her composure. As he watched her and waited, he felt helplessly bound by a past that made it im-possible for him to try to console her.

"I don't believe it," she said finally, turning once more to face him. "Everyone liked Will. Everyone respected him." Her declaration seemed to strengthen her. "Neither Glenn, nor anyone else at the department has ever hinted that Will's death was anything but a horrible accident."

"I'm sure that's what they believe."

"Of course they believe it!" Her face was devoid of color. "Because that's what happened."

He understood how badly she wanted to dispel the doubt. He'd reacted the same way, trying hard not to nurture the seeds of doubt the anonymous caller had planted. It hadn't worked. And here he was, putting Sarah through the same agony. It couldn't be helped. He'd known what he had to do and he was doing it.

"The caller was insistent," he told her. "He swears there's proof. He says the truth is here in the valley." *And if it is, I have to find it,* he finished silently. "We have to know, Sarah." *I owe it to him. I owe it to Will.*

"What does Glenn think about all this?"

He hesitated.

"You *did* tell Glenn about the call, didn't you?"

"Not exactly."

She sat up straighter. "What does that mean, *exactly?*"

"The case of Will's death is officially closed, and without compelling evidence, it will stay closed. You know how the system works. Everyone in this county knows my brothers, either personally or by reputation, and you know as well as I do how the locals dislike outside interference. Most of them consider private investigators a necessary evil, but I've never known any cop who was eager to work with one."

"Cole and Drew are investigating Will's death?"

"Not yet. But they're ready to help if I need them."

"Are you saying you've gone to work for the Spencer Agency?"

"No." Though it wasn't because his brothers hadn't made the offer numerous times in the past year. "But I was trained to be a cop, Sarah, and I still know how to conduct an investigation." In ways he couldn't begin to divulge to her now.

"'Was' is the operative word here. Past tense, Logan. You said you'd quit the force."

It would be so much easier if he could just tell her about his work for the FBI, but that would only complicate matters. Besides, Will's death did not fall under the Bureau's jurisdiction. Not yet, anyway. For the time being, he was on his own. Just as he was when he freelanced cases for the Bureau. This was different. This was strictly personal. "When and if I uncover concrete evidence to either prove or disprove the anonymous tipster's claim, I'll go to Deputy Driscoll. But not before. The guy who called was skittish as a colt. I can't risk scaring him off. Besides, when county officials get involved, they bring a mountain of red tape with them."

She studied him with knowing eyes. "Always the loner, right, Logan?" She didn't wait for an answer to her rhetorical question. "All right, I'll accept your reasons for now. I was married to a cop, after all. I know all about bureaucratic red tape. So, why the line of bull about your coming to work for me?"

The ability to cut to the heart of the matter had always been one of her strongest traits in Logan's view, but it saddened him that she found it so easy to suspect him of harboring an ulterior motive.

"In order to piece together an accurate picture of what was going on in Will's life before his death, I need to be close to the people and things Will was close to."

"Meaning me."

He nodded. "Yes. You. The ranch. His work. All of it."

"Glenn could help with that."

"Not now," he said firmly. At some point he might be forced to reveal to the local authorities his connection to the Bureau, but he hoped it would not come to that. His work had always been covert, on a case-by-case assignment. If things worked out the way he planned, he would be finished with that life forever. But in the event his plans went awry and he was forced to go back to undercover work, he couldn't afford to compromise his anonymity.

Other than his brothers, only a handful of men in the Bureau even knew of his existence as an operative. The success of the highly sensitive assignments the FBI had entrusted to him depended on him staying anonymous, as did the lives of his former colleagues—some of whom were still engaged in undercover activities he had helped design. For their sake, he could ill afford to reveal his Bureau connections to anyone, short of a life-and-death scenario.

"For now, I work on this investigation alone," he said. "Except for any assistance Cole and Drew can give me." He wished he could ask her to simply trust him, but the state of their relationship—their nonrelationship at this point—made that impossible.

To ease her mind, he repeated his conversations with his brothers. "I'll be keeping them up to speed as the case evolves."

Suddenly she smiled.

"What's that for?" he asked.

"Oh, nothing," she said with a dismissive wave of her hand. "It's just that I don't ever recall Logan Spencer asking anyone for help."

"Things change," he told her for the second time. *I've changed,* he tried to tell her with his eyes. "They would both be here now," he explained, "but business is booming at the Spencer Agency, and neither Cole nor Drew has the time it might take to sort this thing out." Besides, the sudden appearance of all three Spencer brothers in their hometown would draw unnecessary suspicion. "Alone, I'll be able to conduct my investigation unnoticed. If someone does have something to hide, they're hiding it from the authorities, not from Sarah and Will's old friend. As far as anyone has to know, I've merely come back to the area to help out a friend." *Can we be friends, Sarah? After all we once meant to each other, can't we at least manage that?*

He watched her mulling over what he'd told her, and after a long minute he said, "How about it, Sarah? Will you help me? Will you let me help you?"

She took a deep breath and stared at him steadily. "Logan, if what you've been told has any basis in fact, then of course I'll do whatever I can to help uncover the truth. If someone intentionally hurt Will, I have to know."

He wanted to hug her, but instead, he merely said, "Good. When do I start?"

She pushed to her feet. "Start? Oh, no. You don't start. Out of the question. You can't work here."

"But you just said—"

"And I will. I'll help you in any way I can. But you can't stay here. It wouldn't work."

"Sarah, be reasonable. This past year must have been hell for you."

She stiffened. "I don't want or need your sympathy, Logan."

Too late, he thought, *you already have it.* "This has nothing to do with pity."

"Then what? Guilt?"

He tamped down the flash of anger her accusation ignited. "Not entirely."

"Then what?"

"What would you say if I told you I'd been considering coming home to the valley?" In truth he'd thought of little else since the day Will died and he realized Sarah was single again. "As I've explained, Cole and Drew have their hands full with the agency, and they aren't always able to look out for our families' ranching interests the way they'd like to. Aunt Bess isn't getting any younger, and although our hired hands are almost like family, one of us needs to be here to oversee the operation.

"I've been thinking that maybe it's time I took up my share of that responsibility. I think it might be time to come home."

Just saying the words made him believe it could work, that he could finally put the past behind him and take up his rightful place as the eldest Spencer brother and head of the family.

But there was skepticism in Sarah's eyes, and he knew she was remembering how he'd once sworn he'd never come back to reclaim his one-third interest in the sprawling Spencer quarter-horse ranch. The ranch his father had felt bound to, trapped in a life he despised by the birth of his first son.

"But I thought—"

"Things change," he told her again. Since his father's death, some of the anger seemed to have seeped out of him. Although proud of his accomplishments, Logan no longer felt the need to prove himself worthy to anyone. Except Sarah.

The irony struck him like a fist. If only he'd spent all his energy on proving himself to her the last time, he might never have lost her.

"All right," she allowed. "So what if you do decide to become involved with the Spencer ranch again? You just said it's a full-time job. What time would you have left for this place?"

"Don't jump the gun, Sarah," he cautioned. "I haven't made a firm commitment to my family's business yet. Who knows, maybe spending the summer here, getting back into the life, working here for you, will help me make that decision."

Her eyes narrowed knowingly. "And maybe you'll decide you miss the excitement of the force. But in any case, you're still keeping your options open, aren't you, Logan?''

It was a cheap shot, using against him the words he'd spoken in the heat of their final argument. Remembering why he'd come here, he tamped down his anger, sensing she'd dragged their past into the mix to blunt the effect of the electricity that had been arcing between them from the moment she'd opened the door and reluctantly let him in.

He knew her well, and although she'd never admit it, he knew she'd felt the pull as strongly as he had.

"Yeah, well," he drawled, "like you said before, some things never change."

"Except my situation *has* changed. This ranch is not a hobby. It's my livelihood, and I need someone who's committed to *this* place. Someone I can count on."

Someone like Will, he imagined she was thinking.

"I'll do what I can to help you uncover the truth about Will's death. But the job is out." She started for the house, a signal that their discussion had come to an end.

"You're making a mistake, Sarah."

Over her shoulder she said, "It wouldn't be the first time."

He didn't follow her, but he wasn't about to let her dismiss him that easily. "I forgot you never believed in taking risks."

She stopped suddenly and walked back to him with her head held high. Anger sparked in her eyes, turning them that hot bright sapphire blue that had always tied his heart in knots.

When she was within arm's length, she said in a low voice, "You let him down, Logan. When he needed you, you were too busy saving the world from bad guys to respond. Now you're feeling guilty. Well, don't expect me to help you out with that. Even if I wanted to, I can't. So you go on, Logan. Go find the truth. Ease your guilt. Play the role of supercop. Find whatever evidence is out there and solve the case. Do whatever you think you have to do to live with yourself. But leave me alone, Logan. You're right about one thing—I don't like taking risks. I took one once, believed I could beat the odds. And I lost.''

Long-suppressed resentment trembled in her voice, and Logan told himself he'd been a fool to come here, to think he'd have a chance of winning her back.

"Goodbye, Sarah," he said quietly. "I'll be in touch."

She turned and headed for the house, anger in every step.

Gut churning, Logan headed for his pickup. Damn it, why had he allowed himself to even hope?

Suddenly a commotion drew his attention to the barn, and he spun around to see danger so imminent and so unthinkable it took his breath away.

For an imperceptible moment, his heart and his mind froze, and at the same time Terri's scream slashed the air. "Jessica!"

Chapter Three

Terri's shouts echoed the panic reverberating in Sarah's chest like a hammer.

"Jessica! Get out of the way!" Sarah screamed. The words tore her throat as she ran, blind to everything but her daughter standing squarely in the path of three runaway horses.

The yearlings! Two of the four young animals Logan had mentioned only moments ago now galloped at breakneck speed toward her precious child. Kicking, bucking and nipping at each other, and the dogs were going crazy, barking and racing to join the fray.

Time froze, even as it spun wildly out of control. "Jessica!" she yelled again. "Jessica, run! Get out of the way!"

As if in slow motion, Jessica turned to look at her mother. She blinked and her mouth opened when she saw the danger bearing down on her. But still she didn't move, didn't utter a sound. Whether she was too startled to run or merely unaware of the kind of disaster heading straight for her, Sarah didn't know. All she knew was that her child, her darling Jessica, was a mere heartbeat away from serious injury. Maybe death. And there was nothing anyone could do.

And then, all at once, miraculously, Jessica was safe.

She'd been scooped up out of the way by two strong arms before the lead horse thundered over the spot where scant seconds before she'd stood rooted to the ground.

Sarah's breath came in gasps as she pulled her daughter out of Logan's arms. Momentarily too shaken to speak, she could only hold Jessica close, trying to catch her breath and still the violent trembling of her body.

When Terri joined them, her face was ashen and her chest heaving. "One minute...she was there," she panted. "Right beside me! The next thing I knew she was gone. I told her to come back, but she wouldn't. Like...like it was some game!" Tears pooled in her eyes. "I—I'm so sorry, Sarah," she stammered.

"It's all right," Sarah managed, realizing she had to calm both the young woman and herself. "She's fine. Aren't you, Jess?" She held Jessica at arm's length. "Oh, Jessica! What am I going to do with you?" This came out on a sob.

The child seemed amazingly unaffected by the danger she'd barely escaped. She pointed past her mother to where the horses now stood grazing contentedly in the backyard. "Look, Mommy! The horses ran into our yard! They came to play with me." She smiled and Sarah felt the terror that had paralyzed her for countless heart-stopping seconds turn to anger.

"Jessica Lynn Breedan!" She put her hands firmly on each small shoulder. "If you ever pull a stunt like that again, I'll...I'll... Listen to me! When Terri or I tell you something, you'd darn well better pay attention! Do you hear me, young lady?"

Unaccustomed to her mother's anger, Jessica looked shell-shocked. When her bottom lip trembled, Sarah knew she had her daughter's full attention. "Don't be mad, Mommy," the little girl cried. "I was only teasing Terri."

Sarah sighed. The tension flowed out of her, sapping what little strength she'd mustered. "I am angry at you, Jessica. I'm really really angry. You must obey adults. We are the ones who take care of you, who make sure you stay safe. Now I want you to understand. You could have been hurt just now. Badly hurt. The animals on this ranch are not your playthings. They don't mean you any harm, but they're so much bigger and stronger than you are. You have to be extra careful around them…" Her voice broke as she stared hard into her child's face and fought the emotions that threatened to overwhelm her at the mere thought of anything bad happening to Jessica. She took a sharp breath. "Do you understand what I'm telling you, Jess?"

Jessica sucked in her bottom lip and nodded. Huge tears began to slip down her small cheeks. "Yes, Mommy. I— I understand."

Emotion clogged Sarah's throat. "Good. I think you should go into the house and take a few minutes to think about what I've told you. Time-out for fifteen minutes. And no riding today."

Sarah turned to Terri. "Take her inside and please close the gate after you. We don't need another rodeo today. I'll go find out how those colts got out and then get them out of the yard."

Terri reached for Jessica's hand and the two of them made their way wordlessly across the yard.

Sarah took a deep breath and turned to Logan. "I don't know what to say."

"You don't have to say anything."

"You saved her life." Thoughts of what could have happened left her weak.

"I just happened to be there." His eyes met and held hers for a long meaningful moment. "Why don't you go take care of your little girl and I'll see if I can find the break in the fence.'' But he didn't make a move to go. He was waiting for her. What else could she do? He'd saved Jessica's life.

"You win, Logan. If you still want it, you've got the job.''

He had the good grace not to smile.

"But it's only temporary,'' she added quickly. Maybe it could work, at least for the summer.

As she started for the barn, he fell into step beside her. "There's a roll of wire and a fence stretcher over there.'' She pointed to the toolshed behind the barn. "I'll grab a couple of halters and put the colts in the corral for the night.''

When they reached the barn, she felt his cool dark gaze moving over her. "You've made the right decision, Sarah. You won't be sorry.''

But even as he assured her, deep down she knew she'd made a mistake. Despite what he'd done for Jessica, allowing Logan Spencer to get this close was just asking for trouble. Now all she had to do was figure out a way to keep him at a distance for the rest of the summer.

"You saved my daughter's life,'' she said. "I owed you.''

"Are you saying this makes us even?''

She shook her head. "You've got what you wanted, Spencer. Let's just leave it at that for now.'' They would never be even, she knew, and if things turned out the way she hoped they would, he would never know why.

"WELL, I THINK he's handsome,'' Terri said as she slid another pan into the sink filled with soapy water. "Sort of a cross between Matthew McConaughey and Alec Baldwin.''

Although she'd never admit it to Terri, Sarah thought

Logan was better-looking than either of those Hollywood heartthrobs. "I think you watch too many movies," she said. "Jessica, put that cat down. He doesn't know how to play Old Maid."

"I love movies," Terri declared dreamily. "The older and sadder the better. Hey, that reminds me, *An Officer and a Gentleman* is on tonight. I just adore that movie, don't you? I mean, when she looks at him, you know, at the end, when he marches in there and sweeps her off her feet, looking all cool and handsome, and then that song starts up in the background. I mean, is that just the most romantic scene or what? Why don't you stay up and watch it with me, Sarah?"

Why? Because the last thing she needed to see, besides Logan Spencer living in her backyard, was a movie where the completely unredeemable hero gets the girl. "Sorry. I've got a date with my check register and bank statement."

Terri wiped her hands on a towel and leaned back against the refrigerator. "Oh, come on, Sarah. We'll make some popcorn and eat chocolate ice cream and have ourselves a good cry. I always feel better after ice cream and a good cry, don't you?"

If only it could be that easy. "Maybe next time," Sarah said. "Come on, Jess. Time for bed."

Two hours later, sitting at the desk in the corner of her bedroom, Sarah did feel like crying, but not because of the movie soundtrack she could hear playing in the next room. She'd avoided reconciling her checkbook for six weeks, knowing it would be a grim experience.

The proceeds from Will's small life-insurance policy had evaporated quickly. On the bright side, if the price of hay stayed high and she could find a buyer by the end of the month, she just might be able to cover her mortgage payments through December. Her check from the school district for weekly riding lessons would help with other expenses, but still there wouldn't be much left over, and little or no cushion against the unexpected.

There had been one bright spot in the past year, she reminded herself. The day her student-loan-payment check had been returned to her with an explanation that her balance had been paid in full. Although she'd talked to three different people at the loan servicing center, she still didn't know how it had happened. All she'd been able to discern was that her loan—the balance of which was more than six thousand dollars—had been anonymously and completely paid in full. At the time it had been nothing short of a miracle.

It bothered her that she didn't know who to thank and probably never would, but she learned to accept the windfall as a blessing, hoping that someday she'd be in a position to return the good deed to someone in similar need.

Thinking back to that anonymous gift buoyed her spirits. Everything would work out, she told herself, and one way or another, she'd be able to hang on to the Breedan ranch. Her ranch was her future. Hers and Jessica's.

From the day she'd discovered she was pregnant, she'd wanted nothing more than to provide her child with the kind of traditional family she'd never known. She hadn't realized at the time just how she would go about accomplishing that feat, but she had been determined nonetheless. Thanks to Will Breedan, Jessica had known the love of two parents, at least for a while.

Sarah leaned back in her chair and sighed as she thought back to her own childhood and the devastating loss of her mother.

Sarah had only been eleven. For years she'd blamed herself, in that way children have of viewing themselves as the center of the universe. If only she'd been better.

Smarter. Prettier. If she'd minded her manners, studied harder, kept her room cleaner, maybe her mother would have cared enough to stay.

With adulthood, those notions disappeared, but the feeling of abandonment never quite left her. And in the smallest corner of her heart, sometimes she still felt like that little girl, grieving the loss of someone she would never fully know or understand.

These days Sarah knew plenty of families where single parents managed to provide loving stable homes for their children, but life with her father had been anything but stable. Johnny Allen had been about as ill prepared as a man could be for the responsibilities Daisy had left him.

Nothing in his rodeo background had prepared him to assume the burden alone. Between bouts with the bottle, he had managed to muddle through somehow. Working odd jobs for area ranchers, at least he'd kept a roof over their heads.

Sarah had learned to fend for herself and keep her wits about her when the county welfare investigators came snooping around. By covering for her dad, she'd been able to remain in the mountain cabin where memories of her mother lingered.

Johnny still lived there and had managed to support himself and stay intermittently sober for the past ten years. After his mother died, Will had suggested that Johnny move into her mobile home behind the ranch house. He'd even offered Johnny a job, but her father had declined Will's offers. He liked his place, he'd said, enjoyed his independence and his privacy.

Sarah hadn't pushed her father to change his mind and move out of the old cabin the elements had reduced to little more than a shack. She sometimes wondered if he stayed there in hopes that someday Daisy might change her mind and come back—not that he'd ever intimated as much.

But even as a child, Sarah knew her father brooded over his lost wife. He'd seemed like a man bedeviled, in constant inner turmoil. Although she knew her father loved her, she couldn't ever remember hearing him say the words. It was as if all the love in him had been lost when his wife walked out the door, and he didn't have the energy or the heart to try to recover it. Or her.

Perhaps it was that emotional distance from her father that had prompted Sarah to eventually try to find her mother. Johnny, on the other hand, had been dead set against the idea. On the rare occasions when she'd attempted to broach the subject, she'd met with cold silence, a disapproving chill that would sometimes last for days.

Finally Sarah had given up, and it wasn't until she had Jessica that she started wondering again what would cause a woman to leave her home, her husband and her only child, to just pick up and leave without a word, without a backward glance. The idea that a mother could abandon her child was incomprehensible. Who could do such a thing? And why? Where had she gone? Was she happy? Was she still alive? And why had she never come back?

When Sarah had first talked to Will about her need to find her mother, he'd reacted much the same way as Johnny.

"It's obvious she doesn't want to be found," he'd said. "If she'd wanted to know you, if she wondered how you were getting along, she always knew where to find you. You have your own family now. Let it go."

But letting go of the deep need to know her mother wasn't that easy, especially now that Sarah knew firsthand the special bond that existed between a mother and her child. Holding her infant in her arms, Sarah's need to know the truth about Daisy's desertion grew stronger.

Eventually Will agreed to help. His position in law enforcement allowed him access to certain records that Sarah would otherwise have needed a court order to view. But in the end, those official records proved useless. All Will had ever been able to discover was that Daisy Allen had never been arrested and that a missing person's report had never been filed on her behalf. Daisy had never closed her meager bank account or renewed her driver's license, and if she'd changed her name, she hadn't done it through legal channels.

Sarah turned her search to the Internet, but again, she'd discovered nothing. Her next step was a private investigator, who, after collecting two thousand dollars of Will and Sarah's hard-earned money, had come to the conclusion that Sarah herself was gradually drawing: The night Daisy Allen left her family, with an overnight bag and fifty dollars she'd taken from the cookie jar, she virtually walked off the face of the earth.

Although the desire to find her mother was still alive, the odds of that happening seemed impossibly slim now. And with the responsibility of the ranch resting solely on her shoulders, Sarah didn't feel she could devote any more time or money to the search.

Almost without realizing it, she turned to gaze at the framed picture of her mother on the dresser across the room. As she'd done countless times in the past, she studied her mother's young face, searching for answers in the wide blue eyes so like hers and Jessica's.

Sighing, she told herself Will had been right. It was way past time for letting go. She would never see her mother, now little more than a stranger, again.

She rose slowly and walked to the dresser and, as if to

cement her decision, pulled a drawer open and placed the picture inside, facedown.

On her way back to the desk, she glanced out the window and caught a glimpse of Logan heading for her back door.

A flutter of anticipation feathered inside her chest. "Now what?" she muttered as she pushed out of her chair again and hurried down the hallway.

She heard a tap on the back door, and when she pulled it open, she found him standing with a towel in one hand and a bar of soap and a razor in the other. His feet were bare beneath the hem of his blue jeans, and his shirt was partially unbuttoned.

"What do you think you're doing?" she demanded.

He offered her the half smile that had served him so well with her in the past. "Seems I've got a water problem," he said.

"What? Oh, no. I completely forgot. A pipe broke under the trailer last winter and I never got around to having someone repair it."

"No problem. I'll take a look at it tomorrow. In the meantime, mind if I use your shower?"

"No. Of course not."

As he headed for the hallway that led to the bathroom, she remembered her underwear drying on the rod. She went after him.

"Logan, wait!"

He stopped so suddenly she almost ran over him. "What's the matter? I brought my own towel."

"Hi, Logan." Sarah spun around to see Jessica standing in the open doorway of her bedroom.

"Hello, Jessica," he said.

"What are you doing out of bed, honey?" Sarah asked her daughter.

"I need a drink."

Sarah put her hand on the child's shoulder and turned her gently back into her room. "There's a glass of water beside your bed."

"But it's all gone. And now I have to go potty," she said, bouncing a little on her toes.

Logan coughed to cover a chuckle, and Sarah felt her patience strain. "All right. Go on, and then right back to bed."

Jessica padded across the hall, smiling up at Logan as she passed him. After she'd closed the bathroom door, Logan turned to Sarah and said, "I hope I'm not inconveniencing anyone."

Inconvenience was hardly the word. With him standing so close to her in the narrow hallway, his open shirt revealing a provocative glimpse of his chest, her nerves were snapping like the frayed ends of a downed power line.

"Look, Logan, I've been thinking—"

"All done," Jessica said, emerging from the bathroom before Sarah could say more. "Can I have another story, Mommy?"

"Oh, Jess. It's late—"

"Pleeease. Just one."

"Well…"

"'Goodnight Moon'!" she declared. "Please, Mommy." She turned to Logan. "It's my favorite."

"Mine, too." He hunkered down so that he and Jessica were eye level. "I read it to my nephew, Andy, sometimes."

Sarah held her breath. Who did he see when he gazed into Jessica's face?

"Come on, Mommy," Jessica pleaded. "Read me 'Goodnight Moon.' It's me and Logan's favorite! I'll be real good and go right to sleep after."

The image of Logan reading to a child did strange things

to Sarah's heart, but before she had time to deal with that unexpected reaction, she had to get him out of her hallway and away from her daughter.

"The bathroom's free," she said pointedly.

"See you, kiddo," he told Jessica, and tousled her curls. The gesture of simple tenderness tugged at Sarah's heart. "Enjoy your story."

"'Night, Logan," Jessica called after him as he headed for the bathroom. "See you in the morning."

He stopped in the doorway and smiled. "I look forward to it."

Sarah suppressed a groan. "Go get your book, honey, and climb back into bed. I'll be right in."

When Jessica went to retrieve her book, Sarah headed for the bathroom door and rapped on it with authority. When it opened, it was just wide enough for her to see that he'd stripped to the waist. The top button of his blue jeans was undone, revealing the tanned taut skin of his flat belly and the tight sprinkling of coarse black hair that thickened as it made its way downward. For a moment she could only stare as long-buried memories came to life, memories of the two of them engaged in other much more interesting late-night encounters.

"Don't tell me someone else needs to potty," he quipped.

For a moment Sarah almost forgot what she'd intended to say. "What? No! No, nothing like that. It's just, well—" she shouldered past him and jerked her panties and bras from the rod "—I have to talk to you."

When he started to push the door closed, she caught the knob. "No! Not now. I'll come over to the trailer after I get Jess settled in."

His eyes sparked with open interest. "It's a date," he said then smiled and closed the door.

Sarah drew a deep breath and forced down the purely physical reaction he'd stirred in her as she moved back across the hall and entered Jessica's room.

What on earth had made her think having him here could lead to anything but disaster? This afternoon she'd made a hasty decision based on emotion, but before another day passed, she would set things right. Logan Spencer had to go, and the sooner the better. For everyone.

HALF AN HOUR LATER Sarah summoned her courage and banged on the metal door that opened into the compact fourteen-by-fifty-foot trailer. This time, to her great relief, Logan was fully dressed when he opened the door and stepped back to let her in.

"Welcome," he said brightly. His lean tanned face was clean-shaven, and he was dressed in a white T-shirt and faded blue jeans that hugged his narrow hips and long powerful legs.

His glossy almost black hair was still slightly damp from his shower, and although he'd greeted her with a smile, there was a spark of sensual awareness in his eyes.

Sarah swallowed hard and clasped her hands in front of her. The moment the door closed, she felt the walls closing in. Already his presence filled the place. On the coffee table, his cell phone and laptop computer sat by a stack of manila file folders. Through the open door at one end of the narrow hallway she could see his clothes spread out on the bed. The scent of leather and citrus—Logan's own distinctively masculine scent—seemed suddenly too tantalizingly reminiscent when mingled with the aroma of coffee brewing on the stove. The man thrived on coffee; she remembered filling a thermos for him to take along on stakeouts.

"Sit down, Sarah," he said and motioned to the couch her late mother-in-law had covered in blue floral chintz.

"Thanks, but I won't be staying that long."

He moved into the galley kitchen and pulled the coffee-pot from the top of the small built-in stove. "I brought some water with me from your kitchen. Didn't think you'd mind."

She shook her head. "Of course not."

He took two cups from the cupboard. "Still take it black?"

"Yes, but I told you, I'm not staying that long."

"Right," he said as he filled his own cup.

"Listen, Logan, we have a problem."

"I know."

"Then I suspect you also know what it is."

"I have an idea, but why don't you tell me, anyway?"

"I've changed my mind. You can't stay here."

Despite the fact that she'd declined his offer of coffee, he filled a second cup and put it down on the table across from him. "We made a deal, Sarah." He sat down on one of the small metal chairs and pushed the one opposite him out to her. "Just how long do you think you'll survive giving half your hay profits to Nick Gallus? I know you've sold your equipment, and that has to have put you in an awkward situation. If I'm working for you, I'll have access to everything we need at the Spencer ranch."

"That's not the point," she said, picking up the cup of coffee she'd decided she needed, after all.

"Then what is it? Maybe you think I'm not qualified. Is that it? You think I've been out of ranching so long I don't remember what it takes."

She set her coffee down so hard it splashed onto the table. "I should have known you would make this diffi-cult." She took a deep breath and told herself she would try once more to reason with him. "Look, Logan, I can never thank you enough for what you did this afternoon, and I know I need help running the ranch, but this... arrangement, well, it just won't work."

He brought his cup to his lips and drank, studying her over the rim in a calm unruffled way she could only envy. "We can make it work," he said finally.

"I don't think so. There's too much...history between us, and I can't..." She groped for the words, feeling more frustrated by the minute.

"Can't stand the sight of me? I promise I'll stay out of your shower if that's the problem." The amused glint in his eyes infuriated and intrigued her at the same time, and she wished she had something to throw at him.

"Darn it, Logan! Will you please be serious?"

Instantly all traces of humor vanished, and his face grew rigid, his expression coolly businesslike. "All right. Let's get serious. I agree, it's high time we cleared the air."

More than a little nervous but determined not to back down, she said, "Fine."

"I'll go first," he said. "You can't stand having me around because I'm selfish, self-centered and egotistical. I'm driven, inflexible..." He lifted one dark brow. "Jump in any time, Sarah. I'm sure you remember the words."

His sarcasm propelled her to the challenge. "And arrogant!" She drew a sharp breath and continued before she lost her nerve. "You take over. You bully people. With you there's no compromise. You think you always know what's best for everyone. You don't know the meaning of the word 'compromise.'"

A muscle worked in his jaw. Perhaps he was not so impervious to her slurs as he would have liked her to believe.

"What if I told you I've changed?" he asked quietly.

I know who I am, Sarah, she remembered him telling

her. *And who I'm not. You have some romantic notion of me that doesn't exist. You don't want me, Sarah. You want a man who wants what you want—the white picket fence, a house full of kids. Much as I love you, I don't know if I can ever be that man.*

"A man can't just change," she declared, voicing the sad echo in her heart. "Isn't that what you told me?"

There was an unexpected softness in his eyes. "I was wrong. I put my career ahead of you. Ahead of us," he admitted solemnly. His eyes held hers until, through sheer force of will, she broke contact.

"I have to go," she said quickly. *Flee* was the better word, before he managed to convince her that the man who sat facing her tonight was any different from the man she'd walked out on five years ago. A changed man from the one she'd dreaded confronting that winter afternoon after a visit to the Westside Health Clinic.

And if that little jaunt down memory lane didn't do the trick, she told herself she could always fall back on the added disappointment of that same night. After drumming up the courage to tell him she'd found out she was pregnant, she'd come home to find his note on the dresser saying he'd been called out on assignment and wouldn't be back until Monday. It was just a few days before Christmas, and they'd planned to spend the evening decorating the tree and wrapping presents. It had been a promise between them, to carve out the time in their schedules for a special night together.

Sitting alone in their apartment, staring at the bare tree, contemplating the future of the fragile life growing inside her, she'd realized there would always be another case, another priority in Logan's life. There would be other holidays, but somehow she knew she wouldn't be spending them with him.

Something else would always compete for his time and attention. And there would always be something more important than his life with her. A high-priority investigation, a partner with a problem, a witness he needed to depose, a shift that needed to be covered, a stakeout no one else could handle—or was willing to endure. His promotion to detective had only made things worse. They hardly saw each other anymore, had become more like roommates than lovers.

To stay with him would have meant exposing their child to the kind of physical and emotional abandonment she had endured.

She'd loved him—dear God, how she'd loved him—but the stakes had become too high. The risk too great. There was someone else, another life, that needed to be respected. The welfare of a child had to be considered, had to come first.

Steeled by those memories and a stab of renewed loss, she stood and walked to the door. "I don't expect you to head back to town in the middle of the night," she said without turning around. "But I'd appreciate it if you left first thing tomorrow."

Chapter Four

"Sarah, wait," he said. "At least hear me out."

She hesitated, although she knew nothing he could say would change their present reality. The sins and decisions of the past had determined their future. "It's late," she said, and opened the door. *Too late for us.*

"You're afraid to be alone with me," he said flatly. "Afraid of what you might feel."

She shoved the door closed and spun around to glare at him. "I'm not afraid of anything." It was a bald-faced lie and she sensed he knew it. She'd been running for her emotional life from the moment she'd laid eyes on him standing on the other side of her front door.

"I won't hurt you, Sarah. I promise."

He had moved around the table and was standing close. Too close.

"We can't change the past, Sarah. What's done is done and we've both had to learn to live with the consequences."

Despite herself, she flinched.

"But it wasn't all bad, was it?" He reached out to cup her chin with his thumb and forefinger, and the gentle pressure sparked unwanted memories of his exquisite lovemaking.

His eyes were dark and sincere, and when he spoke, his

voice was as deep and vulnerable as she'd ever heard it. "I think you have to admit that at times we were downright amazing." A wistful smile curved his mouth, and her heart turned over.

Walk out now, her common sense demanded. *Turn your back on him and walk out, just as you did five years ago. Walk out and don't look back.*

But when he placed his hands on her shoulders and gazed into her eyes, she couldn't move. His breath was soft and sweet against her face, and desire curled in the pit of her stomach, overwhelming all her defenses.

"I know I can't ask you to believe me when I say I've changed. All I'm asking is for the chance to prove it to you. I won't let you down, Sarah. I promise."

The breath solidified in her throat. "Don't promise—"

"Let me finish," he insisted. "If I don't say this now, I know I'll be sorry for the rest of my life, and I've already spent too much time with regret." When he slid his hands down her arms and captured both her hands in his, she felt her heart convulse. The memories of what they'd shared held her.

"I've never cared for anyone or anything more than I cared for you, Sarah. I can't pretend we never happened. Or that I don't still want you."

A current of raw desire shot through her. Together they *had* been amazing, her heart whispered, but damn him for making her remember.

Feeling breathless and torn, she pulled her hands out of his. "It won't work," she told him as she edged to the center of the room. She needed breathing room to gather her wayward senses and still her drumming heart. "I said I would help you uncover the truth about what happened to Will, and I intend to keep my word, but leave our past out of it."

He took a step toward her and she held her breath. "I know you resent me because I didn't come when Will needed my help. I'm sorry, Sarah. You'll never know how much, but it's too late to change things. I'm here now, Sarah," he said pointedly. "And I'm trying to make amends. Not only to Will, but to you."

Amends. How could either of them ever make amends for the pain they'd inflicted on each other? There was no way to make amends to those whose lives she had so irrevocably altered. Will. Jessica. And Logan.

"You don't owe me anything," she said, her voice raspy with the guilt that felt like sandpaper on her heart. "This isn't about you and me—it's about uncovering the truth. It's about Will."

Her words seemed to have a chilling effect on both of them, and for a moment they could only stand staring at each other in strained silence. The tension that stretched between them reverberated with unspoken recriminations.

Finally he sighed and took a step back. "All right, Sarah. If you want me to leave, of course I'll go. But you should realize that when I leave the Breedan ranch, I won't be going back to Denver. I'm not leaving the valley until I've finished what I came here to do."

He turned then and walked back to the table and sat down. Sarah took a deep breath, feeling relieved and drained.

"I'll find a place in Ridgway or Telluride, but I'll still need you to work with me." He lifted his eyes to hers and made one final appeal. "It would make things a whole lot easier for both of us if you'd just allow me to stay here under the terms we agreed to this afternoon."

She opened her mouth to issue a flat refusal, but before she could get the words out, a high-pitched electronic ring from his cell phone interrupted.

They exchanged expectant glances as Logan crossed the room in two strides and brought the phone to his ear.

When his eyes narrowed, Sarah knew she didn't have to ask who was on the other end of the line.

Feeling as if her legs had turned to jelly, she sank onto the couch and waited with hands clenched. Every nerve in her body tensed as she listened to Logan negotiating with the man directly responsible for turning her life upside down. The man who claimed he knew Will had been murdered.

"HOW DO I KNOW you're telling me the truth?" Logan demanded. Sarah sat transfixed, her gaze never leaving his face. His cool reserve turned steely and his eyes blazed like black diamonds. His mouth became a tight determined line and every inch of him had turned cop. The man was a professional, and despite what his unbending devotion to career had cost her, at this moment she was glad to have this powerful intelligent lawman on her side.

"I want proof," he said with authority, and then without warning he punched the disconnect button and stood staring ferociously down at the phone as though it were the face of the enemy.

Half-afraid of the answer, she asked, "What did he say?"

"He said he knows why Will was killed."

The breath came out of her in a gasp.

"He said Will 'got too close' and they had to kill him."

Gooseflesh prickled her arms and a dull throb began behind her eyes. "Wh-what does that mean?"

He ran a hand through his dark hair and glowered as he sat down beside her. "Obviously it means Will was about to uncover something—a piece of evidence. A witness.

Who knows? But whatever it was, they thought it was worth killing for.''

"They?" Her voice was so small and tight she wondered that he even heard it.

"That's what he said. 'He got too close and they had to kill him.' ''

She wrapped her arms around herself in a futile effort to fight the chill that had nothing to do with the room temperature. "But how did he get your number?"

"I'm having my calls forwarded from my apartment." Logan draped his arm around her shoulders, and although she knew she shouldn't she accepted his comfort. Gratefully.

When he turned to look her squarely in the face, he said, "I don't want to frighten you, Sarah, but I'm sure he knows me. I can't place his voice, but I know he knows me. I'm sure he's disguising his voice by putting something over the phone—tissue or cotton maybe. But he chose me for a reason." His eyes held hers for a long meaningful moment.

"And you think you know why." Once again she held her breath, hoping he'd prove her intuition wrong.

He couldn't. "He knows about us, I'm sure of it. About our past relationship. And he knows the personal stake I have in wanting to find Will's murderer. That's why he chose me."

Fear crawled up her spine with icy fingers.

"If what he says is true, he's involved in this up to his ears. He's scared. I can hear it in his voice. He's on the edge."

"And that makes him dangerous."

He nodded. "Very."

Her mouth went dry. "He knows me."

"Yes. I'm sure of it."

"And until we know more about how he's connected to

all this, what his motives are in calling you..." She couldn't bring herself to say more.

"You could be in danger and I won't leave you and Jessica until I know you're safe."

Although she had never lost consciousness in her life, Sarah felt truly faint at the suggestion of Jessica in harm's way. She sank against the couch back and closed her eyes, willing the nightmare to end.

"Tomorrow, I'll check into having a caller-identification service added to my cell phone," he said. "We have to get a fix on this guy. We have to know who he is. Where he is. It seems logical to assume he's somewhere in this area."

Sarah opened her eyes and came to a decision, the only one that made sense. For safety's sake. For Jessica.

She would not feel safe again until the situation was resolved one way or the other. The Breedan ranch was isolated, four long miles from the highway and another ten to the sheriff's substation. "I'd be lying if I said I wouldn't feel safer having you here." Fighting for composure, she braced herself for the promise she was about to make and the courage to keep it.

With legs made strong by her resolve, she rose and crossed the room to stand beside the table, one hand braced on the back of the chair for support. "You'll have to stay here," she said in a voice so firm it surprised her. "We'll just have to find a way to make it work."

When he rose and crossed to her and gently took her hand, the look in his eyes almost made her believe they could make it happen. If he *had* changed, if he did still care, maybe there was a chance. At least to get through this awful summer.

"You're doing the right thing," he said in a firm voice, and without realizing it, she returned his reassuring squeeze.

The simple gesture rocked her. It felt too much like old times, when their every move had seemed in perfect harmony.

With all the strength she could muster she walked to the door. "I'll call the phone company in the morning to see about having the phone line reconnected to the trailer. Just let me know what else I can do to help."

He didn't waste a minute. "Sit down, Sarah, and I'll tell you now."

HE WARMED HER COFFEE and his own before reclaiming his chair. "I want to know everything you know about the cases Will was working on before his death." He pulled a pen and a pad of paper from the drawer and set the pad down in front of him. He'd made the transition from comforting friend to interrogating officer so fast her head spun.

"Was there anyone who'd threatened him, any strange or unusual occurrences he might have mentioned with regard to any case or investigation he was working on?"

She clamped her hands around her coffee cup and tried to remember. "Will was always careful to keep his work and his personal life separate," she began.

"But he must have mentioned something."

She shook her head. "Nothing unusual." *Nothing deadly.* "The night before his...death, there was a fight at the Round-up."

Logan frowned and jotted a few notes. "I'll check it out."

"And I know he'd been following up on the report of a poacher." She sighed, feeling inept and helpless. A poacher. A fight at a cowboy bar. All mundane. Useless. The day-to-day events in the life of a small-town cop. Why would anyone take a life—Will's life—over anything so inconsequential?

"What else, Sarah?" Logan prodded. "What else do you remember?"

She searched her memory again, but couldn't come up with a single significant incident. "Fender benders, drunk drivers—all routine." She felt increasingly exasperated. "He never mentioned anything extraordinary."

With infinite patience developed over years of experience, Logan urged her to tell him everything she remembered about the poaching incident.

She sighed. "It's not much. A rancher found a dead deer in one of his pastures. Will responded to the call and found evidence that at least one more animal had been shot."

"What's the rancher's name?"

She told him, and he made a note before he set the pen down and looked at her. "Well, at least it's a start. What about the fight?"

She shrugged. "He never mentioned it. In fact, I only heard about it later from Nick. He wasn't involved, but he was there. He said something about it in passing, about how Will and Glenn had arrested a couple of Earl's regulars."

He wrote down Nick's name and underlined it twice. "Was there anything else? Something Will couldn't get a handle on that was especially frustrating him or causing him grief?"

She took a sip of coffee and welcomed the warmth it afforded. This was good. She was feeling stronger, more confident, less emotional. Concentrating on details, on facts and dates and names, kept the memories of Logan at bay.

"There was something," she said, and then had second thoughts. "Except..."

"Except what?"

"It was nothing. Not even an official investigation. It was something between Will and me. Personal. Besides, he'd given up on it more than a year before his death."

Logan sat up straighter, and she felt the intensity of his gaze and knew she had no choice but to tell him.

"It could be important," he said.

Again she felt the pressure of his astute gaze. "Listen, Sarah, we can't disregard anything at this point."

There it was again, that patient half-friend half-cop voice that assured and aggravated her at the same time. That reminded her of the job that had torn them apart. "You never know when the smallest detail might reveal a piece of the larger picture, something that would either prove or disprove my anonymous phone caller's claims. I have to know everything that concerned Will. Officially and unofficially. Even if it's personal."

Without emotion she told him about the search for her mother. As she spoke she weighed the complications of confiding this piece of her personal life in the man who had once held and then broken her heart.

"Eventually we gave up," she said finally. "Will did everything he could to try to find out where she'd gone."

"I never knew you were that interested in knowing more about your mother," he said.

"I wasn't," she admitted. "Not until...a few years ago." Again she felt a deep need to protect herself, and she was relieved when he didn't press her to explain her motives. Not that she could have. How could she begin to explain to someone who'd never wanted children how giving birth had sparked such an intense need to find out why her own mother had abandoned her?

"What about your father?" he asked. "Surely Johnny had some idea where she might have gone."

She stared into her coffee. "I'm afraid it's a subject he's never been willing to discuss."

Logan nodded as if he understood, and she supposed he just might. It was pride that kept Johnny from discussing his runaway wife, and pride was a powerful motivator for a man like Logan Spencer. After all, it had kept him from ever truly reconciling his differences with his own father.

"I think he must have suspected she would leave him someday," she said. "According to what little I remember, their marriage was never happy. They fought constantly. After she left, he never even filed a missing-person's report, and as far as I know he never made any attempt to find her. I guess I'll never know why my mother left, where she went, or why she never came back. But it was her choice and I've had to learn to accept it."

The look Logan gave her was one of pure compassion, unsettling and too sincere. Suddenly all she wanted was some distance between them, space to put her emotions on safer ground.

"It's been a long day," she said, feeling genuinely exhausted. "I have students coming for riding lessons in the morning." She explained briefly about the weekly classes for the special-needs kids from the local elementary school.

"Special needs—sounds like a lot of responsibility," he said.

"I guess it is." Sarah resisted the urge to remind him that responsibility and commitment were not dirty words. "But to me it's worth it."

He searched her face as though looking for an answer to some unspoken question.

"The van arrives around nine," she said to break the strangely intimate mood that seemed to have enveloped them again. "I give lessons in the round corral attached to the barn."

"I'll have the fence fixed and the colts out of your way before breakfast."

"Fine." She opened the door and stepped out into the pine-scented darkness, leaving him standing in the doorway as she walked briskly to her own back door. Somehow she knew, without looking back, that his eyes were on her every step of the way.

A moment later, safely inside her own house, she stood in the dark with her back to the door and her eyes closed, feeling inexplicably empty. Alone. And wishing she could feel his arms around her just once more.

He'd been right when he'd called their life together amazing. It had been. Their passion had been an all-consuming magic, and deep down she knew she'd never experience anything like it again.

For one wild irrational heartbeat, she wanted nothing more than to run back to him and grant him that second chance he seemed to want so badly. But reality kept her where she was, standing alone in the darkness with the nip of hot tears reminding her of the past that could never be undone. Of the lies and the pain.

How would he feel about that second chance, she wondered, if he ever found out she was the one who truly needed it?

THE METAL CASING around the pay phone bore the scars and initials of countless vandals. The directory was missing, but the man standing alone in the darkness beside the abandoned gas station didn't need a phone book. He knew the number by heart, and he dialed it quickly before he lost his nerve.

The phone only rang twice before a familiar voice answered with a curt "Hello."

"I have to talk to you," the caller said, knowing he didn't need to identify himself.

"What do you think you're doing calling me here?" the cold voice on the other end demanded.

The caller fumbled with the phone as he searched his

pockets for a cigarette and a match. As always, the thought of direct confrontation with his powerful enemy set the caller's nerves on edge. "I—I had to talk to you, and I didn't think you'd want me coming by your place."

"Yeah, well, at least you got something right. Where are you?"

The glare of headlights from a lone car speeding past swept over him. "South of town, out on the highway. Don't worry, there's no one around."

"This better be important," the cold voice warned.

"It is. I—I need money. I have to get away. I can't take it anymore." The guilt had become increasingly unbearable, especially since the death of Will Breedan. In his own mind, he knew that if he'd put a gun to Will's head, he couldn't have been more responsible for the man's death.

If he could just put distance between himself and the scene of the crime, maybe he could find a way to live with himself.

"You expect *me* to give *you* money?"

"A loan," the caller said quickly. "That's all it would be. Soon as I get settled, I'll pay you back. Every dime."

"And just why the hell should I give you *anything?* You already owe me! Or have you forgotten?"

How could he forget when each day it grew harder to face his own reflection in the mirror? Harder to keep his own tortured counsel. "I haven't forgotten. It's just that, well—" his voice cracked "—I don't know what else to do. I don't know how much more of this I can take."

"I risked everything to save your worthless hide, and this is how you repay me, trying to extort money from me! I don't like this. Not one bit. You're walking on shaky ground, friend. I don't take kindly to threats."

The caller's palms grew slick with sweat despite the evening breeze that moved the high-country air. "No! You've got it wrong. It's no threat. I swear.'' Although no one had ever called him a genius, only a half-wit would be stupid enough to threaten this powerful and dangerous man. "It's just, well, I've been thinking…maybe I should turn myself in.'' He couldn't believe he'd said the words aloud, but now that he had, he found they gave him a measure of relief. "It'd be over then, wouldn't it? I'd tell them it was all my doing. I wouldn't say a word about you, I swear. No one would ever know.''

The man on the other end of the line released a blast of profanity. "Why, I oughta break your friggin' neck! Just how long do you think it would take them to get you to talk? Five minutes? Probably less, and you'd be peeing your pants and begging them to let you tell them everything.''

"But I wouldn't! I swear I wouldn't. But I tell you, I just don't know what else to do. I can't take it anymore. I can't! I have these nightmares, y'know? These awful dreams…'' He swiped at his eyes with the back of his hand.

"You can't take it,'' his enemy said with searing disdain. "Well, I've got news for you, my gutless friend. You *will* take it. You sure as hell will! And you know why? 'Cause I'm the one who's going to make sure you do. Understand?''

The caller understood all too well. He was caught in the same trap from which there had never been any way out, trapped between his own terrible guilt and his enemy's powerful and unrelenting grasp.

"Are you still there?''

"Yeah, s-sure. I'm here.''

"Then you'd better listen to me, and listen good, 'cause we wouldn't want any more bodies turning up in Dove Creek, would we, friend? When you think about it, no one's ever really safe, are they? Men, women, children—you just never know when something terrible could happen. Just look what happened to the sheriff.''

A measured silence allowed the unthinkable implications to sink into the caller's frantic mind.

''Anything can happen,'' the cold voice said again. ''The damnedest accidents. And fast, too. You and I both know how fast.''

The caller almost dropped the phone as fear rose like bad whiskey in his throat. ''Please,'' he sputtered. ''I'll do anything, whatever you say. Just don't hurt them. Do anything to me, but please, just leave them alone.''

''Well, now. It looks like we have an understanding.''

''Yes.''

''You just settle down and remember nothing will happen to anyone as long as you keep your mouth shut. We'll even keep this call between you and me. Forget it ever happened. But the next time you think about running off half-cocked, just remember who you're dealing with. Remember who was there to pull your sorry butt out of the fire. Don't think for one second you can get away with double-crossing me. I'm watching you, friend. Every move you make.'' And with that ominous warning, the line went dead.

Shaken, the caller made his way back to his pickup and fumbled in the dark for another cigarette. Why hadn't he turned himself in when he'd had the chance all those years ago? If he had done the right thing, Will Breedan would still be alive, and innocent people would not be in danger.

He felt older than his years; remorse and self-loathing were taking a heavy toll. Living like an animal perpetually caught in the crosshairs of an unseen telescope. It was a heavy price for freedom.

Especially since the murder of Will Breedan. That one awful event had changed everything. It was then that the past came back to haunt him like never before and he realized nothing was beyond the man. As he'd been reminded only moments ago, no one was safe.

Gunning the pickup to life, he pulled out onto the highway and thought again about turning himself in to the authorities. The prospect of spending the rest of his life in prison didn't really frighten him anymore. There were worse things, he figured. After all, what good was freedom if a man never felt truly free? If only it could be that easy. If only he could purge his conscience without hurting anyone else.

At times he'd considered driving up to the highest peak and sending himself and his truck full-speed over the edge. But ultimately he knew he'd never have the nerve to go through with such a plan. Deep down he was a coward. But on the other hand, suicide might prove less painful than the fate that awaited him if the wrong people found out about his calls to Logan Spencer.

Like the call he'd made tonight, his calls to Spencer had been made in desperation. It seemed like a good plan, calling on Will's old friend, a man who'd once worn a badge and who everyone knew had more than a passing interest in Will's widow, but now he wondered. Had he made a deadly mistake?

"It's up to you, Spencer," the man behind the wheel whispered into the darkness. "There's nothing I can do now."

From now on, the man who'd once loved Sarah would have to be the one to uncover the truth and find her husband's murderer. Put an end to the nightmare that had haunted too many lives for too long.

Taking a drag on his cigarette, he shuddered when he considered the treacherous path he'd chosen in deciding to become Logan Spencer's informant. Like a man running through a minefield, one false step and his world would explode all around him.

Unless Spencer could pull it off. The man was a cop, wasn't he? His brothers had solved sensational crimes. At least now it was out of his hands.

The thought heartened him a little and he told himself he couldn't lose his nerve. One step at a time. And in the end, who could tell? Maybe it would turn out that he wasn't such a coward, after all.

Chapter Five

Logan was up at dawn, and after downing coffee he'd warmed in the small microwave, he made his way to the barn to water and feed the livestock.

He set four new posts and braced the sagging wire along the fence where the colts had escaped yesterday. Next he did a check of Sarah's irrigation system, looking for breaks or clogs on the line that divided her hay fields.

An hour later he headed back to the trailer, feeling more invigorated and alive than he had in months. The fresh air and sunshine seemed to nourish him. He decided to tackle the broken water main next. He had to pry off a section of skirting to get under the trailer. Inching along the ground on his hands and knees, it only took him a minute to locate the damaged pipe and assess what it would take to fix it.

When he crawled out from under his temporary home, he saw Terri in the backyard, dressed in baggy jeans and an oversize T-shirt with the word BABY emblazoned in red and a red arrow pointing downward.

"I saved you some breakfast," she said, walking toward him. "Come on in when you're ready."

He thanked her, pulled a rag from his back pocket to wipe the dirt from his hands, then followed her across the backyard and into Sarah's house.

After he'd washed his hands in the utility sink beside the back door, she told him to sit down. She poured coffee and filled a plate with hotcakes and bacon and brought it over to him. "I can fix you some eggs, too, if you want."

He shook his head and reached for the syrup and butter. "This will be just fine."

She smiled at him and began rinsing the stack of dirty dishes piled in the sink. "We usually have breakfast around six, except on Sundays. Lunch is pretty flexible. If you're working around the house, just drop in whenever. With it staying light so late, Jessica likes to play outside, so we eat supper around seven or eight. I do most of the cooking, except when Sarah decides to make something special."

"Thanks, but I won't be taking my meals here once I get some supplies in and fix that water main."

She seemed disappointed. "But Sarah said—"

"I'll let her know."

"She's outside getting ready for her students."

Terri dried her hands on a dish towel before flipping it over her shoulder. "You know, you might as well eat with us, at least in the evening. No sense both of us cooking. Like my mom used to say, one more doesn't make much difference. And she would know. There were six of us kids, and we were always dragging somebody home."

She brought a cup to the table and sat down opposite him. As he ate, she told him how she'd grown up on a small ranch north of Ridgway. "It wasn't really a ranch, not like this place. Just a few scraggly acres, a couple of horses and some goats. Anyway, when my dad left us, Mom decided to pack us up and move to Denver. I was bummed out, I can tell you! Thought I'd have to sell my horse, but Will said— Hey, did you know Will? I don't remember you being at the funeral."

Her tone wasn't accusatory, merely curious. "Yes, I

knew him. We were friends. I was out of the country when he died.'' He'd told her what he hadn't seemed able to tell Sarah, and he wondered why.

While Logan finished his breakfast, she rattled on, telling him all about her horse and more about the circumstances of her parents' divorce than he wanted to know. He'd been only half listening, until she said, ''When I turned sixteen, I quit school. Mom kicked me out of the house, and I moved in with my boyfriend. It's his baby,'' she said, and smoothed the T-shirt lovingly over her stomach. ''We're getting married soon as he can save enough money.''

''Congratulations.''

''Yes, well.'' She rose and carried his empty plate to the sink, then came back to refill his cup. ''It's not a done deal yet, but I think it will all work out eventually.''

''And in the meantime...''

''I work for Sarah—like you—for room and board. You see, when Hank found out he was going to be a father, he went kind of ballistic. Said he needed time to get used to the idea, you know?'' She sighed and her lashes dipped sadly. ''Anyway, after that I kind of didn't live anywhere for a while.''

The memory pulled the corners of her mouth down, and Logan felt an intense dislike for Hank springing to life inside him.

''Anyway, one thing led to another and I got into some trouble.'' With a wave of her hand, she qualified the statement. ''Nothing really bad, understand, just some stupid stuff, you know? Like, one day I went up to Telluride with some loser friends I used to know, and we got caught shoplifting some makeup and junk. The cops came and took us all to jail. They called my friends' parents, but I gave them Sarah's number. She and Will had always been good to me, you know? So I figured it would be safer calling her than my old man, and what could my mom do all the way over in Denver, you know? Anyway, Sarah worked it all out with the judge so I could stay with her—just until Hank and I can get things worked out," she added quickly.

Due to her own fractured childhood, Sarah had always had a soft spot for kids, Logan remembered, especially kids whose parents had abandoned them, if not physically, then emotionally, as seemed to be the case with Terri. In Denver Sarah had volunteered her time for the Big Sisters program, and one summer she'd coached a girls' softball team made up entirely of kids placed in foster care.

"I help out with Jessica and the housekeeping," Terri said. "When Will's mom got sick, I took care of her, too, did the cleaning and cooked for her, that kind of thing. Hey, did you know Ethel?"

He nodded.

"She was a nice lady. Anyway, Sarah got me hooked up with this GED study program and I'll graduate high school this December. After the baby comes, I'm going to learn to be a nail technician, you know like acrylics and stuff. Of course Hank and I will be married by then, but at least I'll have my high-school diploma and a way to bring in some money."

Discussing her future seemed to lighten her mood, and her smile was bright when she headed back to the sink to finish the dishes. "We're going to have a ranch like this one someday," she said. "Hank's real good with cows."

Logan pushed his chair back and carried his dishes to the sink. "Well, I hope everything works out for you, Terri."

"Thanks."

"And thank you for the great breakfast."

She beamed under his compliment, and Logan decided she'd probably had too few of them in her short life.

"Hey, if you liked the hotcakes, you'll love the lasagna I'm making for supper. I use eggplant, but don't let that scare you. It's Sarah's recipe and it's really good. I'm trying out all her recipes. I figure since I'm going to be a wife and mom, I better learn how to cook nutritious meals. I think that's important for a family, don't you?"

Logan said yes, he thought it was very important, and as he left the house, he decided if pluck counted for anything, Hank-the-reluctant-father and Terri-the-hopeful-mother-to-be just might have a chance, after all.

FROM THE PORCH Logan spotted Sarah leading a horse down the hill from the pasture behind the house. With a backdrop of lush greenery and distant peaks, Sarah couldn't have seemed more at home. The quintessential country girl, he thought with a smile, as fresh as the morning and twice as welcome.

As he left the yard and started up the hill toward her, he thought back to their time together. Even during the happiest moments, he'd sensed her longing to return to the valley. It was the lifestyle she'd romanticized even as a child, a lifestyle he knew had more to do with happy endings than pastoral settings.

He'd never begrudged her her dreams. The hard part had been accepting the fact that he hadn't been made a part of them. But who could blame her?

After all, his life had been cloaked in the shadowy world of criminals and police procedures. His chosen profession, and the intensity with which he'd allowed it to consume him, didn't exactly lend itself to picket fences and the PTA.

He should have known better from the start, should have realized that, despite the deep love they'd shared, their differing dreams would play havoc on their hearts.

It came down to basic differences: Sarah wanted the traditional home and family. Logan knew firsthand it didn't exist—or at least he thought he knew. Later, after Sarah left him, he'd come to realize that his perceptions of life had taken an unhealthy twist. A twist based on his father's bitterness, having little or nothing to do with Logan's own dreams.

What strange turns life took, he thought. Now he was the one praying for a miracle, while Sarah refused to accept anything but the facts. And the fact was, he'd hurt her. Deeply. By putting his career ahead of her, ahead of her dreams for their future together. Letting her down was a mistake he'd regret for as long as he lived. She'd deserved so much better.

"Good morning," she said when she saw him walking toward her.

"It is, isn't it?" Being with her made everything seem better.

"You were up and at it early this morning," she said.

"Just doing my job, ma'am," he drawled.

Her smile was wry. "Yes, I see. Well, I guess I can't complain about that now, can I? I saw you crawling around under the trailer. Were you able to fix the water main?"

"Not yet. Looks like the entire pipe needs to be replaced. I'll go into town later and buy some."

She told him where to find some extra pipe and insulation in the shed behind the house. "I don't know if it's the size you need, but it might save you a trip." As she talked he found it difficult not to stare. She was just so pretty, such a natural beauty.

During their time together, he'd seen her in everything from black silk to his old high-school football jersey, but if she'd ever looked better to him than she did today—in a simple cotton blouse, worn blue jeans and scuffed boots—he couldn't remember when.

Today she wore her thick blond hair in a ponytail threaded through the opening at the back of a faded Denver Broncos ball cap. Seeing the cap reminded him of the weekend he'd surprised her with tickets to a home game. He wondered if it was the same cap, the one he'd bought her at halftime, just before a page from his partner had forced them to leave the stadium.

"If you have to buy more pipe, be sure to save the receipt and I'll reimburse you. By the way, I called the phone company. The service to the trailer will be turned on tomorrow."

"Thanks. I'll have my call forwarding switched from my apartment. Do you have an answering machine?"

Sarah smiled. "Out here? You forget where you are, Spencer. Not many pressing messages or appointments that won't wait."

"Point taken. I'll pick one up next time I'm in town. We want to give our anonymous phone buddy every opportunity to communicate."

Sarah's expression grew somber.

"What about caller ID?" he asked.

"Oh, I almost forgot, I asked about having that option added, but unfortunately that service is not available in this area."

"Thanks for checking."

"No problem. Oh, and I'm sure you noticed the wall phone in the kitchen, but I have an extra desk phone if you'd like one in the bedroom, too."

He said he would, thanks.

"I'll find it for you when we get back to the house. There's an extra directory in the kitchen, as well. Remind me to get it out of the drawer for you."

It all felt so natural, a rhythm so reminiscent of the day-to-day life they'd once shared. The small talk born out of intimacy. *I picked up your shirts at the laundry... We're invited to Drew and Joanna's next Saturday... We're out of milk... Your brother called... The papers say it's going to rain.*

After the initial devastation of losing her had ebbed, it was those little things that caught him unawares and always left him aching. The flowery scent of her shampoo in his shower. The way she folded her towel. The way she turned down his side of the bed every night. The curve of her body beside his in bed. The peace she'd brought into his life. The refuge her love had given him.

He missed it all. He missed her. Missed hearing her say, *I love you.* Missed saying, *I love you, too.*

He wanted it all back.

He wanted her.

"This is Jax," she said, pulling him out of his reverie.

He glanced at the handsome bay walking dutifully behind her. "Nice horse."

"Thanks. Yesterday I rode him up north to move some calves to another pasture. On the way back he started limping." She brought the horse up short so he could take a closer look. "At first I thought it was a cut, but as far as I know he didn't get into any wire. Frankly I'm baffled. I asked my father to haul him to the vet's this morning."

He'd noticed the lack of equipment, and this gave him the opportunity to ask her about it. "You don't have a stock trailer?"

She shook her head. "I needed money and it seemed expendable."

He wanted to ask more to find out about the financial health of the ranch, but he sensed this was not the time. He was, after all, only the hired hand.

"Dad should be here soon, so I thought I'd better get Jax ready."

"What's Johnny up to these days?" Logan asked as he ran his hand down the horse's leg to examine the injury more closely. "Wasn't he working for a stock contractor out of Oklahoma?"

She sighed. "I'm afraid that didn't work out."

He didn't press for more details, nor did he bother asking why her father wasn't working as the hired hand at the Breedan ranch. He knew Sarah loved Johnny and that she could be fiercely loyal to those she held dear, but duty and familial loyalty could only go so far, even for someone as committed to family as Sarah—especially when it came to her livelihood.

Johnny Allen had never held a steady job that Logan knew of. The concept of responsibility just didn't seem to exist for the man. He had often wondered how a woman with Sarah's keen sense of duty and work ethic could have been related to him.

"I can see where the skin was broken, but it seems healed now," he said as he brushed back the hair on the horse's foreleg to get a closer look. "Hard to tell what caused it."

"I know. It looks like there's a burr or some other foreign object imbedded beneath the skin, but I can't feel anything, and he doesn't seem to be in that much pain." She patted the animal's sleek neck and continued walking.

"You always did have a sixth sense when it came to animals," Logan remarked. "Ever think about going back to school?"

"I'm afraid it's a little late for that."

"Why? You're still young."

She rolled her eyes. "Thirty-two is hardly a kid."

"Careful," he warned, "or you'll insult me."

"Ah, yes, the ancient one, closing in on thirty-four this

September, right?'' She quickly averted his gaze, as if letting him know she felt embarrassed about remembering.

He felt heartened that she had.

"If it's something you still want to do, you should look into it. The university has extension programs here on the western slope. You could probably intern locally. Joanna might be able to help." With his sister-in-law splitting her time between her life with Drew in Denver and her practice in Telluride, it seemed logical she might need a partner.

"You're forgetting I have responsibilities now," she said.

"Of course. Jessica."

She shot him a decidedly defensive look. "It's not just Jessica. I have a ranch to run, as well as other commitments vying for my time and attention."

"Like Terri Rhodes, her baby and her horse," he said. He supposed it was none of his business, but the thought of taking on the problems of an unwed teenager seemed to him an overwhelming commitment, especially for a young widow with a child to raise alone.

"Terri's not a problem. I was thinking more about the mortgage on this place."

"And what about Hank? From what I heard at breakfast, he seems to be a problem."

She shot him a sidelong glance. "She doesn't need Hank." The deep disdain in her voice was unexpected and very real.

"He's the father of her child."

He saw her set her jaw. "So?"

"So he deserves some consideration."

"Like the consideration he gave Terri when he found out she was pregnant?" She didn't look at him, but stared straight ahead, her chin tipped stubbornly.

"He's just a kid, Sarah. Maybe you should cut him some slack."

"He was man enough to make a baby," she shot back.

"Last I heard it takes two—"

She stopped short and turned to glare at him. "I'm not saying Terri isn't as much to blame as Hank for her condition."

"Blame? Funny, I thought she seemed happy about her situation."

"Poor choice of words," she muttered. "What I meant was, she's accepted her responsibilities. She is happy about the baby, despite the circumstances. And what's more, she's determined to be a good mother." Sarah made a huffy sound that came from the back of her throat before she started walking again. "Hank, on the other hand, is nothing more than a sperm donor at this point."

"Some people would call that a father." How completely their roles had reversed, he thought, remembering the bitterness he'd felt toward his own father when he'd discovered the real reason behind his parents' marriage.

"There's more to being a father than making a baby," she informed him in a tight voice. After a minute of uncomfortable silence, she added, "And just for the record, I hope I'm wrong about Hank."

Logan nodded, hoping the same thing. "You sound willing to help Terri out for as long as it takes."

"I am. As far as I'm concerned, she has a home here as long as she needs one. Her family is a mess. Will tried to get them into counseling, but it just didn't work. In the meantime he got to know the kids." As she talked about her late husband's involvement in Terri's life, Sarah's expression grew wistful. "I think he'd want me to help her now."

Logan felt something tighten in his chest. Perhaps he'd

been wrong to assume Sarah had married Will on the rebound. Perhaps she'd truly loved Will, had fallen for him head over heels and been the driving force behind their unexpected marriage.

"When we were kids, Will was always dragging home strays or nursing some wounded critter back to life," Logan said. Baby birds that had fallen from their nests, battlescarred barn cats and, once, an orphaned fawn. Logan himself had even been the target of Will's reclamation efforts. The night he'd left home, he called his best friend from a truck stop on the highway. Will had tried to no avail to convince Logan to reconsider leaving home and go back and reconcile with his father.

Remembering that night, recalling the kind of friend Will Breedan had been, Logan reminded himself of what he'd known for some time: Sarah Allen had married the better man.

They'd walked a few more steps when Sarah said, "I still find it hard to believe anyone would have wanted to hurt him."

Logan shared her disbelief. For as long as he'd known Will, he couldn't remember the man ever making a single enemy—no small accomplishment for someone in law enforcement.

"What can I do, Logan? How can I help you get at the truth?"

"For now I just need you to concentrate on remembering anything Will might have told you concerning the cases he was investigating before his death. I still think that's the logical place to start."

"But there must be something else I can do."

This was typical of Sarah, who had never been one to sit idly by and wait for someone else to solve her problems. The woman was nothing if not courageous. Once convinced of a course of action, he'd never seen her do anything but commit herself fully. And after committing, she didn't look back, he thought sadly. Just as she'd never come back to him.

Had she regretted the decision? Had she spent as many sleepless nights as he had wrestling with memories? If she had regrets, they hadn't lasted long, he thought bitterly, as evidenced by her marriage to Will Breedan a short six weeks after their own breakup. If only he could hate her, he thought morosely, knowing even as the thought occurred that he never could. He'd loved her for a long time, and no one since had even come close to making him feel the way she had.

"I want to be a part of this," she said, jolting him out of his thoughts. "Please don't shut me out, Logan."

He realized she was talking about the investigation. "I have no intention of shutting you out, Sarah. As I told you last night, I need your help."

"Then put me to work," she said. "Now. Today."

"All right. There is something I need." He'd considered broaching the subject yesterday, but decided it was too soon. "I want to examine his personal effects."

She stopped so suddenly Jax's nose nudged her back.

"I'd like to get a look at any papers or files he might have kept at the house. And his daily calendar if he had one. Did you keep any of those things?"

Her voice was surprisingly steady when she answered. "Yes, though as far as I know Will didn't keep any sort of day planner. If he did, I guess it would have been at his office in town."

And it, along with all of Will's notes and files, would have been integrated into the county's files by now, Logan suspected.

"We never found his wallet," she said. "I don't know

if he had it with him that day, but it wasn't found at the scene, and I've searched the house." Her expression had turned somber.

"I don't expect you to go through his things. Just point me in the right direction, and I'll do the rest."

When his mother died, dealing with her personal possessions had been an emotionally wrenching experience for him and his brothers. It was an experience he wouldn't have wanted to repeat, and he wasn't about to impose that kind of pain on Sarah.

She gave the lead rope a tug to get Jax's attention, and they started toward the barn again. "It's all right," she said, sounding resolute. "We can start tonight after Jessica goes to bed. It's all up in the attic."

When they reached the barn, Logan pulled one side of the double doors open, and as he did, he made a mental note to contact the Spencer Agency to let Cole and Drew know he would be staying on at the Breedan ranch, at least for the time being.

His brothers' investigative experience and resources could prove invaluable, especially in tracing leads outside the area.

At the sound of an engine in the distance, they both turned to see dust rising off the ranch road in the distance.

"That's probably Dad," Sarah said. "When I spoke to him last night, I asked him to try to swing by early before my students arrived."

"It doesn't look like a truck and trailer," he said.

"It's a van," she said, and Logan took in the disappointed frown and realized nothing had changed. Sarah was still giving her father the benefit of the doubt, and Johnny was still letting her down.

"Would you mind seeing to Jax? The first stall is empty. I'll need to help the teachers get the kids out of the van."

"Sure." He decided he'd give Jax's sore leg a liniment rub and hang around to help Johnny load the animal when he arrived—*if* he arrived. Where Johnny Allen was concerned, one never knew.

Chapter Six

When the bright orange van eased to a stop in front of the barn, the sound of the students' excited chatter drifted into the stall where Logan worked.

He figured the kids were ten or twelve, although he couldn't be sure since he didn't know much about children. It wasn't that he didn't like them, but he'd just never spent much time around them, with the exception of his nephew, Andy, and his niece—Joanna and Drew's daughter—Frani.

When he finished with Jax, he stood outside the stall and watched them unload. He couldn't help wondering whose idea it had been to teach these particular kids to ride. Whoever it had been, it seemed to Logan, they had made an unwise decision.

Two of the kids had to be wheeled off the bus via a special ramp designed to accommodate their wheelchairs. Three others managed to walk on their own, but only with the aid of thick metal braces and leather supports strapped to their legs.

The only child without an obvious disability was a boy he heard someone call Paul. Paul had been the first one out of the van, barging ahead of the two women Logan assumed were teachers. Sporting a buzz haircut and a set of shoulders as wide as he was tall, the kid could have been a linebacker.

As Logan walked toward them, he saw Paul and the woman who'd driven the van assist the last of the kids in leg braces off the bus. When Sarah praised Paul for his helpfulness, the boy's round face beamed with unabashed adoration.

Curiosity drew Logan closer as the small group headed for the long row of stables where the horses waited. "Quite a bunch," he mused as he came up beside Sarah.

In a low voice only the two of them could hear, he asked, "Do you really think it's safe to have these kids around horses?"

"The horses I use for these lessons are well trained and trustworthy," she assured him.

"But accidents happen, even with the most reliable stock. Doesn't it concern you that one of these kids could be hurt?"

"Sure, it's always a concern," she said. "But as long as these kids want to learn, I'm willing to help them."

He merely nodded.

"Look, these kids may have some limitations, but they've accepted their situation, and now they want to test and expand their capabilities."

"And damn the consequences," he said.

A spark of defiance flared in her eyes. "Consequences are a part of life, Logan. We all make choices."

"Yes. When we're given the chance."

She stopped short. The pulse point at her throat beat double time, and he realized his remark held a deeper more personal meaning for both of them. He resented her for leaving him without a word, and she knew it.

"You weren't the only one who was hurt," she said in a low voice. "And as for chances, I don't remember you giving me a choice about spending all those long nights alone, not knowing if I'd ever see you again."

"It was my job, Sarah."

"It was your life," she shot back, and immediately turned her back on him and headed for the stables in long determined strides.

"Sarah," he said, catching up to her, "I didn't mean to upset you."

With her head held high, she stared straight ahead.

"Okay, let's call it a draw. You were wrong. I was wrong, but sniping at each other five years after the fact is not my idea of a great way to start the morning."

She stopped finally, but still wouldn't look at him.

"And it's a lousy way to start our first day working together," he said, and offered her his hand.

She turned to face him and reluctantly took his hand and shook it.

"All right, Logan. If it'll make you feel better, we'll peacefully coexist." She eased her hand out of his. "Now if you'll excuse me, my students are waiting for me."

I didn't mean to hurt you, Sarah, he thought as he watched her walk away from him. *Not now. Not then. Just give me a chance to prove it. I won't let you down. Not this time.*

"If you want, I'd be happy to help out with the kids," he called after her.

"Suit yourself," she replied over her shoulder.

Seizing the small opening she'd given him, Logan headed for the stable. As he made his way down the long center aisle that divided a dozen stalls, he checked on each child and was surprised at how comfortably Sarah's students seemed to be around the horses. Obviously she had drilled them in the basics.

In one of the stalls a red-haired girl in leg braces demonstrated her knowledge when she warned him to move slowly behind the gray mare she was brushing.

"Gracie wouldn't hurt you on purpose," she explained, "but if you surprise her, she just might kick. Nothing personal," she added sagely. "It's just a reflex."

"Thanks," Logan said, and after helping the child arrange Gracie's bridle he moved on to the next stall.

When he'd taken a walk last night to reacquaint himself with the stable and barn areas, he'd noticed the adjustments Sarah had made for her special students. The ramps and handrails allowed the kids in wheelchairs easier access to the horses, and the wooden boxes, filled with currycombs and brushes, had been mounted outside each stall low enough for every child to reach.

Knowing Sarah, it didn't surprise him to see that she'd found a way to help the kids feel independent. He remembered her confiding in him once how she'd hated it as a child when the adults in her life treated her as though she were helpless when, in reality, she'd been taking care of herself and her father.

Logan knew better than anyone what a high premium she placed on independence and respect. Perhaps this time around he could show her he was prepared to give her both. In abundance.

As the kids finished tending the horses, Logan joined Sarah and the teachers in saddling the horses and tightening cinches. Although he found it difficult to hold back, Logan took his cue from Sarah, giving assistance only when asked, encouraging the kids to do as much as they could on their own.

After each child strapped on a helmet, Sarah told them it was time to mount.

As a dozen small hands gathered the reins, Logan couldn't help noticing how the physical limitations that had restricted these young bodies only moments earlier seemed to disappear.

Instead of a bunch of special-needs kids on horseback, Logan began to see only kids eager to get on with their riding lessons. Nothing remarkable or special about any of them, except the joy behind their smiles.

Sarah pushed open the gate and the riders filed into the attached corral. When she walked to the center of the round enclosure, each rider seemed to sit up a little straighter in the saddle.

At her command the riders reined their horses into a single line and moved in a controlled clockwise circle around the ring. Logan was impressed, and Sarah deserved all the credit.

He walked around the outside of the stable and moved up to the fence, where he stood watching with his arms draped over the top rail and one foot resting on the bottom.

From her place in the middle of the ring Sarah kept a steady stream of commands and compliments flowing in equal measure.

"Riders, walk your horses, please. That's it. Good job, Paul. Now, move up a little. Don't let him get away with that, Max. He shouldn't toss his head that way. Pull him in. Use your legs and your hands. That's it. Let him feel the bit and know you're in charge. Andy, check your reins. They look a little uneven."

Each time she asked her students to make minor adjustments in style or form, they did so quickly, and when she praised them, their faces glowed with the pride of their accomplishments.

"Pretty amazing, isn't it?" one of the teachers, a middle-aged woman in stretch pants, noted.

"Yes," he replied without taking his eyes off Sarah. Watching the way she coaxed the best effort from each of her students, Logan felt his considerable admiration for her grow. The teacher had been right; the kids were amazing, but to Logan, it was Sarah who was truly remarkable. Smart, capable, determined. Sarah Breedan was all those things and more. And no one knew better than he.

Although life seemed to have dealt her more than her share of blows, she'd always found a way to land on her feet.

Growing up without a mother, more parent than child to her alcoholic father, she'd never allowed her crippled home life to stand in the way of her goals.

In high school her name topped the honor roll, and although finances had forced her to forgo a degree in veterinary science, she'd made the most of her education and gone on to become a highly skilled assistant.

Fresh out of college she'd gone to work at a veterinary clinic in Denver, and it had been in that setting that Logan met her again for the first time since high school. When a stray dog was hit by a car in front of his apartment building, Logan took the animal to the only twenty-four-hour clinic in town.

The moment he set eyes on Sarah, he recognized her, the fresh-faced beauty he remembered cheering on the sidelines for the home team, the girl everyone admired and respected, the girl he'd planned on asking to the senior prom had his own life not taken such a sudden and irreversible turn.

She'd remembered him, too, and as they worked together to save the injured animal, she talked about the night of the big game when, playing quarterback, Logan had led the Eagles to the district championship.

As they'd reminisced about old times and old friends, he'd sensed her purposefully avoiding the subject of the rift between him and his father.

For more than ten years, Sarah Allen had been a part of the past Logan had done his level best to forget, and suddenly, on that night six years ago, she made him long to remember. Meeting her again felt like going home again.

The next night he took her to dinner, and for ten months—ten amazing months—they'd had a relationship like none he'd ever experienced before or since.

Sarah became his best friend, his confidante and his lover. She'd filled a part of his life he hadn't known was empty.

And then, as unexpectedly as it had begun, their relationship began to crumble. Sarah wanted a home and family, the kind of traditional life she'd missed as a child. Logan, on the other hand, didn't understand why their relationship couldn't go on the way it was forever. The more Sarah's discontent grew, the more his own misgivings about his ability to become the kind of man she deserved ate at him. Resentment grew in both of them.

Their discussions inevitably turned to arguments, and in the end, their differences tore them apart.

Sarah moved out the week before Christmas while he was away on a stakeout he'd volunteered to cover. He knew she'd gone home to the valley, but when he called her at her father's cabin, she refused to talk to him. His letters had all been returned, unopened.

Six weeks later she married his best friend.

"Reverse the circle." The sound of her voice pulled him out of his dark reverie. When she looked his way, their gazes met and held before she broke contact to return full attention to her students.

Whether you like it or not, Sarah, our chemistry is still at work. And working in his favor, Logan sensed, pulling them together in that same irresistible way it always had. Now, all he had to do was convince her to let it happen, to give him a chance to prove to her that he had changed. That the man who had once been willing to sacrifice everything to succeed in his profession now realized that no amount of success had been worth losing her.

"Hi, Logan." At the sound of the young voice, he turned around to see Terri and Jessica coming up behind him. Jessica's hair was braided in two dark shiny plaits, and her smile was as sweet and welcome as sunshine after a storm.

"Good morning, kiddo," he greeted her brightly. "How are you today?"

"I'm great. And I'm going riding. Come see my horse." She surprised him when she reached for his hand. "His name's Sugarfoot, and when Mommy finishes with the other kids, it's my turn for a riding lesson."

When he hesitated, she tugged on his hand.

"Come on, Logan." With her other hand she pulled an apple from the pocket of her bib overalls. "I'll let you feed him this, and when you do, he'll give you a kiss."

Logan smiled at Terri over the child's head. "How could anyone refuse such an offer?"

"Remember what your mother told you, Jess," Terri called after them. "Stay out of the corral until all the other riders have left."

"I *know,* so I won't get runned over," Jessica muttered.

"I'll look after her," Logan promised.

"Yeah. He'll watch me." With her hand still in his, Jessica pulled him toward the small pen behind the barn.

Jessica's pony had been aptly named. His thick coat was the color of dappled butterscotch, and his four stockings were as white as spun sugar. The animal's shaggy mane hung down past his short thick neck, and the flaxen tail nearly touched the ground.

At the sound of their voices Sugarfoot's ears pricked up, and when he spied the apple, he trotted eagerly to the fence.

Just as Jessica had predicted, the pony stuck his face through the rails and nuzzled Logan's hand to get at the apple.

"See!" she exclaimed, giggling. "I told you he gives kisses for apples. I think he likes you! I guess that means you can join our club."

"Your club?"

"Uh-huh. It's mine and Sugarfoot's. Mommy belongs and so does Grandpa Johnny. My friends Dusty and Amy belong, too, and so does Terri—when she's not being bossy. Mr. Orrin said he would join, too, but he lives in Denver and can't come to any meetings."

He was mildly surprised to hear that Sarah and Orrin Fraizer were friends—close friends, evidently, if Jessica had invited him into her special club.

On second thought, in light of Will's position as county sheriff, the link made some sense. Logan experienced an odd relief, readjusting the scenario to make Orrin Fraizer Will's associate rather than Sarah's close friend.

"We go on trail rides and sometimes we even take a picnic," Jessica said. "And you can come to my birthday party, too! It's in a couple of weeks. Mommy's making a cake that looks just like Barney, with purple icing and everything! And we're going to play games and make ice cream, too."

"Sounds great. I'd love to come."

"All the members of our club will be there."

Logan smiled. "Do you have a name for your club?"

"No. Mommy says it doesn't need one. It's just a club for friends. We made up some rules, though—club's gotta have rules, you know."

"Of course." Logan tried to match her serious expression, although inside he smiled. Sarah's child was a delight. Will must have been proud of her.

"You don't have to pay money or anything, but you have to like horses and dogs and all the other animals. That's the rules. And you can't ever be mean to them. Not even to chickens or the mean old turkeys over at Grandpa Johnny's."

Logan made a face. "Chickens? And turkeys, too?"

Jessica nodded vigorously. "Yes. Mommy says they can't help it if they're stupid and moody, and that we have to respect them and take care of them, just like we take care of Shep and Ozzie."

"I think your mom's a pretty smart lady."

"She is. And so's my daddy." Suddenly her face fell and the light in her pretty blue eyes dimmed. "Except he's dead now."

Logan found it difficult to respond. "I know," he said quietly. "I'm sorry."

"Thanks."

Staring down the barrel of a loaded gun couldn't have rendered a more helpless feeling than the one that swept through him as he gazed into the face of this endearing child. If someone had murdered Will Breedan, Logan vowed he would not rest until he brought that individual to justice.

"Where's your saddle, Jessica?"

Her face brightened immediately and she pointed. "Over there. In the tack room, but I'm not big enough to saddle Sugarfoot yet. Mommy still has to help me." She thought a moment. "But you could help me. Could you, Logan?"

"Sure. I think I still remember how."

"Yeah! Hey, you're nice," she declared, "just like my daddy." And without another word she took off for the barn at a run, leaving Logan behind, fighting to breathe around the knot in his throat.

THE ROADSIDE CAFÉ was deserted when the two men entered. The younger and slightly smaller of the two wore a dark brown Stetson, which he took off when he felt the waitress's eyes move over him. She smiled and he nodded, comfortable and accustomed to appreciative glances from the fairer sex.

"This way," he told his companion, and together they walked to a booth at the back of the room.

From the kitchen the noise of clattering dishes and silverware echoed through the empty dining room, jangling his nerves.

The waitress followed them, and when they were seated, the big man asked her about the lunch specials.

"We'll just have coffee," the younger man said before she could respond. When she moved away from the table, he said, "All right. What's this all about?"

The big man scowled. "I just thought you ought to know he called me last night. At home."

There was no need to ask who. "What did he want?"

The big man shook his head. "Money, I think. At least that's what he said. It was hard to know just what he had in mind."

The waitress came up to their table, and the younger man held his remarks until she'd filled their cups and sauntered back to the lunch counter. "He's been scared for twenty years," he said, and reached for his cup to take a tentative sip of the steaming brew.

The big man leaned forward, the weight of his beefy arms causing the metal to creak as the table shifted on its pedestal. "Last night was different. He said something about leaving town and, get this—" he lowered his voice another notch "—he said he'd been thinking about turning himself in."

It was all the younger man could do to not show any

outward sign of the intense reaction his companion's statement evoked in him. He glanced over his shoulder to be sure the waitress had not overheard. "My God. What are we going to do? What did you tell him?"

The big man leaned back against the vinyl seat, an ugly sneer curling one side of his wide mouth, a dangerous glint in his eyes. "Let's just put it this way—I changed his mind." He reached for his coffee again. "But we're not out the woods yet. The man's a loose cannon. Always has been. It's just about time to nail him down once and for all." He set his cup down again and beckoned the waitress.

"Bring me a burger, honey. And a side of your home fries." He glanced at the younger man. "They make a good sandwich here. You hungry?"

"No. Nothing." Sitting here discussing murder as easily as some men discuss a change in the weather had effectively killed his appetite. "Look," he said in a low voice when the waitress left them alone again, "if it's money he wants, maybe—"

"Forget it!" the big man said. "We're not giving him a dime. Just leave him to me. I know how to handle him. He's scared now, too scared to do anything but lay low, and I aim to keep him that way, at least for the time being. I only told you about the call so if anything happens..."

"What could happen?"

The big man sighed. "Nothing, son. Nothing will happen. Just calm down. I just wanted you to know where things stand so you can protect yourself. You know that's all I want—to keep you safe." He reached across the table and chucked the younger man's shoulder good-naturedly. "Think of it as a heads up, that's all."

The younger man could only nod. His mouth had gone dry and the coffee burned his stomach. The last time he'd received this kind of heads up, a body had been found in Dove Creek.

The waitress brought a paper place mat and silverware, and as she arranged them in front of the big man, he smiled. "Thank you, honey. And don't be stingy with those fries, hear?"

The younger man had to leave. He stood and settled his hat on his head. "I have to go. I have to get back to town. I'll call you next week, and in the meantime—"

"Don't worry," the big man said. "Just leave everything to me. When I get through with him, he won't be talking to anyone."

"What about her?"

The other man shrugged. "She won't be a problem. She's given up looking, and she's got her hands full keeping that place afloat. She'll never make it alone, and once she goes bust, she'll leave the valley. Then it'll be over. It takes money to find someone who's been lost that long. Money, or a lawman for a husband. She's already lost one, and soon she'll run out of the other."

But the younger man wasn't so sure. He'd known Sarah Breedan a long time, and he'd seen how determined she could be once she set her mind to something. To his way of thinking, Sarah presented the same threat Will had posed, maybe even a greater threat.

After all, the whole situation had begun with her, hadn't it? And if she kept looking, kept digging...

It was as though his companion had read his mind. "She'll be ruined by winter, trust me. We don't have anything to worry about. She'll be gone and this whole thing will be forgotten. Finally."

"But how—"

The older man cut him off. "Have you ever known me to leave anything to chance?" He smiled confidently. "All you have to worry about is keeping your own nose clean. After all, we can't afford to have you caught in the cross-fire. Understand?''

He understood, all right. Understood that there was no way out and no looking back. The deal had been struck and the damage was done. He'd come out on top just as he'd been promised. He had everything. Money. A bright future. Everything but peace of mind, something he'd traded one night twenty years ago, when he'd sold his soul to the devil.

Chapter Seven

As the van turned around in the drive and pulled onto the ranch road, Sarah waved goodbye to her students and walked back to the stable to give the horses fresh water.

Moving from stall to stall with a hose, she filled each bucket and thought back to the morning's lessons with satisfaction. What she'd told Logan was true. All these kids wanted and needed was a chance.

The same thing he'd asked her for last night. He claimed he wanted to make amends; if only it could be that simple. But nothing had ever been simple where Logan was concerned.

She thought back to that night six years ago when he'd walked into the neighborhood clinic with an injured dog in his arms. Appearing out of nowhere, just as he had this time, to turn her life inside out.

She could still picture him standing there cradling the animal in his arms. The look on his face was like none she'd ever seen before, a mix of quiet desperation and childlike hopefulness. Although she'd known Logan most of her life, that night she'd felt as if she was seeing him for the first time.

The tough exterior that had been so much a part of his persona disappeared as they'd worked side by side through the night to save the dog. Spending that first night together, waiting to see if the dog would survive, she'd been given a glimpse of the man she'd always suspected was there. A good decent man with a big heart. A tender man, with a healthy measure of pride.

Then and there, she'd felt herself falling for him, and for the next ten months they'd shared the kind of love she'd never known existed.

The bittersweet memory brought on a wave of fresh guilt. What kind of woman would give herself in marriage to one man while another held her heart? What woman would bear a man's child without telling him?

A woman who had wanted the best life possible for her daughter, she told herself, remembering how life had been for her as a child.

Inside Sarah there lived the memory of the girl whose mother had abandoned her, the deep humiliation of the child who had been forced to abide pitying looks from social workers, school counselors and even friends. The girl who'd worn hand-me-down clothes and fashioned meals out of government cheese-and-macaroni, except on holidays when area churches sent baskets of donated hams. Growing up in a place where two-parent families were the norm, she was a child whose mother had left her, and whose father was the town drunk.

Although grateful to her benefactors, Sarah's pride had taken a beating. She'd had enough pity and duty-motivated kindness to last a lifetime.

There had never been any doubt in her mind that Logan would have married her to give their child a name, but a marriage based on duty wasn't good enough. Hadn't he told her as much when he'd confided in her the truth about his own family? His father's bitterness about the unplanned family he'd felt was thrust upon him had made an indelible impression on Logan. And although he had never admitted it in so many words, she sensed that his deep need to succeed had somehow gotten all tangled up with his father's regrets.

To see his own life taking the same course as his father's would have been devastating, not only for Logan but for his child, and ultimately for the family they might have tried to sustain.

Logan Spencer was an honorable man, but Sarah hadn't wanted his honor. She'd wanted his love. The kind of love and commitment real families were built on. The kind of love that would have created the home her child deserved. The kind of love he'd told her in a dozen different ways he was incapable of giving.

Will Breedan had offered just that kind of love. Odd as it seemed, their marriage of convenience had taken place for all the right reasons. He'd loved her, and his vision of what a family could and should be dovetailed completely with Sarah's.

In the end she'd found a way to live with herself by knowing with Will there had never been any deception. He'd known when he married her that respect and loyalty were all she could ever give him. And a daughter, a precious child who would love him like the good father he'd become. She'd given Jessica that much—a loving father—at least for a while.

With a heart made heavy by the choices and regrets of the past Sarah moved to the last stall.

"Sarah?" Terri called out from just inside the stable door. "Are you still in here?"

"Back here," Sarah replied.

When she looked up, she saw Terri walking toward her. Peering past the teenager's shoulder she expected to see Jessica.

"Where's Jess?"

"Out there." Terri smiled and pointed. "In the corral with Logan."

Sarah dropped the hose, and Terri jumped back as the water splattered onto the stable floor.

SARAH EMERGED from the stable to see Jessica sliding out of Logan's arms and into her saddle.

"Hi, Mommy," she shouted, all smiles. "Look, Logan saddled Sugarfoot. And he fed him an apple, too. He's in our club now. He's my new friend."

Sarah's stomach tightened at the sight of Jessica in his arms. *This can't happen.* "Jess, you know you're not allowed to ride alone," she scolded, rushing over to them.

"She's not alone, Sarah," Logan said.

"No. Of course not. I just meant—"

"Mommy, watch. Logan showed me how to make Sugarfoot back up."

"She's a quick study."

"Thank you," Sarah said stiffly, edging past. "Come on, honey. Let's start your lesson."

Logan stepped back, but Sarah could feel his eyes on her. To keep from facing him, she fiddled with the pony's bridle.

Out of the corner of her eye she saw him turn to walk away, but before she could breathe a sigh of relief, Jessica called him back. "Stay and watch me ride, Logan."

"He has things to do," Sarah put in quickly. Under his scrutiny she felt transparent.

"Maybe some other time, kiddo," he said, still not taking his eyes off Sarah. "I apologize if I overstepped my bounds."

"It's all right." She tried to sound unconcerned. "I

know how insistent she can be. It's just, well, I always saddle her pony.''

''I understand.'' But she knew he didn't. How could he?

As he walked out of the corral, she could almost hear the questions forming in his mind, and she cursed herself for behaving like an idiot. Logan Spencer was nothing if not astute. She knew him too well to believe he'd buy her simple explanation for what must seem to him irrational behavior. But she also knew that the more she allowed Logan Spencer to insinuate himself into her family, the more likely he was to stumble over the truth.

And that must never happen. Her happiness and, more importantly, Jessica's depended on Logan Spencer believing things were exactly as they appeared.

The decisions and choices of the past had predetermined the future. The time for choices was over, and nothing could change the way things were. From now on the future was all that mattered.

Soon Logan would be gone, and her and Jessica's life would continue. Just as she had been in the beginning, Sarah would be the sole protector of the child that meant more to her than anything or anyone else in the world.

And as long as she could prevent it, nothing would ever hurt Jessica again. No one knew better than Sarah how devastating the loss of a parent was to a child. She ached knowing Jessica would have to live with some of the same emptiness.

But one loss was better than two, she told herself. Her daughter had already been traumatized once, and Sarah knew she still missed her daddy. How could anyone know if a four-year-old truly comprehended the enormity and finality of death?

JOHNNY ALLEN'S PICKUP and the battered two-horse trailer hitched to it rattled down the ranch road, announcing his arrival several minutes before he pulled to a stop in front of the house. Logan emerged from the toolshed to see Sarah's father sliding from behind the wheel.

When Johnny saw him, his face brightened. "Logan!" he called out, and moved forward with his hand extended. "By God, it's been a long time! How are you, son?"

They shook hands. "Can't complain, Johnny. Yourself?"

Johnny said he was "fair to middlin'," but Logan was surprised by how much Sarah's father had aged. His weathered face looked especially drawn, and the crinkles around his pale blue eyes had turned to heavy folds. The evidence of Johnny's lifelong affair with the bottle revealed itself in a dozen ways. None of them good.

Today Johnny seemed as stone-cold sober as Logan ever remembered seeing him, and he wondered if it was because he'd known he would see Sarah.

"I bet your aunt Bess is tickled to have you home. I ran into her the other day at the feed store." As they chatted they walked to the back of the battered horse trailer and unlatched the wide metal door. "I swear that woman gets feistier every day."

Of course Johnny had no way of knowing that Logan hadn't yet contacted his aunt to let her know he'd arrived. He made a mental note to call her that afternoon.

In the barn Johnny bent down to examine Jax's leg. "Don't know what to make of that," he said. "But I think it's a good idea to have the vet check him out."

Logan agreed and within a few minutes Jax was loaded and secured in the trailer.

"Well, I guess that about does it," Johnny said, reaching into the front pocket of his worn jeans for the keys. "Tell her—" he tipped his head in the direction of the house "—I'll call after I talk to the vet."

Logan wondered why Johnny didn't seem to want to speak to Sarah himself and was about to offer to go find her, when the front door opened. Sarah walked across the yard and out through the gate to stand beside them in the driveway.

"Dad."

Johnny's expression was somber and Logan sensed the strain between father and daughter.

"I see you think Jax needs the vet's attention."

Johnny nodded. "Too good a horse to take chances." He turned and walked to the driver's side of his truck and opened the door. "Nice to see you, Logan." He turned the key and the engine came to life after a sputtering hesitation. "I'm still planning on helping tomorrow, Sarah."

"Thanks," she said. "Nick said he wanted to get started around six. Riley Meadows will be helping, too, and possibly another of Earl's hired hands."

Johnny nodded again, then wheeled the truck and trailer around the drive and pulled onto the ranch road.

"What was that all about?" Logan asked as they stood watching Johnny's truck rumble down the road.

"He's going to help Nick bale hay tomorrow."

"I'm not talking about hay, Sarah." And he suspected she knew it. "I'm talking about you and your father. As I recall, the two of you never passed up an opportunity to talk horses."

She pushed the gate open and Logan walked with her into the yard. "We talked," she said simply. "Didn't you hear us?"

"Not much."

She gave him a sidelong glance. "I could tell you it's none of your business."

He shrugged. "And you'd be right."

She sighed and sat down on the porch step. "I suppose you'll find out soon enough, once we start going over what happened." He knew without asking she was referring to the events that occurred the day Will died.

"Dad called that morning and wanted to talk to Will. When I told him Will had gone fishing, he said that sounded like a great idea and that he would grab his gear and try to catch up with him."

Logan recalled that the cabin where Johnny lived was only about a mile and a half west of Tyler Ridge. "And?"

She shrugged. "I guess he changed his mind. When Will didn't come back that night, I tried calling my dad. I even sent someone up to his place, but he wasn't there." Her pale brows drew together in a frown. "It didn't take long to track him down, though. One call to the Round-up and the bartender knew right where to find him—third bar stool to the right of center where he'd been most of the day."

Most of his life, Logan added to himself.

"I guess I should have known."

Logan couldn't remember her ever sounding more bitter. "What did Johnny say when you asked him why he hadn't gone after Will?"

She blinked. "What could he say? He chose to spend the day with a bottle, instead of with his son-in-law."

"So he never went up to the ridge?"

"No." She fiddled with a strand of her hair. "I mean, I guess not."

"You didn't ask him?"

He could almost feel her defenses rising, forming an invisible wall between them. "I didn't have to ask." She picked a stem off a nearby bush and studied it as though it held the secrets to the universe. "Anyway, ever since then, I haven't been able to stop thinking that if Dad had been there, if he'd done what he said he was going to do, things might have turned out differently.'' She tossed the twig aside and turned to face him. ''If he'd been there, he might have been able to do something to help Will.''

Logan didn't know how to respond. Sarah had made a valid point, but nothing could change what had ultimately happened.

''I know what you're thinking,'' she said. ''And I know it's unreasonable to still be angry—he is my father, after all. But I just can't seem to get past it.'' She rested her arms on her knees and gazed at the peaks in the distance. ''It's been a wedge between us ever since. That and the fact that he refused to help when we were trying to locate my mother.''

''You said before that Johnny didn't approve of your search.''

She gave a wry laugh. ''That's an understatement. He was against it from the beginning. Adamantly. Pride, you know?''

Yes, Logan knew all about pride. It had been his intimate for longer than he cared to admit. ''I'm sorry, Sarah.'' *For more than you'll ever know.*

A gloomy silence settled between them until Logan decided to pose the question that was nagging him. ''What if Johnny *was* there?''

She looked at him, confused.

''Up on the ridge, I mean. What if he did go after Will?''

''What are you getting at?''

''If Johnny did try to find Will, he might have seen something.''

Logan could see Sarah mulling over the possibility and then rejecting it. ''If my dad had tried to find Will that day, don't you think he would have told me by now?''

Logan leaned over to pet one of the dogs stretched out

at their feet. "Maybe. But if he did go after Will and he couldn't find him…"

"Or if he tried, but gave up, and decided to go back to town for a drink, then he'd blame himself for not trying harder and possibly being there to save Will's life," she mused. "But if he did try to find Will that day, why hasn't he told me? Why has he allowed me go on believing he went straight to the bar?"

"You said it yourself, Sarah. Pride."

She got to her feet and stood staring down at him. "Logan, do you know what that means? If Will did meet with foul play that morning and my dad was somewhere on the ridge at the same time, he could have become the second victim."

Logan's private conjecture went even further, to an even darker theory, but he knew this was not the time to voice it.

Suddenly dispirited, Sarah sank onto the step again. Despite the warm midday air, she shivered.

Without thinking Logan put his arm around her. When she didn't move away, he felt a bud of hope blossom in his heart.

"You shouldn't jump to any conclusions, Sarah. But I'll talk to Johnny. If he did try to find Will that morning, he might be able to provide some answers."

Finally she pulled away from him. "But even if he was there, it's obvious he didn't find Will."

Obvious, Logan thought, only to a daughter who couldn't allow herself to think otherwise. "I guess we'll just have to find out," he said noncommittally. And pity the man who tried to get in the way of the answer. Even if that man was Johnny Allen.

SARAH FLIPPED a switch, and the light hanging from the center of the sloping ceiling blinked on, driving shadows into every corner. The attic air was warm and smelled of old books and mothballs.

Logan walked to the center of the room, the only place he could stand without ducking. He shifted his weight and the beams creaked. "Sorry."

"It's all right," she told him. "Jessica's a sound sleeper and Terri's watching the late show." As she spoke, she pulled the door closed behind her. The realization that they were alone in this snug little room crept over her.

His touch this afternoon on the porch when he'd put his arm around her had provided an anchor for her reeling emotions. She should have pulled away instantly, but she hadn't, and that reaction—or lack of it—had bothered her ever since.

He said he'd changed, and in many ways it seemed he had, but that didn't mean she could allow herself to start depending on him. She dare not need him, she told herself. She couldn't allow it. Hadn't he told her as much himself? *It's who I am,* he'd said during one of the arguments over children. *I'll never be anyone else. I've been honest with you, and now it's time you were honest with yourself. Are you willing to take the risk of loving me?*

"Sarah." His voice jarred her out of the past. "Are you all right?"

She blinked and moved to where he stood beside a stack of sealed cardboard boxes. "Sure. Fine." Her gaze slid over the battered blue recliner in the corner and the stack of magazines and books piled on the small table beside it. Will had spent a lot of time up here, reading and napping. He'd called it his "poor man's study." Toward the end he'd spent too many nights asleep in the chair. Her fault, she supposed, for not responding to his passion the way he'd hoped she would.

Banishing those grim thoughts, she glanced at the mix of items that crowded the small room: a cedar chest that had belonged to Will's mom, Jessica's crib, an old school desk, a hat box tied with white ribbon that had turned gray with age, the dry cleaner's bag that held her wedding dress.

"Over there," she said, pointing to the stack of boxes against the wall behind him. "Watch your head."

Logan reached for the first box as Sarah made her way around the clutter to join him.

When he set the box marked "Will" on the floor between them, the significance of that simple act seemed to momentarily freeze the breath in Sarah's lungs. She'd been dead wrong. They were not alone in the attic. Will's memory was everywhere.

Forcing herself to breathe, Sarah knelt beside the first box and pulled the tape from one corner. Logan waited as she pulled back each flap to reveal a layer of tissue paper.

When she rocked back on her heels, she could feel his eyes searching her face. "You don't have to do this, Sarah," he reminded her.

She shook her head. "It's all right." She felt like the worst kind of fraud. He no doubt assumed she was biting back grief when, in fact, it was her old nemesis, guilt, that plagued her. "Let's get started," she said.

He sat down beside her, but still he made no move to touch the box.

"Please, Logan. Let's just get this over with," she insisted when she realized he was waiting for her to take the first step. "You know if Will were in your place, he'd be doing the same thing."

That seemed to give him the reassurance he needed to go ahead, and as he peeled back the tissue paper, Sarah saw a framed high-school diploma and a stack of yearbooks. Beneath a stack of uniforms and an extra holster, Sarah withdrew a two-sided picture frame that held Will's diploma from the police academy on one side and a group picture of the graduating cadets on the other.

Her gaze slid immediately to the tall dark-haired rookie in the third row. Realizing she'd sought Logan's face before her husband's made her feel like the worst kind of woman.

Oblivious to the guilt churning inside her, Logan looked over her shoulder. "Oh, there he is. See? Third from the left in the front row." His chuckle was dry. "Would you look at that smile?"

When Sarah finally spotted Will, she said softly, "He looks so young."

"He was. We all were. Young, green and itching to make our mark on the unsuspecting world of crime." He laughed softly, but Sarah felt shaken. How many young widows had gazed at that group picture with tears in their eyes? And how many, she speculated miserably, would have sought first the face of another man? A man whose incidental touch sent desire rushing shamelessly to every corner of her heart.

Self-recriminations whirled through her mind as she and Logan continued to examine Will's mementos. Suddenly the idea of rummaging through his possessions with her former lover seemed unspeakably obscene, especially when each time she looked at Logan, she felt the old attraction burning with a bright new flame.

"I can't do this," she said abruptly, and started for the door. "Everything is in those boxes. Turn the light out when you leave."

She didn't turn around, couldn't face him or spend another moment steeped in Will's memories with thoughts of Logan burning in her brain.

She closed the door behind her and stood alone at the

top of the stairs, gasping for the air she suddenly couldn't seem to get enough of.

Oh, Will, her heart cried. *Forgive me. You deserved so much better.*

IT TOOK TWO LONG fitful hours for Sarah to drift finally into an uneasy sleep. Thoughts of Will and the bizarre twist that had brought Logan Spencer back into her life slid in and out of her dreams in distorted images.

She didn't know how long she slept, but when she awoke it was still dark. "Jess?" she called out tentatively. "Honey, is that you?" There was no answer, and as her fingers fumbled with the lamp beside the bed, an edgy disoriented feeling crept over her. She glanced to the spot on her bedside table where the clock radio should have been, but remembered she'd given it to Logan for the trailer.

She sat up in bed and listened a moment to the silence, then decided that whatever had awakened her must have come from within her own troubled mind. Now fully awake but still feeling slightly alarmed, she swung her legs over the edge of the bed, reached for her robe and crossed the hall to check on Jessica. As expected, her daughter was sleeping soundly with the ever-present Pansy close by.

A glow from a light in the kitchen seeped into the hallway, and Sarah felt all the remaining tension slide out of her.

"Terri," she whispered, and realized the noise that had tugged her from sleep had only been Terri's rummaging through the refrigerator for a snack. Terri's appetite had been fickle lately and these middle-of-the-night kitchen raids were becoming almost a ritual. Sarah remembered her own pregnancy, when her craving for peanut butter had become nearly an obsession.

Thinking a glass of milk would help her go back to sleep, Sarah headed to the kitchen to join her restless housemate.

As she rounded the corner, she stopped short. Someone was in the kitchen, all right, but that someone wasn't Terri.

Chapter Eight

When he heard her in the doorway, Logan looked up from the table and smiled. "Good morning."

Sarah glanced at the clock above the sink and was surprised to see it was almost five. "Yes. I guess it is." Feeling self-conscious, she fumbled for the sash to close her robe over the thigh-skimming nightshirt.

"Did I wake you?"

She shook her head and headed for the refrigerator to keep from staring at him. "I don't think so." How had he gotten in? she wondered. She hadn't given him a key, but perhaps Terri had loaned him hers so he would have access to the kitchen and the bathroom until he could repair the broken water pipe in the trailer.

She held up the milk carton. "Want some?"

"No. But I was just about to make coffee. Do you mind?" He pushed back in his chair and stretched the muscles in his back and shoulders straining the seams of the soft denim shirt, the same shirt he'd worn last night, she noticed.

"No, of course not. And now that you mention it, I think that's what I need." She pulled two cups from the cupboard and set them on the counter. "Wait a minute. You've been here all night?"

"Guilty as charged. I spent most of the night in the attic, but I went out to the barn a few minutes ago to check on something. I probably disturbed you when I came in." He moved up beside her and filled the coffeepot with water as she spooned the aromatic grounds into the metal basket. Such a simple task, and yet with their shoulders almost touching, Sarah felt an unexpected physical awakening.

"Does it bother you?" he asked.

"What?"

"That I've been in your house all night."

"No. Should it?" She realized too late how defensive her answer sounded. *Get a grip, Sarah.* If thoughts of him spending an innocent night under her roof rattled her to this extent, how on earth would she manage the rest of the summer? "I mean, no, why should it. Though I have to admit I am surprised it took you all night to finish going through those few things in the attic."

"I didn't think it would, either," he said as he moved back to the table, "until I ran across this."

She put the coffee on the stove and joined him at the table.

He pulled out a chair for her and pointed to the notebook he'd been reading. "Do you know what this is?"

She glanced down at the familiar faded green ledger. "It belonged to Will's mother. It's one of her journals." She went on to explain how Ethel Breedan had been a fastidious record keeper, dating back to the time she and Will's father had owned the ranch. "She kept the books for the ranch, handled all the finances and tracked the markets. Each morning during breakfast, Ethel listened to the farm and ranch report on the radio and meticulously recorded the ups and downs of grain, hay and cattle markets."

Despite Sarah's willingness to learn, Will had been adamantly opposed to her involving herself in any financial aspect of the ranch. After his death she'd been nearly over-whelmed trying to make up for lost ground. There had been so much to learn, and with the life of the ranch depending on her, she'd had to catch on fast. But even now there were still unpleasant surprises, such as the lien on the property she hadn't known existed until she'd tried to refinance last fall. Little by little she was coming to the realization that Will had kept things from her. It worried her, but at the same time, she felt guilty resenting him.

"This one is different," Logan said. "Take a look."

When she opened the journal and skimmed the first page, it wasn't Ethel's, but Will's familiar scrawl she recognized on every line.

"I didn't know Will had inherited his mother's penchant for record keeping." Although, now that she thought about it, she did remember seeing Will once with a notebook like this one. He'd taken it with him to his office in town, and she also remembered idly wondering why.

"Where did you find this, Logan?"

"Upstairs. After I finished going through the boxes, I noticed a stack of magazines and papers near that recliner in the corner. When I sat down to take a closer look, I found this. Apparently it had slipped beneath the cush-ions."

He told her what she already knew, that there were more journals like this one on a shelf beside the door arranged by date, printed on the spine.

He turned it over to show her the spine. "This one has only a start date—May 1982."

"That's strange," she said. "Ethel and Ralph were living here then. Why do you suppose Will kept this account?" She thought a moment. "1982... Wasn't that the year Will's dad broke his back?"

Logan nodded. "I think you're right. I remember the accident happened in the spring."

Sarah shook her head. "I don't remember that exactly, but I do remember my dad helping out with the chores until Ralph could walk again."

"My family helped out, too," he said. "In fact, I stayed here with Will for a couple of weeks, and later he spent a lot of time at our house. I remember. Will's mom and dad rented an apartment in Denver so Ralph could undergo therapy."

Now Sarah remembered more clearly. "My dad worked for them part-time that year." She also remembered that the Spencers—Cole, Drew, Logan and their father—had harvested the Breedans' hay that season.

"So that explains why Ethel didn't complete this particular journal. She and Ralph weren't here." She thought back to that summer. More than a few times she'd accompanied her father to the Breedan ranch and found herself walking on air every time one of the handsome Spencer boys spoke to her. Especially the eldest Spencer, the tall darkly handsome supremely confident Logan.

"I remember you and your brothers helping Will with the horses."

His expression grew almost wistful. "I remember you, too. Remember the Fourth of July picnic?"

Her breath hitched at the memory, and she found herself unable to break eye contact with him. "The annual Spencer barbecue," she said. "The biggest bash of the summer." She felt a nostalgic glow. She could almost taste the warm night air and smell the fireworks. "The food, the music and the fireworks." *Our first kiss.* "How could I forget?"

The knowing glimmer in his eyes told her he remembered, too.

Without warning he leaned forward and gently cupped

her chin. At his touch the nostalgic glow burst into a flame of pure physical awareness.

His eyes mesmerized her, and when he stroked her cheek with his thumb, she almost moaned with pleasure. She saw his face move over hers, and when her eyelids closed, it seemed as natural as breathing. When his lips touched hers, she felt a rush of golden memories, and for a moment she lost herself in their familiar sweetness. Forgetting everything but the way it felt to be loved by this wonderfully strong maddeningly complex man, she reveled in his kiss.

Her heart swelled with longing for him, long-denied desire she'd never truly forsaken.

The sound of coffee sputtering out of the spout and spilling onto the burner roused Sarah from the sweet oblivion of his kiss.

"Th-the coffee," she stammered, pulling away from him, but when she started to get up, he put a hand on her shoulder.

"I'll get it." The passion in his eyes revealed his own intense reaction to what they'd just shared.

Say something, her common sense urged. *Stop this now before it happens again. You don't want his touch, Sarah. You don't need his kisses. This is madness!*

But even if she had been able to find her voice, what could she have told him? That his touch still moved her like no other man's ever had? That despite everything she still loved him and—damn it all—probably always would?

Flustered and suddenly self-conscious, she ran a hand over her hair and straightened her robe, then sat up straighter and tried not to look at him when he returned with the coffee and sat down.

"Should I apologize?" he asked.

She shook her head. "No. We're both to blame."

He tucked a strand of hair behind her ear and she shivered. "You talk as if we did something wrong."

"We did," she said, fighting the quiver in her voice. "And it can't happen again."

He gazed at her intently. "You're no longer a married woman, Sarah. Will's been gone over a year. You have no reason to feel guilty."

If you only knew. "This has nothing to do with guilt," she lied. "Now, can we please…just get back to the ledger?"

He studied her for a moment before he said, "Sure. Whatever you want."

His demeanor turned cool before her eyes, and she couldn't help wondering how he managed to turn his emotions off and on so easily. Obviously their kiss had held no more meaning to him now than that first stolen kiss so many long summer nights ago. She couldn't decide who she was more angry with—herself or him.

In a steady voice she could only envy, he asked, "So, what do you make of Will's notes?"

She took a deep breath. All right, if he could make the emotional transition with such apparent ease, then so could she—or at least she could try. "I don't know," she began, "except that it would seem Will took over where his mother left off in her record keeping that spring."

His eyes seemed even darker than usual, his gaze even more inscrutable. She felt like screaming. How could she have forgotten how quickly the man could seal off his emotions? Lover one minute, cop the next. His work, his investigations, came first, always taking precedent over his personal life. And this investigation was no different. She should thank him for the reminder, she thought bitterly.

"But there is something I don't understand," she said,

forcing her voice to reflect an inner calm she did not at the moment possess.

"What's that?"

"Well, now that I'm responsible for the running of this ranch, I'm the one listening to those farm and ranch reports, and believe me, I know how deadly dull they can be." *Keep talking,* she told herself. *You're doing fine. You can get through this and then you'll never let it happen again.* "I find it hard to believe you were able to stay awake past the first page, much less sit up all night reading more."

He opened the ledger and slid it toward her. "I think you'd better take a closer look, Sarah. These entries have nothing to do with the price of hay or beef."

She picked up the journal and forced herself to concentrate on what Will had written. After a moment she rocked back in her chair. "I don't understand. This is all about my mother!"

He nodded. "As far as I can tell, it's a complete record of Will's attempt to find her."

Her mouth went dry. "But I didn't know...that is, I had no idea Will had launched such a widespread search."

Logan set down his cup and leaned back in his chair. "You said he considered the attic his study, right?"

She nodded.

"I figure he must have gone up there when he wanted to think through his investigations. At some point he must have just grabbed this book and started making notes."

Sarah had a picture of Will sitting alone in the attic thinking about all those false leads, trying to come up with some new thread that would lead him to the mysterious Daisy Allen.

"Los Angeles, Denver, Tucson," Logan read aloud. "Did you know he'd checked sources in all these places?"

Again she could only nod. All those places and people.

All for nothing. "But I didn't know he'd kept a record," she said softly.

"I'm not surprised. Will was a good cop, and a good investigator lives by his notes. You never know what piece of information might complete the picture." He thumbed through a couple of pages. "I want you to look at this page, Sarah."

If the notes on that page had anything to do with finding her mother, Sarah couldn't have said how. *Albuquerque, Santa Fe, Ruidoso.* "I don't know anything about these places," she said. But it appeared that Will had eliminated the towns in New Mexico with a single line drawn through each name and phone number, just as he'd done on the preceding pages.

Baffled, Sarah could only sit staring at the list, wondering why Will hadn't told her he was still searching.

"Take a closer look, Sarah. Look at the dates."

She shifted in her chair to get a better look and was surprised to see that, according to his notes, Will had been tracing her mother right up to the last week of his life.

"I thought you said you'd given up trying to find her."

"I thought we had." She rubbed her forehead. Why did she feel betrayed? Will had been doing this for her. But why hadn't he told her?

"Two years ago Will insisted I give up any hope of ever finding my mother," she told Logan. "He said we'd done everything we could, exhausted every lead. He said time was money, and he couldn't justify using any more of the county's resources on a case that had no chance of ever being brought to a successful conclusion."

Although disappointed, Sarah had finally agreed to let the matter drop, all the while wondering if they'd stopped too soon. Nothing could explain why Will hadn't told her about his ledger full of notes, or why he'd kept his continuing investigation a secret. "I don't understand," she said almost to herself.

"Maybe he was trying to protect you." Logan brought the coffeepot to the table and refilled their cups. She thanked him without looking up. "Did you see that bit where Will contacted Orrin Fraizer last year when he was in Denver?"

Sarah skimmed the page, found Orrin's name and the notation that indicated a two-hour appointment. She recalled Will's trip to Denver the week before his death. "I can't imagine that Orrin would have been involved in any way with Will's investigation. Maybe it was merely a social call." As she gave it more thought, it didn't seem unusual for Will to drop in on Orrin. They'd been friends for a long time, and she told Logan as much.

She could tell by the look on his face he wasn't totally convinced. "According to his notes, Will went to Orrin's office at the state capital."

"Yes. But it's possible they only met there. Maybe it was nothing more than a lunch date."

"And what about you?"

"Me?"

"Do you see Congressman Fraizer socially?" It sounded strangely like an accusation.

"No—not that it's any of your business."

He gave her a humorless smile. "You're right. It isn't."

"I admire Orrin," she admitted. "He's accomplished a great deal in his life." Earl Fraizer's only son had served the district well. "Orrin is a good man. A friend," she said emphatically, although at times she'd felt slightly overwhelmed by Orrin's friendship, especially during the days between Will's death and his funeral, when Orrin had made a point of calling every day and making special trips to the ranch for seemingly no reason.

The fact that Orrin had lost his own wife three years earlier had given Sarah the perspective she'd needed to accept his sympathy graciously.

Aside from losing a spouse, however, there were no similarities in their circumstances, Sarah thought guiltily. Unlike her own marriage of convenience, Helen and Orrin's marriage had been a good one. Their nearly twenty-year union had been solid, built on trust and mutual respect. Losing Helen after her long and courageous struggle with cancer had nearly destroyed Orrin.

When Will died, Sarah felt the loss of her husband deeply. Will had been a good man, a devoted father and a good friend. She'd respected her husband and grieved his passing. *But not in the way I grieved the end of my relationship with Logan,* she thought. The realization had come out of nowhere, but it struck with a shattering note of truth.

"Okay, so Orrin is an old friend—" Logan said, interrupting Sarah's troubled introspection.

"Forty-nine is hardly ancient," she retorted.

"But he's still old enough to be—"

"An older brother," she finished for him.

His smile was irritatingly indulgent. "All right. So did your not-so-old friend ever talk to you about his meeting with Will?"

"No."

"Don't you find that a little strange now? After all, he saw Will just days before his death."

"I guess he didn't think to mention it. There was so much else going on." She anticipated Logan's next question. "Orrin helped untangle a problem with Will's insurance. He offered his help."

To her relief Logan seemed to have exhausted—at least momentarily—his questions concerning Orrin Fraizer. There were other names besides Orrin's listed in Will's notebook, and Logan read off a few. "Do you know these people?" he asked her.

She shook her head.

When he picked up the notebook again, Sarah studied his face, noting how his features reflected the inner man: strong, well-defined, rugged, yet something around his eyes and mouth hinting at an inner gentleness. Like the man, his face was a study in contrasts. Once again she found herself glad to have him on her side.

"Here's a name you'll recognize," he said, looking up. "Nick Gallus."

"Nick? What could Nick know about my mother? Maybe these notes aren't restricted to my mother's disappearance, after all."

"It shouldn't be hard to find out," he said, and turned his attention back to Will's notes.

At last he looked up from the page again. "Did you notice that Will's last entry was made the day before he died?"

She leaned over to check the date for herself and the notation made in black ink beside it in the margin: D. A. The initials could only stand for one thing—Daisy Allen.

When their gazes met again, the compassion in his eyes touched her. *Don't do that,* she thought. *Don't make me believe you still care, that I can lean on you, that you'll be there if I fall.*

"Well, I think we have our answer, Sarah. The case Will was actively pursuing until the day he died was the case of missing person Daisy Allen."

A sickening realization crept over her, making her heartsick. If Logan was right, that meant Will might have given his life trying to find her mother.

"But we don't know for sure that Will was murdered," she pointed out, clinging to the possibility. "We have no proof. So far all we have is the dubious suggestion of some faceless nameless voice on the other end of a telephone line.''

"We have more than that, Sarah," he said, then reached into his shirt pocket and handed her a photograph. "We have this."

She stared, disbelieving, at the picture of her mother. "Where did you get that?" It was the same picture she'd tucked into her dresser drawer mere hours ago.

"It was in Will's fishing creel."

"His what?"

"Remember I told you I'd gone out to the barn just before you came in?"

She nodded.

"The fact that Will's wallet had never been found really bothered me. Like women with their purses, men don't usually go anywhere without their wallets. Then I remembered you said Jax came back to the house that day still saddled. I had a hunch that in all the confusion no one thought to check Will's fishing gear. I assumed he'd tied his fishing creel to the saddle. When I checked it, I found the picture and this. He handed her a crumpled envelope.

His somber expression sent an ominous message, and even as Sarah accepted the tattered piece of paper, she felt as if the proverbial second shoe was about to drop.

Chapter Nine

Her heart and her hands trembled as she read the words scribbled on the back of the envelope. Incredulous, she read them again.

I know where to find Daisy Allen. Meet me tomorrow.
Tyler Ridge at dawn.
Come alone.

"What does this mean?" she whispered even as the inescapable conclusion slammed into her brain: Will had gone up to Tyler Ridge to find her mother and lost his life.

Sarah rose quickly and walked to the window, determined not to let Logan see her cry. Beyond the glass the first rays of a cloudless morning bathed the jagged peaks in the distance with a pale gold light.

Unfortunately not even the beauty of the mountains or the promise of a new day could soothe her troubled heart.

When she felt him moving up beside her, she didn't turn around. The urge to throw herself into his arms was too strong. Fighting the impulse that would be her undoing, she gripped the counter with both hands and continued to concentrate on the glistening view of the peaks in the distance.

"I'm sorry, Sarah," he said quietly.

She nodded and swallowed the lump in her throat. "What now?" she asked, still not daring to look at him.

"I'll do some backtracking through Will's notes, talk to the people he contacted. Eventually I'll ride up to Tyler Ridge myself."

The idea startled her, and she spun around to face him. "But why? What do you hope to accomplish by going up there?" Her rational mind told her there was nothing to fear, but her heart convulsed at the thought of something happening to him. "You said you'd found what you were looking for," she reminded him even as she headed for the phone on the wall across the room. "Now it's time to turn everything over to the proper authorities. I'll call Glenn Driscoll now," she said. "When he gets here, we'll explain all of this together."

Somehow he beat her across the room. "No, Sarah." He insinuated himself between her and the telephone. "We can't call Glenn yet."

"What are you talking about? Of course we can. That note makes it clear that someone lured Will to the ridge the morning he died." She tried to reach around him for the phone, but he stood fast.

"Get out of my way, Logan." She tried to push past him, but he captured her wrist and held it.

"Let me go!" She shoved him hard, but failed to move him even an inch.

"Sarah, listen to me. Calm down."

"I am calm," she lied, and jerked her hand out of his grasp.

He took a deep breath and she knew he was fighting for patience. "We can't call Glenn. Not until we know what we're dealing with."

To Sarah it was all too clear. "We know your anony-mous tipster is right. Will's death was no accident. Isn't that what you wanted to know? It's obvious someone set him up.'' The words seemed to drain the reserves of her inner strength. ''Murder,'' she whispered. ''That's what we're dealing with.''

Tears threatened again, and she swiped at her eyes with the back of her hand and fought to compose herself. ''And that's a matter for the police. They have to find whoever is responsible and punish him for what he did to Will.''

''You're right,'' he said. ''And I promise you I'll do everything to see that it happens. But on their own, the note and the photograph of your mother don't prove anything. It's merely the first step. We have a lot more work to do before we can bring Glenn Driscoll the evidence that would justify the kind of investigation I plan to begin immediately.'' His eyes begged her to understand. ''Sarah, you were a cop's wife. You know how the system works.''

Despite the fact that she wanted desperately to turn the whole matter over to the sheriff's department, she had to admit he was probably right. When viewed objectively, a note and an old photograph were not enough to reopen an investigation that had been officially closed.

The system had decreed Will's death an accident, and the men who made the system work would require rock-solid evidence before they'd admit they'd made a mistake—especially with regard to one of their own. Much as she hated thinking in those terms, she knew the situation was wrought with political implications, as well.

Glenn had been appointed as the interim replacement for Will's position, but in the fall, he was planning to win the sheriff's office in his own right. Having to admit that the department, under his leadership, had bungled the case of his boss's death wouldn't be a good start to his first political campaign.

"Couldn't we approach Glen unofficially?" she asked. "At least let him know what we've found?"

Logan answered her question with a question. "When it comes to murder, how can any cop be less than official?"

Of course he was right, and when she told him so, gratitude flickered across his face and he sighed.

"The minute we turn this over to the authorities, my hands will be tied. Glenn won't allow my involvement, Sarah. I think you know that. And now, more than ever, I have to be able to proceed in my own way, on my own.

On his own, she thought, turning the familiar phrase over in her mind. That much, at least, had not changed. Alone was how he'd always operated best.

"Besides," he went on, "if we've learned anything from Will's notes, it's that he took pains to keep this investigation secret. He must have had a good reason."

"Are you saying he didn't trust Glenn?"

"I have no way of knowing that yet. There could be other explanations." He walked to the table and picked up the envelope. "But any cop worth his salt would have seen a setup the minute he read this note. Don't you think it strange that Will didn't ask Glenn to back him up that morning?"

"But it said for him to come alone."

He shook his head. "Not good enough. Not for a professional." He folded the note and slipped it inside the cover of Will's journal. "No, there's more to it than that. A lot more. Something else is missing, and until we find out what it is, I'm not taking any chances. This whole thing could blow up in our faces if the wrong person knows we suspect foul play."

She remembered what he'd said about the potential danger from the anonymous caller. Now it seemed he suspected everyone. "You sound as if you believe Glenn might have had something to do with Will's death."

"Think a minute," he said, crossing to her. "Consider what we know. Whoever wrote that note knew Will was still trying to locate Daisy. The note was the bait they knew without a doubt Will couldn't resist."

Everything he said made sense, but she still couldn't make herself believe Glenn Driscoll could have done anything to hurt Will. Glenn and Roberta had been frequent visitors to the Breedan ranch. Their kids had ridden her horses and played tag in the yard with Jessica.

Feeling frustrated, she ran a hand through her hair. "Glenn couldn't possibly be involved. I trust him."

"That's good. Eventually we'll have to go to the authorities and it might as well be Glenn."

"But until that time you're bent on handling this alone? Do you really think that's wise? For all we know, the man calling you is the one who wrote the note. You said yourself that note was an invitation to an ambush. So, what about the meeting you plan to set up with him? Isn't that exactly what Will did?" The skin on the back of her neck tingled as she considered the very real potential for danger.

"But I won't be working alone," he said. "In fact, I plan to send a copy of Will's notes to Cole and Drew. They'll be able to run a check on every name. Who knows, with my brothers' help we might be able to identify our anonymous caller before the meeting. In the meantime I want to ride up to Tyler Ridge. I'll need a good trail horse."

She told him finding a suitable mount would not be a problem, but a chill raced along her spine at the thought of something happening to Logan up on that ridge. She reassured herself by remembering that Will had been lured to Tyler Ridge. Logan was going on his own terms. He would not be ambushed. He would have his eyes wide open for danger. But still, her uneasiness refused to go away. There was no use telling herself she didn't still care. She did. The man had never been farther than a few thoughts away.

"You shouldn't go up there alone," she said. "My dad could ride with you."

His expression softened. "I'll be fine, Sarah."

"On second thought, why don't I go with you?"

"No." He shook his head. "Out of the question."

Sarah opened her mouth to remind him that she sat a horse as well or better than any man, and that if it was too dangerous for her, it was too dangerous for him.

But before she could pose her arguments, the sound of a vehicle pulling up to the house interrupted her.

She glanced at the clock and remembered the hay that was supposed to be baled this morning. "That's either my dad or Nick and Riley. I've got to go get dressed."

"I'll go out and meet them," Logan said, and headed for the door.

"We need copies of Will's journal," he said from the door. "Can you take care of that?"

She nodded.

"Good. I want to overnight them to Drew and Cole. Oh, and, Sarah—it will all work out. I promise. Don't worry." He was halfway out the door, when her entreaty called him back. "Yes?"

"It's just...I know it isn't much in light of what you're trying to do, but, well, thank you," she said softly.

His gaze reached out to her across the room and held her. "Don't thank me, Sarah," he said in a voice unexpectedly gruff. "It's the least I can do."

A moment later he was gone, and Sarah could only stand staring after him.

AFTER SHE'D DRESSED and returned to the kitchen to fix Jessica's breakfast, Sarah prepared a basket of sandwiches and a thermos of iced tea to take to the men working in the hay field.

"Cereal, bananas, apples," Terri called out as she worked on a grocery list at the table. "How about Logan?"

Sarah had been only half listening, but at the mention of his name, her head shot up. "What about him?"

"Groceries. Do you think we ought to see if he needs anything?"

Knowing all he had to think about today, Sarah told Terri just to pick up whatever she thought he might need, then she tightened the lid on the thermos and headed for the door. "I'm going to run this food over to the guys. Could you take Jessica with you to town?"

Terri said she'd be glad to have the company, but Jessica, who normally would have jumped at the chance to go shopping, balked. "No! I want to go with you, Mommy! I want to see Grandpa and Logan."

"Not today, honey." She tried to force a lightness into her voice that belied her inner turmoil. If Logan had had this much impact on the child after only a couple of days, how much deeper would Jessica's attachment be by the end of the summer?

"Seems your Mr. Spencer has made quite an impression on the ladies in this house," Terri teased.

Sarah spun around to confront her. "He's not *my* anything."

Both Terri and Jessica gaped at her.

"Sorry, Sarah," Terri said sheepishly. "I heard voices in the kitchen this morning and I thought, that is... Gosh, I didn't mean anything. I was just kidding, you know?"

One look at the young woman's hurt expression, and Sarah immediately regretted her outburst. She crossed to Terri and laid a hand on her shoulder. "I'm the one who should apologize, Terri. I'm sorry. I shouldn't have snapped at you. I didn't sleep very well last night, and I guess I'm just…feeling a little edgy this morning."

"No problem," Terri said. "I know I haven't exactly been a joy to be around lately, either."

"You're fine," Sarah assured her. During her own pregnancy she'd been emotional and ridiculously weepy. Remembering Will's seemingly endless patience made her feel even more ashamed of the way she'd barked at Terri.

"Jessica, I want you to go with Terri this morning, and when you get back, we'll saddle Sugarfoot. All right, honey?" She bent to kiss her daughter's cheek before heading for the door.

"But I want to go with you, Mommy. I want to see Logan and Grandpa," she insisted.

"Grandpa will be here when you get back," Sarah said, then gathered the food and the thermos and walked out the door.

THE FOUR MEN WORKING in the hay field all turned at the sound of Sarah's pickup. When she pulled to a stop and climbed out of the cab, Logan took in her puzzled expression. She'd noticed the bailing equipment sitting idly on the road at the side of the field.

As she approached, Nick and Riley set their shovels aside.

"She isn't going to be happy about this," Nick said.

"You can say that again," Johnny muttered.

Logan left the men to meet her, his boots sinking into the soupy mud with each step.

"Logan? What's happened here? Where did all this water come from?"

He hated having to tell her. "One of the main shutoff valves on your irrigation system broke. I can't tell when it happened, but by the amount of water in these fields, I'd say it ran all night."

She set the thermos and basket down and stared at first one side of the field and then the other. "But that's impossible! Valves don't just break!"

She was right. Cast steel was built to last. The only other time Logan had seen a valve ruined so completely was when a hired hand had accidentally backed over it with a tractor.

"I don't know what happened," he said. But he had some ideas, none of which he was willing to discuss in front of the other men. "I located the main shutoff valve as soon as we arrived."

But the damage had already been done. The water had been allowed to flow unchecked into the fields for no telling how long, and three hundred acres of prime alfalfa hay, which had been cut six days earlier and lay waiting in neatly raked rows to be baled, had been saturated, making it unfit to bale.

"I should have found a way to get it baled sooner," she declared miserably.

"It's not your fault, Sarah. No one could have predicted this. Besides, Nick said he couldn't have come any sooner."

She took a deep breath. "How bad is it?"

"Hard to say. It might not be a total loss." His optimism was for her sake. "We dug trenches to divert the runoff. Now all we can do is pray the weather holds. If it stays warm and dry, we'll turn the hay at the end of the week and let the other side dry." With luck the harvest would not be a complete loss, unless the moisture had done too much damage and mold was already setting in—which it certainly would if they tried to bale it now.

"What about the field on the other side of the irrigation line?"

"It looks the same. Completely flooded. It'll take several days of hot sunny weather to dry." And even if the weather did hold, the bales from both fields would be less than top-quality hay.

With the quiet dignity he'd always admired, she tipped her chin and started off through the mud. "I want to see that valve."

Logan led the way, and Johnny, Nick and Riley fell in behind them.

"Damn shame," Johnny said.

"Yeah," she muttered without breaking stride. "A shame."

As they walked, Nick and Riley added their condolences for the ruined crop.

"These trenches should help some," Riley, a large red-faced man, said. "Not much else to do now but wait."

"Thanks, guys," Sarah said. "I'll call you when I think we can try again."

Grim-faced, Riley nodded and started for the road, where his white pickup was parked.

"Nick, will your equipment be available in a week or so?"

Nick nodded. "Just say the word, Sarah, and I'll bring everything back over. And I'd be happy to fix that valve for you," he added. "I've got the tools in my truck."

Logan cut in before Sarah could respond. "That won't be necessary."

Nick's blue eyes shifted to Sarah's for confirmation.

"Thanks, Nick," she said. "I appreciate the offer, but it looks like we can take it from here."

"Whatever you say," he muttered, yet he still hung back. "You might want to check the pressure tolerance on that valve," he said. "Could be you need to replace it with something stronger. I could check out your whole system if you'd like."

Again Logan intervened. "The system's fine," he said, feeling suddenly churlish. "I checked everything yesterday."

Nick's eyes narrowed. "I see. Yesterday. Well." He turned to Sarah, and she thanked him again for his help and his advice.

It was decent of Nick to offer his help, Logan thought, but it was his motives that bothered him. Any fool could see the man had trouble keeping his eyes off Sarah—and who could blame him? But what bothered Logan was not knowing whether or not Sarah was similarly attracted to the tall blond rancher.

"Well, I guess I'll head out, then," Nick said. "But, Sarah, if you need anything at all, just call me, okay?" When he gave her shoulder a reassuring squeeze, Logan ground his teeth. When Sarah returned Nick's smile, a jolt of raw jealousy shot through Logan's veins like lightning.

"Thanks, Nick," she said. "I'll be sure to check the specs on the replacement valve."

"I'll swing by in a few days to see if the hay has dried out enough to turn. Take care of yourself, Sarah," he said. "See you around, Spencer." With that he strode off.

Logan muttered a curt goodbye as he picked up the ruined valve and handed it to Sarah. More than anything he wished he could do something to dispel the worry that clouded her eyes.

"What on earth could have caused this?" she asked, staring at the heavy metal valve in her hand.

Logan glanced at Johnny, but the older man only shrugged.

"That valve is made to handle twice the pressure your

system demands," Logan said, negating Nick's earlier suggestion. "There's nothing wrong with your system, Sarah."

"Look at that," Johnny said, pointing to the jagged metal where the valve had broken from its stem. "Looks like it took a hefty hit. Like someone just reared back and teed off on the thing!"

With a damn big hammer, Logan thought, but kept his opinion to himself.

The three of them walked solemnly to the road. When they reached it, Johnny said goodbye and moved toward his pickup with his shoulders hunched. As he opened the door to step inside, he seemed to remember something and walked back to where Sarah and Logan stood looking out at the flooded hay fields.

"I'll be bringing Jax back tomorrow morning," he said. "The vet said his leg should heal just fine."

"Did he say what caused the swelling?" Sarah asked.

"Aw, not really. When I talked to him last night, he said the leg was already looking better."

"Thanks, Dad. I'm glad it wasn't anything serious."

When Johnny left Sarah turned to Logan. "All right, tell me what you're thinking. I know you have some ideas about what happened to that valve. What I don't know is why you're not telling me."

"You're right," he admitted. "I do have some ideas, but I didn't want to talk about them out in front of the others."

"Well, there's no one here now. Spill it, Logan. What are you thinking?" She leaned back against the fender of her truck and crossed her arms, waiting for his reply.

Logan took a deep breath, wishing he could come up with any other explanation. "It looks to me like someone broke that valve intentionally."

She didn't even blink.

"You're not surprised that I suspect foul play?" he asked.

"No. I'm just...angry!" She blew out an exasperated breath. "And confused."

"I'm sorry, Sarah," he said, needing desperately to comfort her.

"What I can't figure out is why anyone would do something like this to me." She turned her back on the ruined fields to stare at the peaks in the distance. "Will and I— we never hurt anyone. Why is this happening? Why would someone want to hurt him? Or me?" Her voice broke, and when she turned around to face him, he could see she was fighting to maintain her composure. "What's the answer, Logan?"

He couldn't stop himself from reaching for her. When he pulled her into his arms and she didn't resist, he felt his heart leap. "Oh, Sarah," he murmured against her hair, "I only wish I could do something to make it all go away."

He held her for a long quiet moment, nestled against his chest. Her hair smelled like sunshine and her body felt warm and welcome against his. Holding her felt right, as if a part of him that had been missing had been returned to him at last.

When she finally eased out of his arms, she said, "Seems all I've done for the past forty-eight hours is thank you, and here I am ready to thank you again." She offered him a weak smile.

"There's no need for thanks. I said I wanted to be here for you, and I'm just glad you're allowing me to help."

She gazed past him at the ruined fields.

"It'll be all right," he said gently, laying a hand on her shoulder. "I promise. Somehow, some way, it will all work out."

And when she turned and looked into his eyes, he knew that she wanted to believe him.

Chapter Ten

After Sarah left, Logan walked the length of the irrigation ditch, checking and rechecking every connection and valve, before driving into town to buy a replacement for the ruined valve. On his way, he decided it was time to confront Nick Gallus.

He hadn't wanted to question Nick in front of Johnny and Riley Meadows, but now more than ever he needed to know why Nick's name had been listed in Will's notes.

Remembering that Sarah had told him Nick had recently made an arrangement to purchase a thousand acres of the old Bailey ranch from Earl Fraizer, Logan pulled onto the highway and headed east.

Fifteen minutes later he steered his truck onto the half mile of paved road that led to Nick Gallus's place. When he pulled into the yard, Logan was surprised to see that the Baileys' old ranch house had been completely remodeled. It now looked almost stately. Apparently Nick's cattle venture was doing well, Logan thought, noting the well-manicured lawn and the newly constructed three-car garage north of the house.

When he knocked on the front door, no one answered. Thinking perhaps Nick was working, Logan made his way around the house and made a quick check of both barns, but saw no sign of Nick. On his way back to his pickup, he ran into one of Nick's hired hands, who told him Nick usually had his lunch in town.

"Might catch him at Earl's place," he suggested.

After thanking the man for the information, Logan left and five minutes later, he was back on the highway, headed for the Round-up and what he hoped would be an informative conversation with Nick Gallus.

A DOZEN PICKUPS were parked in front of the bar, but when Logan realized Nick's wasn't among them, he decided to go in anyway, to see if he could ferret out some bit of information about the fight that had taken place here the night before Will's death.

With his eyes still adjusting to the dimly lit interior Logan let the heavy wooden door close behind him, then moved to the nearest booth and sat down.

Over the heads of the men hunkered over their drinks at the bar, a haze of blue-gray smoke mingled with the scent of Tex-Mex and beer. The sounds of a pool game and good-natured ribbing drifted from the alcove in the back, while a familiar country voice coming from the jukebox promised to keep his love "One Step Ahead of the Storm."

He'd barely settled onto the black vinyl booth when Gaylene Fraizer spotted him. Wearing a pair of tight blue jeans and a Western-cut shirt, she smiled warmly as she made her way around the end of the bar and approached his table.

Gaylene was a small birdlike woman, as animated and effusive as her husband, Earl, was large and lumbering. Her hands fluttered when she spoke. "Well, if it isn't my favorite Spencer! Hey, there, Logan—I heard you'd come back to the valley." She stood with her hands on her slim hips, a feigned pout pulling down the corners of her scarlet mouth. "Now, what I want to know is, how come it took you so long to come by to see me?"

"You know how it goes, Gaylene," he drawled. "Never enough hours."

She rolled her eyes and batted her lashes. Although heading down the long side of sixty, Earl's wife could still flirt with the best of them. "Don't I know it! This place keeps me so busy, I hardly know what day it is." The lighted beer signs behind the bar glinted a garish red off her dyed black hair. "Chili *relleños* on special today, with a side of rice and beans. What'll it be, Logan? Are you eating or drinking your lunch today?"

He declined the *relleños* and ordered a beer, and when she brought it, he asked her if Earl was around.

"Won't be in till tonight," she told him, and set a basket of tortilla chips and salsa beside his beer. "I handle the day shift on my own now that he's decided to play rancher."

"I heard he'd bought some land," Logan said before he took a long swallow of his beer.

"Yeah. He's even talking about building a house and moving out to the country."

Logan pictured the small frame house behind the bar where the Fraizers had lived for as long as he could remember.

"You wouldn't know him, Logan. He's gone and got all respectable on me!" Her green eyes narrowed. "All that shoulder rubbing and glad handing might be all right for Orrin, but not for me. Like I always tell Earl, that house and this bar was good enough for my folks, and it's good enough for me. Why, I raised a congressman in that house, didn't I? And he didn't turn out too bad now, did he? Besides, can you imagine me stuck out in the middle of nowhere, up every morning with the chickens?"

Logan couldn't help chuckling. "No, ma'am, that I cannot imagine."

"Me, neither. But don't worry, I won't let him get away with it. I just tell him if I go, this place goes under, and he'll change his tune."

"Business is good, then?"

"Never better," she replied proudly. "We've got live music six nights a week now, and it's bringing in a younger crowd. Lots of rhinestone cowboys moving in. You know the type, just give 'em five acres and a horse in the back-yard and they think they're John Wayne." Her eyes twinkled mischievously. "Some of the old-timers get kind of ornery about all the new blood, but I say let 'em come. As long as their money's green."

"Does this new crowd cause you much trouble?" He was angling the conversation toward the fight that had taken place a year ago, but he knew he had to move carefully. Gaylene Fraizer could play the part of the good-natured redneck barmaid to the hilt, but she was nobody's fool.

"They're a good bunch mostly. They just like to get a little tight, sometimes. Lots of pretty girls coming in." She smiled knowingly and winked at him. "You ought to come by some night, check out the neighborhood."

He feigned surprise. "Are you telling me the Round-up has turned into a singles bar?"

She laughed. "Is that what they're calling it these days? All I know is there's romance in the air come closing time on a Saturday night. Nothing new about that, though some folks would rather I didn't notice."

He shook his head and said he guessed times really hadn't changed all that much. "I suppose you and Earl must know just about everyone who's ever lived in this valley."

"I reckon," she said absently. "Although there are some I'd just as soon forget."

"Like Daisy Allen?"

She blinked. The mention of Daisy's name had obviously caught her off guard. "Daisy Allen?"

"Yes. Did you know her?"

"Yeah," she admitted with some reluctance. "I knew her. So?"

He shrugged. "Just curious."

When a red-haired waitress passed by balancing two platters of burritos and a tray of drinks, Gaylene turned to her. "Watch the bar for a few minutes, will you, honey?"

When the waitress moved out of earshot, Gaylene slid into the other side of the booth and said, "Daisy Allen is a name I haven't heard mentioned in some time. What's this all about, Logan?"

He took a drink of his beer before he replied, "Like I said, I'm curious."

"Sarah isn't still trying to find her mother, is she?" Gaylene leaned across the table and her voice dropped a notch. "'Cause if she is, someone ought to discourage her."

Logan's instincts went on red alert, but he remained casually sprawled in his seat, sipping his beer. "Oh? Why's that?"

When Gaylene's eyes narrowed, she looked every minute of her sixty-plus years. "Because Daisy Allen is nothing but trouble. Always was, always will be. Best thing she ever did for that child was leave."

"You act as if you have a personal ax to grind with the lady."

Gaylene snorted and sat up straight. "Believe me, that woman was *no* lady."

Logan accepted her assessment of Daisy's character without comment.

"Say, you wouldn't be working for your brothers, would you?"

He shook his head. "It's a purely personal interest at this point."

She seemed unconvinced.

"Do you know what happened to Daisy after she left the valley?"

Her reply came back a quick, almost angry, "No."

"Any guesses?"

"Look, Logan, I don't know what this is all about, but I'm going to tell you what I told Will Breedan when he asked me the same question. I don't know anything about that woman. Nothing. Understand?" She stood abruptly and looked down at Logan with hard determined eyes, all pretense of good humor gone. "Now, if you'll excuse me, I have to get back to work. Lunchtime, you know?"

Before she could walk away, he pressed her for one more answer. "Nick Gallus been here today?"

She stopped and turned around to face him, not even bothering to hide the suspicion flickering in her eyes. "No. Is he supposed to be?"

"That's what I heard. If you see him, would you tell him I need to talk to him?"

She gave him an uncertain nod. "Sure." Then she bustled back to the bar.

Five minutes later Logan laid two dollars on the table and walked out—just in time to see Nick Gallus's pickup pulling away from behind the building.

Logan ran to his pickup and was behind the wheel in a heartbeat. Jamming the engine into reverse, he glanced in the rearview mirror and slammed on the brakes to avoid the truck that had pulled up without warning behind him seemingly out of nowhere.

Muttering a curse under his breath, he glared in the rearview mirror as he watched Riley Meadows climb out.

"Hey, Spencer," Riley called out genially as he sauntered up to the window with a relaxed smile on his face. "Got time for a beer?"

"Actually I was just leaving," Logan ground out between clenched teeth. "That is, until you blocked me in."

Confusion skittered across Riley's face, and then he glanced over his shoulder and smiled sheepishly. "Oh, hey, sorry about that. Hang on, I'll back up and let you get out of here." He started to walk away, but stopped. "You sure about that beer?"

"I'm sure. Maybe next time," Logan said with barely restrained anger.

Logan mentally ticked off the seconds as he watched the big man get behind the wheel and put his pickup into reverse.

With a friendly wave Riley gave an all-clear sign and then smiled as Logan gunned his engine and sped out of the parking lot, knowing even as he floored the accelerator that Nick Gallus was long gone.

NOT KNOWING which way Nick had gone, Logan vowed to catch up with Sarah's illusive business partner another time. His anger subsiding, he pulled onto the highway and headed back to Sarah's, wondering as he drove why Gaylene Fraizer had lied to him.

And she had lied, he was certain of that. Nothing happened at the Round-up that passed her notice. But why she'd lied about seeing Nick was a question Logan couldn't readily answer. And then there was the question of why Nick had been so anxious to avoid him.

Obviously the mention of Daisy Allen had disturbed Gaylene—unnecessarily, it seemed. And that led to other questions. What was the connection? What, if anything, could Nick Gallus—a man closer to his own age than either Daisy or Gaylene—tell him about a woman who'd left the valley twenty years ago? And why didn't Gaylene want him asking the questions?

His gut told him if there was a link between Nick Gallus and Daisy Allen, it could be traced through Will's journal. But where did Gaylene figure in? Her name hadn't been mentioned. Then again, maybe Will hadn't gotten that far.

As Logan sped back to the Breedan ranch, he barely noticed the miles, his mind too preoccupied with trying to fit together the pieces of this increasingly complex puzzle.

From everything he'd managed to unearth so far, he was solidly convinced Will Breedan's death was somehow linked to the disappearance of Sarah's mother. But what had Sarah's hay crop to do with Daisy Allen? Why would anyone want to obliterate the Breedan ranch's main source of income for the year? Was there a link, and if so, what?

Reaching for the cell phone on the seat beside him, he punched in the number for the Spencer Agency. After two rings he heard the sound of Cole's mellow baritone.

After exchanging pleasantries, Logan gave his younger brother a brief summation of the journal he'd found in Sarah's attic.

"I'm sending you a list of names," he said. "I need to know what link there is to Daisy Allen." He switched on his blinker to pass a semi. "The more we know about Daisy, the better our chances of finding Will's murderer."

"Consider it done," Cole said in his characteristically confident way.

"Start with Orrin Fraizer."

"Orrin? What's his connection to any of this?"

"Good question," Logan replied. "Will met with Fraizer just a few days before he died. If he was as deeply into this investigation as I believe he was, he might have mentioned something to Orrin."

"I didn't know congressmen dealt in missing-persons cases," Cole admitted wryly.

"Neither did I." But if this one had, Logan thought, he intended to find out why. "And while you're at it, run a background check on Nick Gallus."

"Hollywood Nick," Cole said.

"The same. He's come back to the valley, and judging by appearances, he's acquired the Midas touch. Check out his finances and his associates. He's involved with Earl Fraizer in a lease/purchase deal on some land, but I want to know more. Keep it behind the scenes, will you? My instincts say our boy Nick has something to hide. He's already avoiding me. I don't want to spook him into hiding."

After assuring Cole he would have the list of names in front of him within the next twenty-four hours, Logan thanked his brother for his help and prepared to hang up. Before he could, Cole asked, "So how's Sarah?"

"Pretty upset at this point. Hearing that her husband might have fallen victim to foul play came as quite a shock."

"I can imagine," Cole said solemnly.

"And there's more." He explained about the broken valve and the flooded fields. "I can't prove it yet, but I know that valve was ruined intentionally." He remembered Nick saying he carried tools in his truck, not unusual for a rancher. Unless one of those tools happened to be a sledge-hammer.

"Watch yourself, Logan," Cole admonished. "Sounds as if someone has it in for the Breedans in a big way. First Will and now this. For all we know, Sarah might be next."

Cole had confirmed Logan's own mounting suspicions, and he felt chilled at the prospect of anything happening to her. "I'm going to try to set up a meeting with the anonymous caller," he said. "And when I do, this thing could start to unravel fast. I doubt I can talk her into it, but I'd like to send Sarah and her daughter over to stay with you and Anne for a few days. Would that be a problem?"

"Are you kidding? Anne would love the company, and Andy can always use another playmate. Besides, it'd be good to see Sarah again." There was a brief silence before Cole added, "Take good care of her, Logan. She's a special lady, but then, I don't have to tell you that, do I?"

Logan knew full well how his siblings felt about the woman they'd both assumed would someday be part of the family.

"If she won't abide my shipping her out of the county, you can bet I won't let her out of my sight." Not now, and not later, if she'd have him.

"And while you're at it, watch your back," Cole warned.

"You can bank on it, buddy. Give my love to that gorgeous wife of yours and tell my nephew his uncle Logan misses him."

"Will do," Cole promised. "And, Logan, remember you're not in this alone. I won't try to tell you we don't have our hands full here at the agency, but whatever concerns you and Sarah concerns us. We're family, you know? And that means we're never too busy to look out for each other."

Logan knew, but he wondered what had taken him so long to truly understand. "I'll be in touch," he said, his voice unusually husky. "In the meantime I can be reached at this number."

"Where are you staying?"

"At Sarah's," he said simply, and pictured his brother's dark brows lifting.

"I approve," Cole said heartily.

"Somehow I knew you would, but before you go jumping to conclusions, you should know I'm bunking in the trailer behind the house."

The warmth in Cole's chuckle resonated over the line. "Well, at least it's a start."

It *was* a start, Logan thought, albeit a shaky one, in what he hoped would be the next chapter in his relationship with Sarah. But unlike the past, this time he wouldn't settle for an unhappy ending.

As he neared the turnoff for the Breedan-ranch road, Logan said goodbye to his brother and tossed the cell phone onto the seat, then grabbed the steering wheel with both hands in order to avoid the four cows standing squarely in the middle of the two-lane highway.

With a glance in his rearview mirror to make sure no one was behind him, he pulled to the side of the road and quickly herded the animals back into the pasture through the gaping hole in the fence he'd repaired himself just yesterday.

Within minutes he'd twisted the ends of the broken strands together, but the mystery of how they'd broken again followed him as he climbed back behind the wheel.

It was easy to see the wire had been cut. The only question was, who had done the cutting? And why?

After bumping over the ranch road, he finally pulled up in front of Sarah's house and spotted her in the corral with Jessica and her pony.

He turned off the ignition and sat gazing at mother and child. From this distance Jessica seemed hardly more than a baby. Even Sarah seemed small and achingly vulnerable.

Just the thought of anyone intentionally hurting either of them made his blood boil. How Will must have loved this life, he thought.

What did you find, friend? Whose skeletons did you

rattle? What cruel twist of fate or man had taken Will Breedan from his family?

"Logan!" the sound of Jessica's small but insistent voice
jerked him from his thoughts, and as he climbed out of his
truck, he waved at her. When she laughed and waved back,
her enthusiastic welcome warmed him.

Sarah's daughter was a delightful child, bright, inquisitive and loving. Almost without him knowing, Jessica Lynn
Breedan, four-going-on-five, had stolen his heart.

And if he had to move heaven and earth, he would do
both to make sure nothing evil ever touched her young life
again. After all, as he'd told Sarah, it was the least he could
do. For the child's sake. For Sarah's. For Will. And, in
some strange way he couldn't yet explain, for himself.

Chapter Eleven

Johnny called the next afternoon to say he couldn't pick up Jax at the vet clinic. Familiar disappointment thudded through Sarah as she listened to her father's slurred excuses about a broken axle. He promised to bring the animal home as soon as he had time to fix his trailer, but knowing her father, Sarah realized if she ever wanted her horse back, she'd have to go get him herself.

The way some kids grew up with swing sets, Johnny Allen's daughter grew up with junked cars in the backyard—in the front yard, too, such as it was, all weed-choked and rocky.

For as long as she could remember, her father had been waiting for parts to come in, or good weather, or time. The battered vehicles that littered their property were all diamonds in the rough, according to Johnny.

"That Chevy'll be good as the day it rolled off the line," he'd say, or "That old Dodge will be right as rain," and he'd prove it to her, he swore, just as soon as he found time and the right part.

After talking to Johnny, Sarah called the clinic.

Dr. Tyson, the vet who split his time between his offices in Ridgway and Grand Junction, wasn't in, but his assistant assured Sarah she could borrow a trailer to take her horse home.

Half an hour later with Jessica seated beside her Sarah pulled onto the ranch road. As they drove toward the highway, the child chattered like a jaybird, happily absorbed in plans for her upcoming birthday party.

At the end of the ranch road, Sarah glanced to the right to make her turn and spotted Logan walking along the fence line, a wire stretcher in one hand and roll of barbed wire in the other.

The unexpected sight of him, dressed in a white T-shirt and snug-fitting jeans caused a little flutter of awareness in her chest. Determined to pretend she hadn't seen him, she glanced quickly away, signaled to make her turn and eased off the brake.

Thanks to her observant passenger, however, Sarah's getaway plan failed.

"Mommy, stop!" Jessica exclaimed. "It's Logan. Stop! He's waving and he wants us to wait for him."

Sarah sighed and stepped on the brake. As Jessica rolled her window down, he was already walking toward the pickup, covering the ground between them in long confident strides.

When he reached the passenger side of the truck and leaned in the open window, he was smiling. "Hi, kiddo," he said brightly, and ruffled Jessica's hair. "How's the girl?"

"Great! We're going to pick up Jax, 'cause Grandpa Johnny's trailer got broke."

Over the child's head Logan's eyes posed the question.

"Broken axle. I made arrangements to borrow a trailer from the clinic."

"And on the way we're going to City Market and pick

up party stuff for my birthday," Jessica informed him. "Hats and balloons and grape paper, too."

"Crepe paper," Sarah corrected.

"Oh, yeah." Jessica giggled. "Come with us, Logan. You can help pick out balloons."

Logan lifted his gaze to meet Sarah's as he made his excuses to her daughter. "I was just on my way back to the trailer to have some lunch. Maybe next time."

Sarah opened her mouth to say they should be going when once again Jessica foiled her escape. "We're going to lunch, too, aren't we, Mommy? At my favorite place. Whitey's. It's sort of like McDonald's, but they don't got Happy Meals."

"They don't *have* Happy Meals," Sarah said automatically.

"Right, but they got really good hamburgers and cherry colas, too. You could go eat lunch with us, couldn't you, Logan?"

Sarah held her breath, and when she saw him smile, she knew she was lost.

"I guess I could do that," he said. "That is, if it's all right with my boss." There was a playful note in his voice that tugged at a corner of Sarah's heart.

Jessica laughed. "You don't have a boss, silly. You work for us."

"Your mom's my boss, kiddo, so that makes it her call."

Jessica frowned. "My mommy's not bossy. She's nice. She'll let you go with us, won't you, Mommy?"

Sarah groaned and tried her best not to smile. "I'm not sure I have a choice."

"Does that mean Logan can come with us?" Jessica was already unfastening her seat belt so that she could scoot over and make room for him.

Sarah sighed, resigned. "Sure. Why not."

"Great," Logan said, effortlessly tossing the roll of wire and the stretcher into the back of the truck. "It's hot out here and an ice-cold cherry cola sounds good."

"Yeah! This is gonna to be fun!" Jessica declared as Logan pulled the door open and slid in beside her.

Within minutes they were on the highway headed for Whitey's for a late lunch. Crowded together in the cab, Sarah fought an acute awareness of the man whose arm was draped casually across the back of the seat. When she leaned back and felt his fingers graze her shoulder, one glance in his direction told her the touch had not been inadvertent.

The fresh air, hard work and sunshine was agreeing with him. His face was deeply tanned and his hair provocatively tousled by the air that swept through the open windows. His T-shirt was stretched tight across his broad chest, and the short sleeves revealed tanned well-muscled arms—arms that felt too good wrapped around her.

"I'm not exactly dressed for a lunch date," Logan said, knocking the dust off his jeans.

"You're fine," Sarah shot back curtly. Then, slightly embarrassed by her brusque remark, she added, "Lots of ranchers drop by Whitey's straight from the field. It's definitely come as you are."

"I've got a better idea," he said, turning in the seat. "Why don't we pick up the burgers and drinks and go for a picnic?"

Jessica clapped and squealed her delight, but Sarah sensed trouble. She couldn't deny that watching Logan interact with his daughter in such a positive and loving way moved her, but another part of her worried that Jessica was already far too attached to him for her own good.

A day in the park, spinning more memories, would only

strengthen that attachment, making the loss all the worse when he left at the end of the summer.

Her deeper fear was even more troubling. Allowing him to spend the afternoon this close to Jessica was an invitation to disaster. How much longer could he look at the little girl without realizing she was his daughter? Would today be the day? Would it be Jessica's smile that finally exposed the truth? Or maybe her frown? Or would it be something more subtle that finally triggered some instinctual response in Logan? Something no more significant than a lift of a brow or a hint of a familial expression. The possibility that any moment her deception might be revealed made Sarah's stomach churn.

"Can we do it, Mommy?" Jessica asked. "Can we have a picnic with Logan?"

Feeling the weight of her lies pressing like a hand on her heart, Sarah shook her head. "I don't know if that's a good idea today, sweetheart. After all, we have so much to do. After we pick up the party supplies at the store, we have to go get Jax, remember?"

"But we have to eat lunch, anyway," Logan said. "And there's a little park near the supermarket. You know the place, don't you, Sarah? It has a stream running through it and a playground. It's right off the road."

Of course she knew it, just like she knew it was right on the way to the clinic.

"I know where it is!" Jessica said excitedly. "We went there with Grandpa Johnny one time and fed popcorn to the ducks."

Jessica and Logan swung their gazes to Sarah at the same time, and their expectant expressions were so hauntingly similar, she thought her heart would stop.

"Okay, but we can't stay long," she said, forcing her

focus back to the road. "We have errands to run and chores waiting at home and—"

"All right!" Jessica cheered. "We're going on a picnic!"

"Thanks, boss," Logan teased, and gave her shoulder a gentle squeeze.

And then, in that startlingly wonderful way children have of speaking their hearts, Jessica looked up at Logan and said, "I like you, Logan. You're nice."

"I like you, too, kiddo," he replied, his voice unusually husky. "In fact, you're just about the nicest little girl I've ever known."

PICKING OUT BALLOONS proved an easy task, especially after Jessica decided they should all be pink. From the supermarket Sarah angled her truck beside the drive-up window at Whitey's, and within minutes they were on their way to the park, with the smell of burgers and fries filling the cab and whetting everyone's appetite.

Almost before they stopped, Jessica spied an empty picnic table and scrambled out of the truck to claim it. It was a beautiful day, cloudless and warm. A gentle breeze wafted through the aspen and pine, taking the edge off the midday heat. The sounds of children laughing drifted through the pine-scented air like music.

Jessica finished her lunch in short order when she spotted a friend from preschool by the swings.

"Can I go play with Amy now?" she asked.

Sarah wiped a smudge of ketchup from her daughter's chin and gave her permission.

She watched as her daughter ran to join Amy and Amy's father, Vince Patterson. Sarah remembered that Vince had been raising Amy alone since his wife's fatal car accident last year. She made a mental note to invite him to Jessica's party. Maybe he'd enjoy the festivities, too.

Seeing Vince made her consider, for the first time in earnest, what would become of Jessica if anything should happen to her. The thought sobered her, and with a startling flash of self-awareness, she realized there really was only one person in all the world to whom she would entrust the care of her precious child. And, ironically, that person was Jessica's father.

"Mommy!" Jessica called from the swings, interrupting Sarah's disturbing insights. "Will you come give me a push?"

Logan rose from the bench before Sarah could answer. "I'll go," he said as he crumpled his wrapper. "You stay and finish your lunch."

As he strode over to the swing set, Sarah finished her hamburger and cleaned up the remnants of their picnic. Across the way Amy's father and Logan took turns pushing the girls on the swings. The sounds of the girls' squeals and chatter filled the air, and despite the constant strain of her own guilt and the shadow of the investigation into Will's death, Sarah couldn't remember enjoying a more pleasant moment.

When the children ran to feed the ducks the bun Sarah had ordered at Whitey's expressly for that purpose, Logan walked back to her and shocked her by reaching for her hand.

"How long has it been since you went wading?"

Before she could answer, he pulled her to her feet. His smile was a gentle entreaty that obliterated her defenses. "Too long," she admitted with a sigh.

Within minutes Logan's boots and Sarah's sneakers were sitting side by side on the bank. With her jeans rolled up to her calves, Sarah took the first tentative step. "Ooh, that's cold!"

Logan charged ahead of her, seemingly immune to the icy sting. "It *is* a little cool—" he gave an endearingly crooked smile "—but it's not so bad once you get used to it. Come on in."

Sarah held her breath and plunged both feet in the water. The water stung and invigorated at the same time. But Logan had been right, and after a minute, the water felt wonderful.

The stones that lined the creek bed were slippery, and Sarah extended her arms like a tightrope walker to keep her balance. She edged cautiously to the middle of the shallow stream and settled atop a flat boulder that was just the right height to allow her feet to dangle in the creek. With the sun warming her back and her feet cooled by the creek, Sarah felt more relaxed than she had in days.

Logan bent over to dip his forearms in the water and sighed. "This is great, isn't it? Makes me feel like a kid again."

And there was a childlike sparkle in his eyes, she thought. His face seemed smooth and young and totally carefree. She couldn't remember when she'd seen him look this happy.

He waded over to her and sat down on the boulder so that their shoulders touched. "Thank you, Sarah. I think I needed a day like this more than I knew."

She found herself strangely unable to do anything but smile and nod. When he returned her smile and reached out to push a strand of hair away from her face, she suddenly saw in him all the qualities that had drawn her to him in the first place. He had so much passion for life. He was such a strong and vital man, and yet at times he could seem so vulnerable. A proud man, and yet more needy than she'd realized. He was tough but tender, also, as evidenced by his friendship with Jessica. The man was a walking contradiction, a puzzle that had always intrigued her and probably always would.

"Hey, kiddo!" Logan called to Jessica. "Why don't you join us?"

He didn't have to offer twice. Jessica tugged off her shoes and was edging down the bank and into the shallow water. Logan got off the boulder and waded toward her to take her hand and help her keep her balance. For several minutes he stayed with her, walking her around in the water and pointing out the wonders of the streambed. The child looked up at him adoringly, seemingly unable to get enough of his attention.

Watching them together, Sarah felt moved but at the same time guilty as sin. How could she keep denying her child the love of this wonderfully complex man?

"Hey, look, Mommy! Look at what I found," Jessica exclaimed, and held out a piece of white quartz she'd found on the streambed. "Do you think it's a diamond?"

"It could be, sweetheart. Bring it over and let me take a closer look." Absorbed in watching Jessica wade through the water, Sarah was caught by surprise when Logan moved up beside her, put his arm around her waist and said in a low voice, "You're a good mom, Sarah. You've raised one fantastic kid."

Nearly overcome with emotion, Sarah could only look at him. He returned her gaze and for a long warm moment, she almost let herself believe things could work out between them. That the three of them could somehow become a family.

Lost in each other's eyes, they didn't see Jessica coming up behind them, but when the icy water hit Logan in the back, he jumped up with a roar and shook his head, sending a shower of sparkling droplets in all directions.

Exhilarated by the success of her surprise attack, Jessica exploded with laughter and jumped up and down in the stream and clapped her hands. "I got him!" She giggled. "Did you see, Mommy? I really got Logan!"

He spun around with a playful growling noise and charged toward the child. "You sure did, kiddo, but now it's your turn!"

Jessica gasped when he scooped her up and threatened to dunk her headfirst in the stream. Her eyes were wide and shining and completely devoid of anything but sheer delight. Her shrieks of laughter echoed around them as she clung to his neck, begging him, between gasping giggles, to let her go.

Amy joined the fun, and Logan endured many more surprise attacks from both children, until his clothes were soaked and they were all breathless with laughter.

Eventually they finally waded to the bank, and they sat together in the grass for a while, allowing the sun to dry and warm them.

"All right, guys," Sarah said finally. "It's time to go." She handed Jessica her shoes, and the child surprised her by climbing into Logan's lap and asking him to help her tie the laces.

Sarah's heart contracted at the sight of Jessica on her father's lap, his big hands fumbling with the small striped strings. The affection between them was real, and as natural as breathing. The realization that some bonds could not be denied caused emotion to swell in Sarah's throat.

For her, their carefree afternoon had come to an end.

With a heavy heart she stood and told them again it was time to leave. The look on Jessica's face said she wasn't ready for the fun to end, but just as her face began to fall,

Logan challenged her to see which one of them could win a footrace to the truck. Like the sun coming out from behind a cloud, Jessica's face brightened and she took off at a dead run.

Watching Amy and her father walk to their car, and Logan running after Jessica, Sarah felt gutted.

Five years and what now seemed like a lifetime ago, she'd made a choice based on what she'd believed was the best interest of her child. But since Logan had swept back into her life, all the justifications of the past seemed to be crumbling.

The only father Jessica had ever known was gone, and suddenly, it seemed despicably selfish of Sarah to deprive her child of Logan's love. Although he hadn't loved her, Sarah, enough to change his life to fit her dreams, maybe now he would find room and time in his life for his daughter.

If she did decide to tell him the truth, he would never forgive her, of that she had no doubt. This was the same man who had held a grudge against his own father for most of his adult life, all because of the lie Josh Spencer had allowed his son to believe for too long.

Logan was nothing if not an honorable man, and he'd shown that he would not abide a liar. And that was what she was, Sarah knew. A *liar*. The ugly truth pierced her heart.

As she walked to the pickup and slid in beside her daughter and her former lover, she felt the tug and pull of her conscience. It tore at the fabric of her heart.

SARAH LINED THE back of her truck to the trailer parked in front of the clinic. Logan watched with admiration as she made just the right adjustments and the hitch and tongue aligned perfectly.

"You're pretty good at that," he told her, but instead of receiving his compliment with a smile, she merely nodded.

Something had happened at the park, something he didn't understand. Her mood had changed, and Logan was at a loss to understand why.

Dr. Tyson's assistant, a jeans-clad young man who introduced himself as Gary Burnes, came out of the office and led them to where Jax was waiting.

Jessica was glad to see her mother's horse and she marched up to him fearlessly. Logan watched how smoothly Sarah insinuated herself between her daughter and the big animal. Although Jax was a gentle horse, calm and dependable, it was obvious Sarah wasn't taking any chances with her daughter's safety.

She lifted Jessica and let the child stroke the big bay's neck. "Do you think he's glad to see me, Mommy?"

"Yes, honey, I'm sure he is."

Sarah was so good with her child, Logan thought. Always instructing and protecting, while at the same time loving and nurturing. Regret for what might have been filled him.

When Sarah took her daughter's hand and moved her out of the way, Logan attached a lead to Jax's halter and brought the animal out of the stall.

Logan was shocked to see the large bandage wound thickly around what had appeared to be only a small irritation the other day. Sarah must have been equally surprised because she turned to Gary and said, "My goodness. Is all that really necessary?"

"Dr. Tyson had to do a fair amount of digging to get at the source of the irritation," Gary explained. "It'd worked itself in pretty deep, almost to the bone. It took a dozen stitches to close the wound." He patted the horse's neck.

"I've been looking after him since the surgery, and he seems to be healing just fine."

He handed Sarah a bottle of white pills.

"Doc says he'll be good as new in a couple of weeks. Just be sure to keep him in a clean stall and give him one of those antibiotics twice a day."

"Did Dr. Tyson discover what caused the problem?" Logan asked.

The young man seemed surprised. "I guess I thought you knew. I was sure Doc explained everything to Sarah's father."

Sarah and Logan exchanged glances. "I guess it must have slipped Dad's mind," Sarah said.

"What was it?" Logan asked. "Do you know?"

"Yeah, sure I know. I helped Doc with the procedure." Gary shook his head. "Darnedest thing, too. Doc said he'd never seen anything like it— Wait a minute, I think he saved it. Why don't you load your horse and I'll go check in the office and see if I can find it. You're not going to believe it."

By the time they'd loaded Jax and secured the trailer door, Gary rejoined them. "Look at this." He handed something to Sarah.

Sarah's face paled and when Logan looked down at what she held in her palm, he understood why.

"Buckshot," Gary said. "It's no wonder you didn't notice. Something that small probably wouldn't leave much of a mark. In all likelihood, it would barely break the skin, and by the time it started bothering him, the initial entry wound would've healed over."

But Logan hardly heard the assistant's explanation. He was too busy trying to figure out how the animal had been shot, and why, in light of such an unusual circumstance, Johnny Allen hadn't told Sarah about the vet's find.

As they headed back to the ranch, Sarah seemed unusually quiet. Jessica, too, seemed finally to have run out of steam. In fact, Logan felt her body sag against his side and he guessed she'd fallen asleep.

He glanced down to be sure, and when he was satisfied that she was deep in the throes of sleep and not merely dozing, he said, "How do you suppose Jax got himself shot, Sarah?"

"Poachers," she said, her one-word declaration surprising him.

He shook his head. "No. A poacher hunting deer would have used a rifle. That pellet came from a shotgun."

Sarah sighed. "Of course you're right. But then, I have no other ideas of how it might have happened."

"There might be another explanation, Sarah. But I need to go over the events of the day Will died. Are you up to it?"

He saw her tighten her grip on the wheel. "Sure, if you think it's necessary."

"It could help."

"All right," she said softly, "but let's keep our voices down. I don't want to upset Jessica."

"You said Jax must have been spooked that day to come home without Will."

She nodded. "Yes. Now that you've been around him, you've seen for yourself that he's not a skittish horse by nature."

"Right. So, what if it was a shotgun blast that spooked him that morning on the ridge?"

He heard her sharp intake of breath. "Yes, I guess it's possible. But it's been almost a year."

"Right, but Gary did say the pellet had worked its way almost to the bone. In all the confusion of that day and the weeks after, you might not have noticed such a small wound.''

She sighed. ''I admit, Jax was the last thing on my mind.'' When she glanced over at him, her eyes were wide. ''In fact, now that I think about it, I remember I turned him out to pasture that day, and until this spring I hadn't ridden him.''

''That might explain why the pellet just now started to irritate. Without any stress on his leg, it just stayed there, fairly benign. When you started riding him and he was forced to use his muscles, the piece of buckshot began to rub and irritate.''

The turnoff for the ranch road came into view, and Sarah signaled to pull off the highway. ''You can drop me at the gate,'' Logan told her. ''My pickup is still in the field.''

Besides, he wasn't coming back to the house just yet. There were too many questions that needed answering, questions he couldn't wait to get to a phone to start asking.

''Sarah, I'm planning to ride up to Tyler Ridge the day after tomorrow. Do you have a horse I can use?'' If not, he would swing by the Spencer ranch and find a suitable mount.

''Of course. What time should we plan to head out?'' Sarah asked as she pulled to a stop.

Not wanting to get into a discussion about her going with him, he merely said, ''Early.'' He would make it clear to her later that he would be riding up to Tyler Ridge alone. Right now he had more pressing concerns, most notably, the conversation he planned to have with Johnny Allen.

Chapter Twelve

When Logan returned to the trailer, he headed for the phone and dialed Johnny's number. As he waited for Sarah's father to answer, he activated the playback mechanism on the answering machine. There were two messages, one a hang-up and the other from Cole.

When no one answered in the little cabin near Tyler Ridge, Logan punched the disconnect button and returned his brother's call.

After a pleasant exchange with Anne, Logan asked her to put Cole on the line. Just as he'd suspected, his brother had pounced on the information Logan had sent him.

"I spoke to Orrin Fraizer," Cole said. "He claims his meeting with Will in Denver last year was purely social."

"And you believed him?"

Cole hesitated a moment before he answered. "Well, yes. At least I believed him when he said he considered Will a friend. He thinks a lot of Sarah, too."

Something that could only be called jealousy sliced through Logan, and he moved on to the subject of Daisy Allen.

"He said he wasn't aware of Will's search and couldn't recall ever discussing Sarah's mother with Will. He seems to have a lot of affection for Sarah. Seems genuinely concerned about her welfare.''

As Cole went down the list of other names he'd checked out, Logan made notes on the pad beside the phone.

''All dead ends, I'm afraid,'' Cole reported. ''Will covered a lot of miles, but it didn't seem to produce any results. It's not that unusual to have this kind of response to a search. The world is full of well-meaning people wanting to help in situations like this one. They see a flyer about a missing woman, spot a blond woman in her fifties and pick up the phone.''

''What about Nick?'' Logan asked.

''No rich uncles that I could uncover,'' Cole replied. ''And no employment record, either. He's been ranching for a little less than a year and seems to be doing well. I ran a routine check on his finances, and let's just say he's extremely solvent. Not bad for a man who spent two of the last four years in a Texas jail.''

Logan's interest piqued as Cole went on to report what he'd discovered, detailing the charges Nick had been convicted of. ''For a few years he tried his luck on the tour.''

Logan knew his brother was referring to the PRCA— Professional Rodeo Cowboys' Association circuit.

''One year he took top honors in calf roping in Tulsa and again in Scottsdale. He earned some serious money in other regional competitions, as well. Four years ago he was even in the running for the world finals, but in Amarillo, he tried to improve his chances by other means. The night before the final round, he drugged his closest competitor's horse.''

Logan released a low whistle. ''I take it he got caught.''

Cole confirmed his assumption. ''He was lucky he got out of town alive. The horse had a violent reaction to the drug and nearly died.''

"So that explains the lack of an employment record, but how does an ex-con, just a couple of years out of jail, come by a stake big enough to buy land and cattle?"

"That's what I wondered," Cole said. "So I did more checking."

Logan knew Cole had his way of discovering such things, but his own close ties to law enforcement made him reluctant to ask for specifics.

"I remembered that you told me Nick was living on the old Bailey place, so I decided to give Stan Bailey a call and find out why he decided to sell. Come to find out, Stan didn't have much choice."

"Are you saying Earl or Nick forced him out?"

Cole sighed. "Well someone did. The year before Stan packed it in, he suffered an unbelievable string of unlucky coincidences. Lost cattle, numerous calves stillborn, a barn fire and—get this—flooded hay fields."

Logan felt a muscle tense in his jaw. Unbelievable was the operative word. "Thanks, Cole," Logan said. "You've given me a lot to work with."

Even before he hung up the phone, Logan was planning his next conversation with Nick Gallus. In light of this latest information, Nick's disappearing act from the Roundup the other day seemed even more suspicious.

He walked to the rear of the trailer to take a shower before going over to Sarah's. With the water running he didn't hear the phone ring, but when he finished his shower, he noticed the light on his answering machine flashing.

He hit the playback button, and as the tape rewound, he pulled on his jeans and reached for his shirt. When the muffled voice started talking, his hands froze on the buttons.

"This is it, Spencer. I can't call you anymore. It's too

dangerous. I've told you what I know. If you want the proof, it's up there. Up on Tyler Ridge. Good luck.''

Logan stood staring down at the machine, his mind reeling. Though the tipster had muffled his voice in the same way he had before, this time the ruse didn't work. This time Logan recognized the voice.

THE NEXT MORNING dawned clear and bright, and by eight Sarah reined in her horse behind Logan's and they started the steep ascent of the narrow trail to Tyler Ridge.

He turned around in the saddle to look back at her. "How are you doing?"

"Don't worry about me, Spencer. Diva knows this trail like the inside of her stall and so do I. We'll be right behind you."

Despite the grim circumstances that had brought them to the mountain, she couldn't resist an inner smile. Logan hadn't been happy about her insistence on coming along, but after she'd reminded him that her stakes in this investigation were even higher than his, he'd had no choice but to relent. She'd bolstered her argument by reminding him that, between the two of them, she was the only one who had actually read the official report of Will's so-called accident. She knew where Will's body had been found, and she knew approximately where he'd been injured when Jax kicked him.

Logan hadn't been the only one grumbling this morning. Unable to understand why she wasn't being allowed to go along on what she thought was merely a trail ride, Jessica had been difficult and whiny from the time she'd rolled out of bed. She'd tried Sarah's patience, but thankfully, Terri stepped in to save the day by promising to give Jessica a grown-up manicure while Logan and Sarah were gone. By the time they rode out, Jessica was all smiles and looking forward to picking out just the right nail color.

"Which way?" Logan asked when they came to the trailhead.

"Bear right," Sarah told him. "The left fork takes you straight down to the creek."

"Ah, yes. Now I remember," Logan said.

Sarah nodded and remembered the countless times she'd encountered the Spencer boys riding past the cabin where she'd grown up. Sometimes they'd drop by to discuss with Johnny which flies the trout were taking that particular day.

On their way back they'd swing by again and stay awhile, lounging on the front step, swapping rodeo tales and fish stories with Johnny. Drew, the youngest of the three, was the most outgoing, with Cole adding his two cents from time to time, often embellishing his brother's fish stories.

But Sarah's attention had always been riveted on Logan, the tall darkly handsome oldest brother, who commented sparingly, but seemed—to Sarah, anyway—infinitely more interesting.

Just as he was to her now. She stared at his broad back and admired how he sat a horse. He rode tall and proud, and his subtle hand and leg cues made it seem as if he and the horse were one.

This morning, he was riding a horse named Porter, a sleek black gelding that Sarah considered one of her best trail horses. Her own mount, the white mare she'd named Diva, was as surefooted and nimble as the gelding, but slightly smaller.

The trail twisted and turned and the incline grew steeper. The horses picked their way around large rocks and fallen timber. As Sarah adjusted to the jostling she found her thoughts drifting to Will and the circumstances that had brought him to the ridge that fateful morning a little more than a year ago.

Had he sensed the danger awaiting him? she wondered. As he'd ridden toward the top of the mountain, had his mind been too troubled to take in the awesome view, too preoccupied to hear the soothing sounds of snow-fed waters rushing through the canyon below or the gentle chirping of the birds in the forest? Had he thought of her and Jessica, and worried that he might never see them again?

Sadness made her heart heavy as she contemplated that awful morning and the unknown circumstances of Will's death. Life could be so unfair, so unpredictable. There really were no guarantees.

If losing Will had taught her anything, it was that. Life was precious but fickle. And too short to waste a moment with regret.

A half hour later Logan pulled Porter to a stop and said, "We're nearing the top. We'll leave the horses here and walk the rest of the way."

After they'd loosened the cinches and tied their horses to a tree, they walked the last few yards to the top of the ridge.

"Over there," Sarah said, pointing to the edge of the trail where the ground fell away sharply. Despite the warmth of the midday sun streaming through the pines, Sarah felt a chill as she walked toward the spot where Will had lost his life. Her insides trembled.

"Are you going to be all right?" Logan asked.

She nodded and murmured, "I'm okay. Let's just get this over with."

They walked slowly to the edge of the steep bank and stood together staring down at the white-capped waters of Dove Creek. The water chasing through the canyon some two hundred feet below had once seemed magnificent and thrilling, but to Sarah, Dove Creek would never be anything but malevolent and sinister from now on.

"They found him over there," she said quietly, pointing down to the place along the creek bank that Glenn and the official report had described. "Near that cluster of aspen."

When Logan put his arm around her waist and drew her close, there was nothing sexual about the contact. The gesture was one of friendship and caring, just one human being comforting another in the midst of an unthinkable situation.

"I'm sorry, Sarah," he said in a low voice.

She found she couldn't speak around the lump in her throat, and her chest hurt with the emotion pressing against it. After a few minutes and a long last look, she sighed and turned her back on the ledge.

"All right," she said, taking a deep breath. "Now what?"

"Can you find the spot where they think he was thrown from the saddle?"

Sarah shaded her eyes with the back of her hand and looked back down the trail.

"I think it must have been someplace over there." She started walking down the trail. "I remember Glenn mentioned something about a huge blue spruce and a thick stand of scrub oak. He mentioned that boulder," she said, pointing.

Logan followed her, but she sensed his reluctance.

When she stopped near the spruce tree, she turned to see him walking back up the trail to the edge of the cliff. "Logan? What is it?"

When he didn't reply immediately, she went after him.

"What are you doing over here?" she asked. "There's no blue spruce here. According to the report, Jax injured Will down there."

He seemed lost in thought for a moment, then he turned

slowly and walked back to the spot Sarah had pointed out to him just moments ago.

"Logan? What are you doing?"

"I think the report is wrong," he said as he walked and she hurried to catch up with him.

When he stopped to stare at the spruce tree, she felt her patience wearing thin. "I wish you'd tell me what this is all about." Exasperated, she stood a few feet away with her hands on her hips.

He continued to stare at the tree for another maddening moment before turning slowly to face her. His eyes were very dark, and she could almost hear his mental gears spinning.

"A man receives a serious blow to the head. He staggers to his feet. He's dazed and disoriented. He's hurt, half-blind with pain."

Sarah's heart convulsed with the image of Will's suffering he'd drawn.

"He manages to get to his feet and he stumbles forward. Now tell me, where does he go?"

The horrific image was not one she cared to contemplate, but she had to know where this was leading. "Up there." She pointed to edge of the ravine. "We already know that."

"Do we? Think again, Sarah. Carefully this time. Which way does he go?"

She hated not knowing what point he was trying to make, and her frayed nerves felt dangerously close to snapping. "Logan, please. What are you trying to say?"

He blinked and it was as though he'd come out of a trance. His expression softened and she knew he had suddenly become acutely sensitive to her discomfort. "Sarah, I'm sorry. I know this isn't easy for you. Forgive me, I'm so used to working alone. Sometimes I tend to think out loud.''

''I know you didn't want me come, but I had to. I thought you understood I have to be part of this. I want to help bring Will's murderer to justice.''

''I understand,'' he said. ''And you have every right to be here. I didn't want you to go through this, but now I'm glad you're here,'' he admitted. ''We're in this together, Sarah. I needed you to show me the way.''

His admission surprised her more than he could know. The old Logan, the one she'd run away from, had always been a loner. This man wasn't too proud to admit he needed help. He needed her.

''I was afraid of what coming here would do to you, knowing what happened,'' he went on. ''But I know now what a strong and special woman you are, Sarah Breedan.'' A tender smile curved his lips. ''Sweet, loving, feminine— and strong as steel.''

His compliment warmed her, touching her deeply, showing her in ways she could never have imagined possible just how much he really had changed. ''Go on, Logan,'' she said quietly. ''Tell me what you're thinking. What's so special about that tree?'' She took a step toward him.

His eyes moved over her face almost lovingly. For the first time, it seemed Logan the cop and Logan the man had merged. ''All right,'' he said finally. ''But I think it might be easier to show you. Close your eyes, Sarah.''

''What?''

''Just do it, Sarah. Trust me. You'll understand in a minute. Close your eyes.''

She shook her head doubtfully, but did as he ordered.

''Don't open them until I tell you, okay?''

She nodded. ''Whatever you say.''

''Good. Now turn around.''

When she hesitated, he put his hands on her shoulders and turned her himself. She gasped and nearly stumbled over the brush that tangled at her feet. "Enough!" she cried, when he continued to turn her around and around. "Logan, stop! I'm getting dizzy."

"That's the idea," he told her. "Just keep your eyes closed."

Finally his hands fell away from her shoulders and he said, "All right. Now, walk. But be sure to keep your eyes closed."

"I—I can't! I'm so dizzy."

"Keep your eyes closed," he reminded her. "And don't worry, I won't let you fall or walk into a tree. Go on, Sarah. Start walking."

His command was not all that easily obeyed; the world seemed to have tilted and she'd lost all sense of direction. As she shuffled blindly forward, twice she nearly fell over the brush and rocks in her path. But just as he'd promised, Logan was there to catch her and keep her moving.

After a few more clumsy steps he said, "All right. Open your eyes and see where you are."

Gratefully, Sarah opened her eyes and realized with a jolt that she was nowhere near the edge of the ridge. In fact, she had gone in the opposite direction, farther down the trail, away from the place where Will had ultimately fallen to his death.

He gave her a shy smile. "Sorry to put you through that, but I wanted to prove a point." He took her hand and pulled her down to sit beside him on a boulder at the edge of the trail. "You're a good sport, Sarah. Did I ever tell you that?" He pushed a strand of wayward hair behind her ear.

Despite the situation, she couldn't resist leaning into his touch. "Yeah, maybe a time or two. Now, tell me what just happened here, besides a very weird game of blind-man's bluff.''

"You walked downhill, Sarah."

She blinked and stared at him, as understanding dawned.

"Back down the trail," he said. "Downhill, not up. If Will had been thrown from the saddle here, he would have had to walk uphill in order to fall off that ledge."

When he paused, Sarah continued his line of thought, suddenly understanding fully what he'd been trying to say. "And a man who's dazed, disoriented and injured would do just what I did. He'd follow the path of least resistance. He'd walk downhill. And I just proved it!"

"Exactly." He smiled.

"But they know Will fell over the edge of the ravine up there," she insisted. "There was never any doubt about that."

His smile faded. "Right. But they never found any evidence of *how* he got to the edge, did they?"

She almost gasped. "Oh, Logan, you're right. The report was very vague about that. I guess since everyone assumed it was an accident, they were more concerned with where the fall occurred than where he was thrown from the saddle and injured when Jax kicked him."

Logan's face was solemn—the cop face she knew so well—but somehow he seemed different. Changed.

"Come with me," he said, pulling her to her feet. "I want to show you something else.

"Look at that," he said pointing to the spruce. "What do you make of it? Up there where the bark is all splintered?"

She stared at the damaged tree trunk and shrugged. "I don't know. Obviously something tore the bark away, but I couldn't begin to guess what. An ax, maybe?"

"Too high."

"Some sort of animal, then?"

He shook his head. "You don't like guns, do you, Sarah?"

"No," she replied quickly. "They make me nervous." She supposed it sounded silly coming from a woman who had been intimately involved with two men who were cops.

"Then you've probably never gone target shooting."

She wrapped her arms around herself, remembering how the crack of a gun's retort always unnerved her. "No. That's definitely *not* something I've ever had the desire to do."

"Well, if you had, you would know what damaged that tree trunk."

"A bullet?"

"Buckshot. Someone peppered that trunk with buckshot. At least two blasts, maybe three."

The implication of what he was suggesting rocked her. "You're saying someone shot at Will that morning?"

"Yes. I think that's probably what spooked Jax."

When he reached up to peel a piece of bark from the tree, her eyes followed his movements. "And I'm also guessing that there is still a fair amount of buckshot in the trunk." He rolled a rock over to the tree and climbed onto it, his pocketknife in his hand.

"Someone ambushed him here," Logan said when he stepped down and showed her the buckshot he'd dug out of the trunk—the same kind of pellets as the one the vet had removed from Jax's leg.

Sarah felt her stomach roll as the scenario played through in her mind. "Jax spooked when that piece of buckshot hit him. Will was struck by a hoof when Jax reared or bucked, and while he was down and disabled, his attackers moved in and..." She was too shocked to finish the sentence.

When she met Logan's gaze, she knew they'd come to the same conclusion.

Will hadn't stumbled over the edge of Tyler Ridge. He'd been pushed.

Chapter Thirteen

As far as Sarah could determine, no one had seen or heard from her father for at least two days. She'd called the cabin countless times over the past twenty-four hours, but Johnny never answered.

Her father's unannounced absences were nothing new. When Sarah was a teenager, he was always disappearing, sometimes for weeks on end. She'd learned the words "bender" and "binge" at an early age, incorporating them into her grim understanding of her father's alcoholic lifestyle.

The last time he'd disappeared he ended up behind bars in Albuquerque. It had been right after Will's death, and Sarah had spent money she didn't have on bail and bus fare. Afterward she served notice on her father that she'd come to his rescue for the last time. If he wanted to drink himself to death, she told him she wouldn't stand in his way, but she also let him know she didn't have the stomach to watch him destroy himself.

It seemed that her ultimatum had a positive effect, at least for a while. For the past five months Johnny had seemed more in control of his life than he'd been in years. Until now.

And now, if he had gone on a bender, there was no way

to know when, or even if, he'd be coming back. Laying down the ground rules had been a necessary step for Sarah's own sanity, but not knowing where her father was or if he was all right was worrisome. Despite everything, she loved the old man, and the thought that he might be hurt or in some kind of terrible trouble disturbed her deeply.

Maybe this time, when he resurfaced, she could convince him to check into a treatment facility for some real help. She'd always maintained that deep down her father was a decent man, tenderhearted and kind. Her greatest hope was that someday he would get his life together and make a real commitment to sobriety.

Logan was less sympathetic, especially since now more than ever he wanted to confront Johnny about his whereabouts the day of Will's death. Last night, when they'd returned from Tyler Ridge, he'd insisted they drive up to the cabin, but when they arrived, there was no sign of Johnny, nor any indication that he had been there all day.

Sarah finished the breakfast dishes and was picking up the phone to call Johnny again when Logan walked in the back door.

"I'm going to try the cabin again," she said. "There's coffee on the stove. Help yourself."

"Thanks."

He was dressed in a navy blue polo shirt, the dark color perfectly complimenting his ruddy skin and dark eyes. The soft cotton hugged his broad chest and tapered waist to perfection. He smelled clean and citrusy, and his dark hair was combed away from his face, the ends still damp from his shower. His handsome essence invaded Sarah's senses, and she found she had to force herself to concentrate to remember her father's phone number.

"Have you heard from Nick?" he asked.

She shook her head as she listened to the phone ringing

on the other end of the line. "His hired man said he was still in Denver. He said he expects him home day after tomorrow. Late."

"That hay is ready to be turned," he told her. "We can't wait for Nick another day. I'll make arrangements to borrow the necessary equipment from the Spencer ranch."

Sarah counted three more rings and then replaced the receiver.

"Still no Johnny?"

She shook her head and tried to look unconcerned. "He'll turn up."

His expression said he didn't share her optimism. "Yeah. Well, I'd better go see about getting that hay turned. I'll see you later this afternoon."

He set down his cup and headed for the door, but he stopped when she said, "Do you plan to tell Glenn Driscoll what we found up on the ridge?"

"No," he said flatly.

"Don't you think he ought to know, at least about the buckshot?"

"Not yet," he said firmly. "I spoke to Cole the other night, and he gave me some interesting leads I need to follow up on before I go to Glenn."

The mention of leads intrigued her, and she started to ask him to tell her more, but Jessica burst into the kitchen, forcing Sarah to put her curiosity on hold.

"Hey, kiddo," Logan said, his hand still on the door, "how are the party plans coming along?"

"Great!" Jessica replied gaily. "Today we're making place mats with everybody's name on them."

"Sounds like fun. Too bad I'm going to miss out. Have a good time," he said, and then shifted his eyes to Sarah's. "We'll talk later," he promised, and then he was gone.

THAT AFTERNOON Logan, with the help of a crew and equipment borrowed from the Spencer ranch, turned the hay in both fields. Sarah made lunch and took it out to the men, with an extra thermos of iced tea. The temperature had peaked, hitting almost eighty.

By five o'clock the men had finished working, and for the first time Sarah allowed herself to believe that most of her hay crop would be salvaged, after all.

After supper she and Jessica finished decorating the party place mats, but even as she listened to her daughter's happy chatter, her mind was on the man across the way, working alone in the trailer.

He'd gone straight from turning the hay in the fields to finishing the repair of the fence near the highway, and by the time he'd driven back to the trailer, it had been after nine. When she called to ask him if he wanted her to warm up the supper he'd missed, he'd declined, explaining that he had calls to make and he'd be tied up most of the evening. She knew he was intent on finding Nick and demanding to know why he'd abandoned his promise to turn the hay.

Although she'd wanted to press him to give her the details he'd mentioned this morning, she resisted. He'd put in a long hard day, and he sounded exhausted.

Two hours later sleep eluded Sarah. Though her body was tired from a long day of chores, her mind refused to be stilled. The questions that had nagged her all day seemed to loom larger in the darkness, like a nightmare waiting for her at the edge of sleep.

Where was her father? Why hadn't he told her about the buckshot in Jax's leg? Had he gone after Will that fateful morning? And if he had, why hadn't he told her? Was the information Logan had obtained from his brother in any way related to their find on the ridge? And if it was, how?

For some reason the soft glow of the light from the living room in the trailer seemed to intensify her restlessness. And imagining the man sitting alone by the lamplight only made matters worse.

She closed her eyes to block out the light filtering through the sheer curtains at her window, but she couldn't block out the image of the man in her mind's eye. She tried to stifle her thoughts of him, to tell herself she would survive this aching need she had denied for so long. She told herself she could live without him, that loving him amounted to emotional suicide.

The answers to the mystery surrounding Will's death would be found. The end of the summer would come. Logan Spencer would walk out of her life and back to his career. Knowing he would soon be out of her life forever, she should have felt relieved, even glad. Instead, she was dying inside. Aching and brokenhearted all over again at the thought of losing that which she'd never really possessed.

She groaned, rolled over and punched her pillow, and noticed that the light had finally gone out in the trailer.

IT WAS JUST AFTER midnight when the sound of thunder reverberating off the peaks in the distance pulled Sarah from her fitful sleep. By the time she opened the front door and stepped out onto the porch, the heavens had opened and the rain had begun. With a vengeance.

Standing alone in the midst of the storm, listening to the rain hammer everything in its path, knowing that all the hard work of the previous day had been for nothing, Sarah felt too numbed and too disbelieving to even cry.

''Sarah!'' She thought she'd imagined his shout, a trick of nature and the storm, but when she spun around, he was there, right behind her, the rain sluicing down his face and onto his T-shirt.

"What in hell?" he gasped, and then without giving her a chance to speak, he swept her up and into his arms and carried her across the porch and through the front door.

"The storm woke me," he explained before she could ask. "I came over to make sure you were all right."

As he whisked her down the hall and into the bathroom, she felt the chill creeping over her body, and by the time she was standing on her own two feet again, she was shivering so violently her teeth chattered.

He pushed the door closed with the toe of his boot and ordered, "Lift your arms," and proceeded to grab the hem of the sodden T-shirt and pull it unceremoniously over her head. She was naked for only as long as it took him to yank a towel from the bar and wrap it and his arms around her at the same time.

Swaddled in the protective cocoon of strong arms and dry terry cloth, Sarah felt the damn of her emotions cracking. "The hay," she sputtered. "I-it'll be ruined."

"I know," he said softly. "I'm sorry."

"Damn it!" She balled her fists and planted them on his chest, then pressed her face against them. "Oh, Logan!" she cried. "What am I going to do?"

"Shh, Sarah. Not now. Just let it out."

When the first shuddery sigh shook her, he tightened his embrace. "Let it go, Sarah. Let it go."

"N-no," she whispered raggedly. "I—I'll w-wake Jess."

With one swift motion he reached behind him and turned the shower on full blast.

"It's all right," he murmured against her hair. "Now no one will hear."

With his arms still around her and the sound of the water muffling her sobs, Sarah gave in to the tears in soft gulping sobs. As the emotion poured out of her, he murmured, "It's all right, Sarah. It's okay. Let it go," against her cheek and hair.

Gradually her tears subsided and she became aware—achingly aware—of her acute need for him. Suddenly her mouth was on his cheek, and her hands moved up his back and slid through the thick soft hair at his nape.

He brushed his lips across her wet cheek, and she thrilled to the sensation that rippled through her body. She forgot about the pain they'd caused each other. She forgot about the rain and the ruined crops and even—God help her—the child sleeping just across the hall. All she thought about was him, and the way it felt to be in his arms again.

The taste of his lips was honeyed with his desire, and with the steam swirling around them, she reveled in the familiar taste of his mouth. When his hands moved under the towel, she whimpered and with her body and her lips begged him to go on touching her forever.

Her hands moved over his body, shamelessly reacquainting themselves with the flesh and sinew of the only man she'd ever truly loved. Breathless, they clung to each other, savoring the taste of a desire too long denied.

He kissed her deeply, and when he finally drew his mouth from hers, his breath was ragged. "Come back to the trailer with me, Sarah, and let me make love to you. You don't know how much I want you."

But she did know, and she remembered with exquisite detail how it had been between them. How his lovemaking had made her feel like the most cherished woman in the world. How he had filled her and satisfied her, body and soul. His kisses had made her oblivious to any other sensation, and his touch chased every care from her mind. But that had been before. Before Jessica.

She opened her mouth to tell him that their recklessness

had already cost them more than he'd ever know, but before she could form the words, his lips captured hers again and he kissed her with such tenderness she felt her knees go weak.

Liquid fire coursed through her veins, and her body trembled beneath his touch, but without warning he dragged his mouth from hers and pressed his finger to her moist lips.

She blinked. "Logan. What's—"

"Shh," he warned, even as he feathered a kiss across her cheek. "Listen," he murmured just beneath her ear, and reached behind her to turn off the shower.

In the silence Sarah strained to hear what had alerted him.

"Mommy?" the sound of Jessica's tentative voice drifted across the hall and into the bathroom.

He grabbed the robe hanging on the back of the door and held it for her. Fighting to steady the breath made ragged from his kisses, she dropped the towel and shoved her arms into the robe as he pulled the sides closed over her nakedness and tied the sash.

"Go," he whispered, and pressed a quick hot kiss to her still-tingling lips. "I'll see you tomorrow."

"Mommy!"

"It's all right, sweetheart," she said, her voice shaky, as she opened the door. "I'm coming."

And with the taste of his lips still clinging to hers and her heart aching with desire, she slipped out of the bathroom and across the hall to her child.

THE NEXT DAY dawned bright and clear, the murky puddles in the drive the only evidence of the previous night's ruinous storm. Sarah didn't have the heart to drive out to the hay fields. There was no point. After two soakings the crop would be ruined.

Still feeling drained by last night's emotional onslaught, she moved through her morning chores with a heavy heart and tired limbs. Glancing out the kitchen window, she noticed with a mix of relief and disappointment that Logan's pickup was gone.

"He left real early," Terri said as she brought the last of the dishes from the table. "I woke up before dawn and saw him leave."

"Up at dawn?" Sarah asked idly. "Why so early?"

"I don't know. It's the weirdest thing. I woke up feeling like I could climb Mount Sneffels." She edged Sarah away from the sink. "Let me finish. I have all this energy to burn and you look like you're dead on your feet."

"The storm," Sarah muttered. "It woke Jess, and I guess I didn't sleep all that well, either."

"I talked to him before he left," Terri volunteered.

"Oh?" Although Sarah tried to sound uninterested, she sensed Terri knew better.

"Yeah. He said he was going to take the borrowed equipment back to the Spencer ranch. Said not to count on him for lunch."

Sarah sat down at the table and Jessica climbed onto her lap with a brush and comb in her hand. As Sarah brushed and braided her daughter's hair, Terri chatted about a sale at some children's shop she'd noticed in the morning paper.

Sarah's attention drifted as her hands moved automatically through Jessica's hair and she marveled at its lustrous darkness. So like her father's.

Then her mind wandered back to what had transpired between Logan and her last night and she groaned inwardly. She knew she'd always worn her emotions close to the surface, but there was no excuse for the way she'd lost control with him last night.

Remembering the way his body had felt beneath her

hands provoked an unwanted shiver of desire. She cursed the sensation, mortified by thoughts of how much further they might have gone had Jessica's cries not interrupted them.

It must not happen again, she told herself with firm resolve. No matter how much she wanted him, no matter how badly she longed to seek comfort again in the shelter of his all-too-welcoming arms.

And he did welcome her, she knew that. Just as she knew he still wanted her. And in some ways she knew he had changed. Although he was still the tough confident Logan Spencer who'd made detective before he'd turned thirty, there seemed to be a gentleness about him now, a sensitivity and a thoughtfulness she'd sensed in him from the beginning but never before seen so overtly demonstrated.

And he was wonderful with Jessica. But wonderful in the way that an uncle or a family friend might indulge a child. It wasn't the same as being a full-time father, she told herself.

And even if he had changed, it didn't change their situation or the deception that would always keep them apart—no matter how strong the physical attraction that drew them together.

He'd said he wanted her, not once, but twice. But wanting and loving weren't the same. Five years ago he'd told her he loved her, but in the end it had not been enough. He hadn't loved her enough to change his life for her or to temper his obsession with his career. A career that, for all she knew, still waited for him in Denver. He'd said he'd stay for the summer. That he'd uncover the truth behind Will's death. And then he'd be gone, back to a way of life that didn't include a wife and child.

For Jessica's sake, and for the sake of her own heart, she had to get a rein on her emotions. She had to remember the past and think about the future. Jessica's and her own.

Chapter Fourteen

It seemed strange to Logan to realize how little the house he'd grown up in had changed—especially in light of the changes that had occurred in his own life since that day seven years ago when he'd come home to say goodbye to his mother for the last time.

The Spencer ranch house, with its sturdy log walls and wide wraparound porch, looked exactly as Logan remembered. Even the flower beds, lush with columbine, impatiens and petunias, were the same. The massive spruce in the side yard emitted the same scent, that same clean sharp aroma that would always remind him of home.

When he was halfway up the walk the front door opened and Bess Spencer, her small oval face split in a wide smile, made her way down the front steps to meet him. Although he couldn't remember her hair when it had been anything but gray, Logan had never thought of his aunt as old. With her indomitable spirit and laughing brown eyes, the woman seemed wonderfully ageless.

"Just in time," she declared merrily, wiping her hands on her apron before giving him a quick hug. "I made a pie. It's just about ready to come out of the oven." Bess's pies were legendary.

"Peach pie, I hope."

She looped her arm through his and gave it a squeeze. "Peach it is." She smiled up at him. "You didn't really think I'd forget it was your favorite, did you?"

"I never knew anyone with a better memory," he said, and dropped a kiss on her cheek as they made their way to the front door. "It's really good to see you, Bess."

She smiled and pushed open the front door.

"Well, don't just stand there, honey. Shall we have our pie now or save it for after lunch?"

"I'm afraid I can't stay for lunch." Cole was scheduled to call back this afternoon, and Logan planned to track down Nick as soon as he got back to the trailer. "Maybe some other time."

"I'll hold you to that," she promised. "And now I'll go see about that pie. Go on in and make yourself comfortable."

Left alone in the spacious living room, he found himself bombarded with memories. As he stood in front of the mantel and gazed at his parents' eighteenth-wedding-anniversary picture, his thoughts drifted back to the celebration, and the argument he'd inadvertently overheard drifting out of his parents' bedroom that evening. The words that he'd allowed to redefine and shape his life for too long.

I won't have it! his father's voice had boomed from beyond the bedroom door. *He's taking that scholarship and that's the end of it!*

He hadn't heard his mother's reply, but he'd always imagined her trying to calm him. It apparently hadn't worked, however, for whatever she'd said seemed only to add even more fuel to his father's emotional fire.

Regrets? How can you talk to me about regrets? I did the right thing by you, didn't I? I married you and gave our son a name. I quit law school, swallowed my pride and

*came crawling back here just like my father always said I
would. And I did it all for my son, damn it! And now he
owes me. I traded my future for him. And, by God, he's not
going to cheat me out of my dreams again.*

The rest of that night was nearly lost in a blur of even
more painful memories. His mother running out into the
yard. His father cursing him from the doorway. Cole and
Drew standing wide-eyed and confused on the stairs.

Please, Logan, she'd cried. *He didn't mean it.*

Logan had slammed the front door so hard the windows
had rattled. He could still picture his mother coming after
him, dressed in her favorite summer dress, the one with the
yellow roses embroidered on the collar and hem.

*You're wrong, Ma. He meant every word. For the first
time in seventeen years, he told the truth.* And the truth had
explained everything. *He didn't want me. Hell, he didn't
want you! He gave up his dreams for a son who's been
disappointing him ever since.*

He could still feel her hand on his arm, desperate and
clutching. *Don't do this, Logan. Don't leave. This is your
home. You belong here.*

*I don't belong, Ma. And neither does he. He had to stay
here, for you, for me. But he's never wanted either of us.*

The memories of that night drove him from the living
room. He wandered like a sleepwalker through the house,
and before he realized it, he was standing in the doorway
of the room that had been his father's study.

At the sound of Bess's voice behind him, he gave a start.
"It's quite a room, isn't it?"

Josh Spencer had been an impressive man. Logan felt
his stomach clench as his gaze moved over the rows of
leather-bound law books on the shelves opposite the desk.
"I think this is where he was happiest, surrounded by his
books, absorbed in his fascination for the law."

She walked past him to stand beside the massive mahogany desk that sat opposite a bay window offering an unobstructed view of the San Juan Mountains.

"I remember the first time he laid eyes on this desk. That was quite a day, remember? All the way from Venezuela!" Bess mused. "It took four men to get it through the front door."

He remembered vividly. His mother had talked him into coming home for the celebration. Once he'd arrived she'd enlisted his help in distracting his father. Somehow, Logan and his brothers had convinced their father to take the day off and go fishing with them, which allowed their mother time to arrange the surprise.

It had been a fine spring day, cloudless and warm. By noon they'd each caught their limit of rainbows and brookies. Lazing on the bank, eating sandwiches and drinking beer, the bitterness of the past had seemed like a bad dream. He and his father had not only been cordial to each other, but at times almost friendly.

He remembered how it had seemed that the day would stretch on forever, and that the past that had kept them distant from each other for more than ten years had never happened.

Halfway through their lunch, Drew had jumped to his feet and pulled Cole into the river. Never one to be bested, Cole had quickly retaliated. It had taken both of them to dunk Logan, and it had been all the three of them could do to pull their father into the water. Josh Spencer had been a big man, strong as a bull and twice as stubborn.

Within minutes they'd all been happily soaked, chest-deep in water so icy it stung. Splashing and laughing, they'd played like children, and by the time they'd dragged themselves home that evening, they'd all been too tired and happy to do much of anything but smile.

Running a hand over the desk's gleaming surface, Bess said, "I still remember the look on his face. I don't recall my brother ever at a loss for words, but when he saw what she'd done, he was positively dumbstruck."

"And do you remember what he said when he finally found his voice?" Logan smiled at the memory.

"I sure do. He just looked at her and said, 'I guess this means you expect me to learn to read and write?'"

They both laughed long and hard, but as their laughter faded, it was replaced by a melancholy silence that seemed to descend over both of them at the same time.

"It's good to have you home, Logan," Bess said softly.

He put his arm around her shoulders and they walked together to the kitchen. "I'm glad to be here," Logan said. "It feels..."

"Like home?" Bess supplied.

"Yes." The way he felt at Sarah's.

She brought the pie to the small oak breakfast table and sat down across from him. He took his first bite and smiled. "Delicious. Even better than I remembered."

"It was your father's favorite, too, remember?"

He did.

"The two of you always had so much in common. Your father was a proud man, Logan. He didn't know how to bend, and in the end it almost broke him. But he loved you, that much I know for sure. No matter what else you think, you need to remember that. It meant a lot that you were with him those last days in the hospital, though he couldn't tell you."

Dear Bess, always the mediator. "I believe you," he assured her as he reached over and patted her hand. He might not have accepted her assurances five years ago, but the changes in his own life made him believe her now.

Losing Sarah had forced him to confront his own fatal

flaws, and in doing so, he'd somehow gained insight into his father—the man from whom he seemed to have inherited so many of them.

"Did I ever tell you what he did the day you were born?"

She had, many times, but he didn't stop her when she launched into the tale again.

"He gave everyone the day off. By then your grandpa had retired and your dad was running the place. Oh, but he was proud! And right from the start he had so many plans for you."

Logan winced. "Yes. He certainly did."

She frowned. "And he was wrong."

Inexplicably Logan felt compelled to defend his father. "He couldn't help himself. He felt trapped by the things he'd done. He felt he'd wasted his life, and he didn't want the same thing to happen to me."

Bess sat up straighter in her chair. "Now that's just plain hogwash!" Her derisive tone shocked him. "Your father gave up his dreams because his dreams changed, not because he had a wife and son before he was ready. He loved this ranch, took pride in being known as one of the top breeders of quarter horses in the country. Believe me, nothing ever stopped Josh Spencer from doing exactly what he wanted."

Logan wasn't convinced, but he took another bite of pie rather than contradict her.

"Just think about it," she urged. "Do you really believe that if he'd wanted that law degree badly enough, anything would have stopped him from getting it?"

She'd made a good point. If the old man had ever encountered an obstacle he couldn't overcome, Logan couldn't remember it. "Then why—"

"That damn Spencer pride," she interrupted almost angrily, "that's why! It's a blessing and a curse, and so darn thick in our blood it's a wonder anyone puts up with us. When your dad told his father he was going to law school, your grandpa pitched a fit, just the way your own dad did when you told him you weren't accepting that scholarship."

"I never knew."

"He had no right to try to force his dreams on you," she said. "But you're wrong if you think he wasn't proud of you. Did you know he kept a scrapbook of all your accomplishments?"

Logan couldn't conceal his surprise.

Bess pushed away from the table and stood. "Hang on. I'll go get it."

In minutes she returned and handed him a leather-bound album.

As he leafed through it, Logan shook his head in disbelief.

Bess looked hard into his eyes. "In some ways I think you made him prouder than even Cole and Drew." She gave him a wry smile. "You know, you're more like him than either of them."

As he turned the pages, he was amazed to see that the entire album was filled with mementos of his days with the Denver P.D., some he hardly remembered.

Opposite the photograph taken the day he'd graduated from the police academy was a newspaper clipping. "Oh, that one made him especially proud," Bess said. It described how Logan had saved his partner during a drug bust gone awry. "And there's your picture with the police chief."

Emotion clogged Logan's throat as he turned the pages and came to the picture of Sarah and him in front of the apartment they'd shared in Denver, the old dog he'd rescued sitting happily between them.

He gazed at Sarah's pretty face and then closed the book. He leaned back in his chair and sighed. "I just wish I'd known him better..."

Bess patted his shoulder. "Life's too short for regrets, Logan. Just learn from them. Don't allow history to repeat itself in your own life. When you care for someone, let them know it before it's too late. Change and compromise won't kill a man, but loneliness sure can."

Her simple wisdom resonated in his heart. If he didn't set things right with Sarah, he knew he'd regret it for the rest of his life.

Chapter Fifteen

Logan opened the scrapbook again and gazed down at the picture of Sarah. Life didn't always offer a man a second chance, but when it did, only a fool would be too proud to grab it.

"Such a special girl," Bess said wistfully. "You know, I always thought the two of you made the perfect match."

"We did," Logan said. *We still do.*

Lifting his gaze from the page, he felt his aunt's assessing gaze and decided to shift the subject.

"Bess, what do you know about Sarah's mother?"

"Daisy."

He nodded.

"Well, not much really. I knew her of course—in a community this small, everyone knows everyone."

"What was she like?"

Bess's gray eyebrows drew together in concentration. "Like Sarah, she was beautiful. And that figure..." She rolled her eyes. "Let's just say she didn't hesitate to use all her charms to get what she wanted." She sighed. "She was a charmer, no denying that." She rose to bring a pitcher of lemonade to the table and fill their glasses. "A real party girl. She just couldn't seem to settle down. Not even after Sarah was born."

"What about Johnny? Where did he figure in?"

"Johnny was out of his mind in love with the woman, no doubt about that, and when she left him, we all feared he might finally drink himself to death."

"You remember when she left?"

"Oh, my, yes. It was all the talk for a while. Poor Sarah." Bess made a clucking sound with her tongue.

"Then you weren't surprised?"

"Oh, no, not really. Daisy had her faults, but not many women would have put up with Johnny, what with his drinking and never knowing from one week to the next if they'd have food on the table or a roof over their heads." She scowled. "But to just walk away from her child...well, that was what I never could understand."

"So, you think she left of her own free will?"

The suggestion seemed to shock Bess. "Of course she did. Never any question about that, I don't think. Leastwise, not to any of us who knew her."

"Was there another man?"

Bess sat up straighter in her chair. "That's what they said."

Logan leaned forward in his chair. "Did they say who?"

Her brows knitted. "I don't abide gossip, Logan Spencer," she informed him tersely.

"And I respect that," he said flatly. He could not remember if he'd ever heard his aunt pass on a snippet of rumor or say an unkind word about anyone. "And neither do I. But this is important, Bess."

"What's this all about, Logan? Why the sudden interest in Daisy Allen?"

When Logan hesitated, her scowl turned to a knowing smile. "Never mind. You don't have to tell me. I think I understand, and if this has anything to do with you and Sarah getting back together, I'm all for it."

He opened his mouth to tell her not to get her hopes up, but somehow the words wouldn't come. After what had happened between Sarah and him last night, his own hopes were riding high.

"You probably think you've grown too old to ask for my blessing, but that's where you're wrong. Besides, you've already got it. Sarah was the best thing that ever happened to you, if you don't mind my saying."

He stood and walked around the table and kissed her on the cheek. She smelled of peaches and cinnamon. "Believe me, I don't mind, sweetheart. Not in the least."

"Well, I guess I know you well enough to know you wouldn't be asking about Daisy Allen without good reason."

He thanked her for her confidence and waited for her to give him a name.

"All right," she said finally, inclining her head as if to impart state secrets. "But keep in mind, dear, it was only a rumor."

WHEN LOGAN TOLD his aunt he had to leave, she walked with him to the door. "Oh, wait a minute," she said, putting a hand on his arm. "I meant to send the rest of that pie home to Sarah, Jessica and Terri."

Before he could stop her, she'd headed back to the kitchen.

Logan stayed in the living room, and as he waited, he wandered over to the group of framed family pictures arranged on a side table beside the couch.

His attention was drawn to the recent picture of Cole, Anne and little Andy.

Smiling, he picked up the photograph and stared at his nephew's face. With Anne's sweet nature and Cole's keen intelligence, their two-year-old was already very special.

From the shape of his face to the determined tilt of his sculpted chin, he had Spencer written all over him. And yet he hadn't inherited the Spencer hair—that dark, almost black-brown hair that Logan and his brothers had. Andy's hair was light, almost strawberry blond, like Anne's.

Studying Andy's image more intensely, Logan marveled at how, within that small distinctive face, there seemed to reside so many elements of all of them—Cole's eyes, Anne's chin, Grandpa Josh's nose and, when he smiled, Drew's dimples.

And yet, with all those inherited traits, Andy still possessed a completely distinctive look.

Just like Jessica, he thought idly, whose eyes were replicas of her mother's, but who didn't resemble Sarah in any other way.

Nor Will, now that he thought about it. Will's face had been round. Jessica's was a near-perfect oval. Will's nose had been broad and short. Jessica's was small and fine. Will's coloring had been nearly as fair as Sarah's, and yet Jessica's complexion was definitely ruddy. Like his. The thought stopped him cold.

With his mind flicking back and forth between his mental image of Jessica and his nephew's picture, he felt for a moment as if his eyes were playing tricks on him.

The longer he stared, the harder he stared, the more he began to see an uncanny resemblance. But how was that possible? How? Unless…

And you can come to my birthday party, too! It's in a couple of weeks…

A couple of weeks. That meant the first of July. Jessica Lynn Breedan, four years old going on five. In July. Five years ago Sarah had left him. It had been just before Christmas. He'd given the turkey she'd purchased for their dinner to a homeless shelter. His mind raced back in time to the empty apartment, to the unanswered calls, all his letters returned unopened.

He'd driven home to the valley but she'd refused to see him—wouldn't see anyone, according to what his aunt had later told him. And then, that February, the shocking news that she'd married Will Breedan.

December to July, with a wedding in February.

His heart froze while his mind did the math. December to July, seven months, with a wedding in between. And then, a baby. His baby! His and Sarah's. Jessica! His daughter. His child.

Dear God, Sarah! What had she done to them?

SARAH HAD JUST FINISHED putting clean towels in the linen closet when she heard footsteps on the porch. As much as she tried to deny the feeling, thoughts of seeing Logan again set her senses thrumming.

He hadn't come to the house for breakfast, and when she returned from taking Jessica to the dentist this afternoon, his pickup was gone. For the rest of the day her nerves had been on constant edge with the anticipation of seeing him again. The memories of last night, of their intimate exchange, distracted her, kept her feeling vaguely disoriented and wistful.

It would be hard enough facing him after what had happened, and the waiting had only made it worse. Torturous.

She'd heard his truck pulling into the drive this evening just before supper. But when Terri called to invite him to join them for dinner, he told her he'd eaten in town. And then, less than an hour later, she'd seen him driving away again.

The most she'd seen of him all day was a glimpse of his back as he'd headed to the barn just before sunset to feed and water the livestock. And seeing him then had only been by chance. *Chance, my foot,* she thought miserably. It had not been by chance that she'd agreed to play Old Maid with Jessica and then talked her into moving their game into the living room where she'd have a clear view of the barn.

Watching him steer a wide path around the house had told Sarah everything she needed to know. He was avoiding her. There was no other explanation. Since the day he'd appeared out of the blue on her doorstep, she'd found herself literally tripping over the man at every turn.

And it wasn't difficult to guess what made today different. He didn't want to see her; he regretted what had transpired between them last night. Despite what he'd said about changing, her emotional outburst had given him pause.

The realization hurt. Deeply. Last night, wrapped in his arms and blinded by her deep need, Sarah had almost allowed herself to believe that he really had changed. That he truly was capable of the kind of emotional commitment she'd always wanted and needed from him.

By the clear light of day, however, she discovered she'd been wrong. Again.

At the sound of his knock on the front door she said, "I'll get it," loud enough to be heard over the sound of the television coming from the living room.

Out of habit she ran a hand through her hair on her way out of the bedroom. At the door she stopped and took a deep breath in a futile effort to steady her jangled nerves. Her hand shook as she turned the knob and opened the door.

"Evening, Sarah."

Like a startled deer, she stood staring wide-eyed at the man standing in the pool of light from the porch lamp. The man who was not Logan.

THAT NIGHT Logan was waiting in Nick's driveway when the man they'd once called Hollywood Nick drove in.

"Logan," Nick said as he climbed out of his truck and slammed the door behind him. "What are you doing out here this time of night?" The yard light illuminated Nick's face and revealed an expression that told Logan he was the last person he wanted to see.

"I've been waiting for you, Nick. I tried to buy you a beer the other day at the Round-up, but seems you were in a big hurry to leave."

Nick shrugged.

"I don't like it when people avoid me," Logan went on. "I start taking it kind of personal."

Nick tried to laugh off Logan's accusation, but there was no humor in the sound and he didn't seem able to make eye contact. "Well, hell, come on in," he drawled. "Let's have us that beer now. No use standing out here in the dark."

"I don't want a beer, Nick," Logan said. "I want answers."

All pretense of geniality faded and Nick's blue eyes narrowed. "About what?"

"Daisy Allen," Logan said evenly. "What do you know about her disappearance?"

This time Nick's laugh was loud. "Daisy Allen? Hell, Logan, I was just a kid when she took off. What makes you think I'd know anything about that?" Nick leaned back against his pickup's left fender and folded his arms.

"Just a hunch," Logan said. "I want to find her, and I thought a guy like you might know where to start looking."

"Sorry, friend. She was way before my time. Now if you ask me about her daughter…"

It was all Logan could do to keep from lunging at the man and wiping the lascivious smile off his face. "Let's get something straight. First, I'm not your friend. And second, as far as Sarah is concerned, I think we've had this conversation before. Do you really want a replay?''

Nick's hand went to his nose as he edged away from the truck, putting a little distance between himself and the fist he sensed was just itching to make his face a target.

"Hey, I didn't mean anything by that. No disrespect, Spencer. So just simmer down.''

"What do you know about that broken valve in Sarah's hay field?'' Logan asked. "And before you answer, I should tell you I'm aware of what you did to Stan Bailey.''

Nick stood up straighter. "I don't know what you're talking about.''

"I think you do,'' Logan said. "In fact, I think all those things that drove the Baileys out of business have your signature on them. And what's more, I think Glenn Driscoll might see it the same way.''

Nick's eyes turned a steely blue. "Get the hell off my property, Spencer,'' he spat, then turned and started for the house.

Before he could take another step, Logan caught his shoulder and spun him around, snagged a fistful of shirt and slammed the ex-rodeo rider against the fender of his shiny new pickup.

"I know all about Amarillo, Gallus. How you drugged that horse and spent two years in jail for your trouble. Did you use the same drug to kill Bailey's cattle or have you moved on to something stronger?''

Nick was tall and athletic, and in one fluid motion, he jerked free of Logan's grasp. There was hatred in his eyes when he cocked his arm, but before his fist could connect with Logan's jaw, Nick found himself facedown in the driveway with his right arm bent painfully behind him and Logan's knee in his back.

"You always did prefer to do things the hard way," Logan drawled. "Now, start talking, Gallus. And keep it interesting."

"EARL! SARAH GASPED. "What are you doing here?"

The stomach that bulged over his belt shook when he laughed and pushed his old gray Stetson a little farther back on his balding head. "Now, ain't that a heck of a greeting for an old friend!" His pale almost translucent eyes twinkled.

Flustered, Sarah stammered out an apology. "Oh, I— I'm sorry, Earl. You surprised me, that's all. I wasn't expecting anyone this late."

"I drove over to Grand Junction for an auction this afternoon and decided to swing by on my way home and see how you're doing." He glanced past her into the hallway. "Hope I haven't interrupted anything." He shifted his weight from one booted foot to the other, and Sarah realized with a flush of embarrassment that she hadn't even asked him to come in.

"No, you're not interrupting anything. Come in, Earl. It's nice to see you."

Still adjusting to the shock of finding Earl Fraizer on her front porch, instead of Logan, she almost stumbled stepping aside to let him in. Then she noticed that he was carrying an oblong pan.

"Gaylene sent these," he said, handing it to her. "Our grandkids are crazy about her sticky buns, and she made an extra batch for your little one when she found out I was planning to come by your place today."

Regardless of what Logan thought of the Fraizers, Earl and his wife and their son, Orrin, had never been anything but kind to her, as evidenced by this latest gesture.

Sarah smiled her appreciation. "I'll give her a call and

thank her tomorrow. Say, I was just about to fix myself a glass of iced tea. Won't you join me?''

"Sounds good," he said, and followed her into the living room where Jessica was watching a Barney video, and Terri was doing her nails.

Earl and Terri exchanged greetings, but when Earl said, "Hey there, Jessica, how's the girl?" Jessica was too absorbed in her video to be bothered with anything but an absent nod.

"Jess, say hello to Mr. Fraizer," Sarah prodded.

Without taking her eyes off the television, Jessica muttered, "Hi."

"Sorry, Earl. I swear that purple dinosaur has hypnotic powers."

"No problem," Earl replied genially.

"Come into the kitchen, and I'll get our tea."

As Sarah filled their glasses from the gallon jar on the countertop, Earl lowered himself onto one of the kitchen chairs.

"Helluva storm last night," he said. "We measured an inch up at our place, but by the condition of your road, I'd say it rained even harder here."

"I wouldn't doubt it," she replied gravely.

When she brought their tea to the table, she felt his eyes searching her face.

"Sorry about your hay crop, Sarah."

She sighed and sat down on the chair opposite his. "After the incident with the broken valve last week, we knew it would be a dicey proposition getting the hay dried and turned again before it rained."

"Damn shame, anyway," he said as he measured a couple of teaspoons of sugar into his glass and stirred. "Reckon you'll get a third cutting?"

The question jarred her. She should have been asking

herself the same question today, instead of wasting her energy moping, worrying about whether or not she would run into Logan Spencer. Whether there really was a possibility for a second chance between them.

"I don't know," she said. "It will depend on the weather of course and if the water hasn't done too much damage to the root systems. We might have to wait and replant in the spring."

Earl tried to cheer her. "Well, you've still got your cattle." But despite his optimism, she knew they both realized the financial ramifications of losing the income the second cutting of alfalfa hay would have ensured.

"Ever figure out what caused that break?"

She shook her head. "Not yet." She thought about what Logan had said about the damage to the irrigation system having been done maliciously, but for some reason she felt reluctant to share that with Earl.

"You know, Sarah, a place like this would bring a good price in today's market."

Sarah rose to refill their glasses. "But I don't want to sell," she said. "We'll get by. Every rancher goes through a bad season now and then."

"True enough. Trouble is, one season has a way of turning into another."

She didn't come back to the table, but stood leaning against the counter, sipping her tea without tasting. Hearing Earl give voice to her own fears made them seem suddenly more ominous.

"I know Will was struggling to make ends meet, even with his sheriff's salary. The ranch was heavily indebted when he took over, but it's too bad he had to resort to a second mortgage."

Resentment stung her when she realized Will had confided in Earl something he hadn't seen fit to confide in her.

A dull ache began behind her eyes, and she wished she could think of a way to change the subject.

The grim look on Earl's face, however, and his constant fidgeting with the sugar spoon told her that he wouldn't be sidetracked. That this visit had been planned and was not social.

"I know it's none of my business, Sarah," he drawled, "but I can't help wondering how long you're going to be able to hang on."

She had been wondering—and worrying about—the same thing. With her hay crop all but obliterated, she had no idea how she would deal with the creditors she'd stalled with promises of payment from the proceeds of her second cutting—the second harvest that was now nonexistent.

"I'll get by," she said, trying to sound more hopeful than she felt. "Like you said, I've got cattle I can sell, and if it comes down to it, half a dozen nice colts."

"I admire your spirit, Sarah. Always have." He dragged his hat from his head and rubbed his wide forehead. "And I want to help."

"I appreciate that, Earl. But right now I just need to assess my losses and go from there." And pray the bank would agree to help her through until spring, she thought grimly.

"I have a better idea," he said, and then paused long enough to drain his glass. "Why don't I make you an offer right now. This minute. You can get out from under this burden just that easy."

Nothing he could have said would have shocked her more, and for a moment she couldn't find her voice.

"Now don't go getting all proud on me, Sarah," he said in such a fatherly way she felt disarmed. "I'm not doing this as a favor. This ranch has a lot of potential, and taking it on doesn't hurt me one bit. If it makes it any easier, you and your little gal can stay here through the end of the summer. I wouldn't need to take possession right away. That will give you time to look around Denver and find yourself another job, like that one you had when you lived there before—a vet's clinic, wasn't it? I bet you're real good at that. You always did have a way with animals.''

This was happening too fast. He had his checkbook in front of him and was pulling a pen from his shirt pocket.

"Earl," she said, her voice surprisingly firm, "I don't want to sell."

He held up his hand and smiled. "I know. No one likes to give up. And you weren't expecting my offer. But believe me, prolonging this is only going to make it harder when the time comes. Now, we don't have to talk numbers tonight. In the meantime ten thousand ought to qualify as earnest money, shouldn't it?"

Flatly astonished, Sarah had to clear her throat to speak. "Earl, I don't think you're listening. I said I don't want to sell. I don't want to go back to Denver." She snagged a breath. "This is my home and I'm staying."

He stared, the look on his face incredulous. "Sarah, do you understand what I'm offering?"

"Yes. Completely. And I'm saying no."

His expression turned hard, strangely almost threatening. "Sarah, you're not acting rational. How do you expect to make that second-mortgage payment this fall?"

Anger and indignation fought for possession of her emotions. "How do you know about that?"

The smile that curved his colorless lips was devoid of humor. "Because I arranged for Will to get it."

His declaration shocked her.

"Just after the two of you were married, Will nearly lost this place. The bank turned him down flat. In fact, they were threatening to foreclose on the first note. He came to me for help. He knew how much this place meant to you and, well, frankly, Sarah—'' Earl leaned back in his chair and rubbed his chin ''—he was afraid if he lost this place, you'd leave him. He never had any illusions about why you married him—you know, what with the little one on the way and all.''

A sense of sickening betrayal coiled in the pit of her stomach at the thought of Will discussing their personal life with this man. Out of her humiliation came a flood of white-hot anger. ''I think you'd better go, Earl,'' she said, fighting to control her temper.

He blinked and stared at her almost as if he hadn't heard right.

''Now,'' she said, and started for the back door.

''You're making a big mistake, Sarah.''

Sarah took a step toward him, to tell him again to leave, but the sound of Jessica's animated exclamations coming from the living room stopped her.

Chapter Sixteen

"Logan!" Jessica's excited voice echoed through the hallway and into the kitchen. "You're back!"

"Hi there, kiddo." Sarah couldn't remember Logan's voice ever sounding so buoyant or more welcome.

"Is that for me?" Jessica asked.

"Sure is. Try it on for size."

In the next instant Jessica dashed into the kitchen sporting a child-size Stetson. It was pale pink with a thin leather band and three white feathers dangling down the back.

"Mommy! Mommy! Look what I got! Logan got me a hat. A real cowboy hat!" She twirled to properly show it off. "And it's all pink! My favorite color!"

Logan sidled into the doorway and stood leaning with his arms crossed beaming at the child whose heart he'd just stolen.

"Mommy!" Jessica cried. "Will you *look* at my hat? I'm a real cowgirl, aren't I?"

Sarah's eyes met Logan's over the top of Jessica's new prized possession. "Yes, sweetheart. I guess you are." It took every ounce of strength she possessed to put on a good face for her daughter. "A real cowgirl. But I think you might have forgotten to tell Logan something?"

"Oops!" Jessica whirled around and launched herself

into Logan's arms. "Thank you, Logan!" She planted a noisy kiss on his beard-stubbled cheek. "Thank you so much!" Then she wriggled out of his arms to run back into the living room.

Logan turned to look after her with a smile that sent Sarah's heart into complete meltdown. When he turned back to her, however, his smile disappeared so fast she felt as though she'd been drenched in ice water.

"Logan," Earl said, coming to his feet. "It's been a long time." He crossed to Logan with his hand extended. "How are you, son?"

Logan's expression remained flat and unreadable as he shook Earl's hand.

"Nick and Riley told me they'd seen you the other day," Earl went on. "What brings you back to the valley? No problems with the family, I hope? Bess doing okay?"

"Family's all well," Logan said through lips that barely moved.

Seemingly oblivious to the animosity coming off the other man in waves, Earl smiled. "Well, now, that's good to hear. Just visiting, then?"

"He's working for me, Earl."

The older man took a step back and his gaze traveled between the two of them. "That a fact?" His eyes narrowed and a knowing grin curled into an ugly smile.

"Yes," Logan said. He glanced at the checkbook still lying open on the table and then at Sarah. "That's a fact."

"Living right here, are you?"

"Yes."

Earl's smile dimmed. "Well, hell, why not? You're both over twenty-one."

Logan took a measured step toward the older man. "I don't think I care for what you're implying, Fraizer."

"Logan, please…" Sarah interjected, moving across the kitchen to impose herself between the two men.

"Hey, Spencer," Earl said smoothly, backing up a step. "Hell, I didn't mean anything. Everyone knows the two of you had something going once."

Sarah watched Logan's jaw clench and unclench.

"Don't get me wrong, boy." Earl's response was strained, not nearly as good-natured as he tried to make it sound. He was a big man—in more ways than one, for he was a respected and successful member of the community—and Sarah knew he wasn't accustomed to being challenged or forced to back down. "I'm all for anything that helps our little Sarah. Which brings us back to the point of my visit." He shifted his attention to Sarah. "So how much did we say?"

"We didn't," Sarah reminded him. "Earl was just leaving," she told Logan pointedly.

"Not quite," the older man said. "Say, Spencer, you're a businessman. What would you say this place is worth?"

Sarah's patience snapped. "Stop it, Earl! I told you I'm not interested in selling, and that's the end of it."

She stood glaring at the man, so angry her chest was heaving, so near the edge of control she didn't know what she would do if he touched her. "I asked you twice to leave. And now I'm telling you again. Get out, Earl!"

She could feel Logan's eyes on her back and wanted more than anything to know that he would back her up. How could she have guessed what was on his mind? How could she have predicted the next startling event or the words that would come out of his mouth, words that would shock and betray at the same time?

"Hang on a minute, Sarah," he said. "Maybe you're being too hasty. Let's hear him out. Sit down, Earl. I have a few questions I'd like to ask."

When Logan turned to her, his expression was inscrutable and cold. "Sit down, Sarah," he said evenly.

It felt as though her world had tilted, as though he'd crushed her pride and her heart beneath his boot heel and ground them both to dust. How could she have believed he'd changed, that he'd come to recognize how much her dreams meant to her?

"Sit down, Sarah," he said again.

Earl beamed. "Well, now. That's just fine. Glad to see someone around here has some common sense."

If there had been any way the hatred she felt for Logan at that moment could somehow have been transferred to her glare, the man would be picking himself up off the floor.

When he took a step toward her, she stiffened. "Trust me, Sarah," he said in a low voice. "Just sit down and listen."

The anger sluicing through her veins made it impossible to think straight, but something in his eyes warned her that there was more going on here than met the eye. On blind trust and still almost too stunned to think, she moved woodenly to the chair opposite Earl and sat down.

Earl reclaimed his chair, but Logan remained standing, his arms folded over his chest, his feet braced wide.

"Now, Earl, you were saying?"

Earl settled himself in his chair and charged on with the business at hand. "All right. Here's the deal. I know the financial situation of this place. Like I was just about to explain to Sarah, I co-signed on that second note for Will. Anyway, we all know there's no way she can make both mortgage payments this fall, what with that rain ruining her crop, coming the way it did on the heels of that accident with the irrigation system and all—"

"And the damaged fence," Logan put in.

Earl blinked, and it seemed to Sarah a little color seeped out of his face. "Fence? Well, I guess I didn't hear about that."

"Oh, you remember, don't you Earl?" Logan said with a lightness Sarah recognized as feigned. "The five-hundred-dollar fence?"

This time it was Sarah who was taken aback. "Logan? What are you taking about? What five-hundred-dollar fence?"

He held up a hand, asking her for patience. "Wasn't that the price you and Nick agreed on? Five hundred?"

Earl started to get up out of his chair, but Logan's hand moved swiftly and pushed him back down. "Sit tight, Earl. And don't make a scene." His voice was hard-edged and dangerous. "There's a little girl and a very pregnant woman in the next room, and if you do anything to upset either one of them, I'll break you in half without even thinking."

"Why you..." Again Earl attempted to get up out of his chair, but again, Logan's hand stopped him.

"Listen to me, Fraizer." He bent down close and stared directly into Earl's eyes. "Your boy Nick and I just had a little conversation about broken irrigation valves and fence lines. After that we had a chat with Glenn Driscoll. The good deputy is waiting right now to have a similar chat with you."

Sarah was on her feet. "Logan! What's going on? What's this all about?"

He ignored her. "Now, Earl, I'm giving you a choice. Do I call Driscoll and tell him you're here, or do you want to drive to the sheriff's substation and turn yourself in?"

The big man's face was a mask of rage. "Go to hell, Spencer." He knocked Logan's hand off his shoulder and rose so fast the chair almost tipped over.

"It seems you've chosen the latter," Logan said. "All right." With a cool professionalism that chilled her, Logan walked with him to the door. "But just in case you plan on going anywhere besides the sheriff's substation, you should know that the minute you walk out that door I'll be on the phone to Deputy Driscoll." The lethal light in his eyes left no doubt that he would do precisely as he promised.

"You don't know who you're dealing with, Spencer." There was venom in every word. "When my lawyers get finished with you, I'll not only hold title to this place, but to that fancy quarter-horse spread next door, as well. I'm not finished with you! Either of you!" he promised.

And just when Sarah thought she couldn't have been more bewildered by the strange turn of events taking place in her kitchen, Earl, propelled by pure rage, stomped out her back door.

THE SOUND of the back door slamming seemed to echo endlessly between them. Feeling considerably less angry now but more thoroughly confused, Sarah could only stand staring at Logan, deciding which question to ask first.

Taking a deep breath, she walked up to him and stood with her hands planted on her hips. "Would you please tell me what that was all about?"

When he didn't answer, she felt singed by the heat in his glare. "Logan? What is it? What on earth has gotten into you? And what just happened here?"

"I have a phone call to make," he said, and grabbed the receiver from the wall phone and dialed. She heard him tell Glenn Driscoll that Earl had just left the ranch. Then he replaced the receiver and turned back to her.

"Come with me, Sarah," he said, his voice so low it rumbled. He left the room to head down the hallway. Sarah gasped, as if his leaving had sucked all the air out of the room.

Who did he think he was, anyway? Marching into her house and ordering her around like some errant child? Still, she followed him out into the hallway and saw him waiting for her at the front door.

"Outside," he said quietly.

"Why?"

"We need to talk, but not here."

When she hesitated, he grabbed her hand.

"Let go of me!" she demanded, struggling in vain to free herself from his grasp. "Logan! What's come over you? What do you think…"

His gaze flicked toward the living room, reminding her of the pair of small ears waiting around the corner to absorb every angry word.

"I'm not taking another step until you tell me what this is all about," she informed him in a voice only the two of them could hear.

A dark unfathomable stare was his only reply, and with her hand still firmly in his grasp, he leaned his head into the living room.

"Terri," he said in a surprisingly calm voice, "would you mind keeping an eye on Jessica for a little while? Sarah and I are going for a walk."

Sarah tugged again to try to free her hand from his unrelenting grip. "I'm not going…"

The declaration died on her lips when he gave her hand a meaningful squeeze, a clear warning that brooked no argument.

Her mind raced, and it occurred to her that perhaps he had heard from the anonymous tipster, or maybe there had been some news of her father.

"Sure, no problem. Have a nice time," Terri replied, her

tone telling Sarah she was oblivious to the drama being played out in the hallway.

"We shouldn't be too long," Sarah said, her eyes moving to Logan's for confirmation. When she received none, she added, "But if we're not back by the time Jessica's video ends, would you see that she gets a bath and goes to bed?"

Terri glanced up at her. "Sure. Take your time."

"Fine," Sarah managed to say before she addressed her daughter. "Terri will tuck you in tonight, Jess. I'll come kiss you good-night when I get back."

Barney seemed to have worked his magic again. Without looking up, Jessica said, "Uh-huh." She blinked and seemed for a moment to come out of her trance. "Can I sleep with my hat?"

"Sure," Logan put in before Sarah could answer.

"Bye, Logan," Sarah heard Jessica call out as he pulled her toward the door.

"Bye, kiddo. See you in the morning."

And in the next heartbeat Sarah found herself half running to keep up with the man who hauled her out of the house and into the pine-scented darkness.

A MINUTE LATER, Sarah and Logan were sitting opposite each other at the picnic table at the edge of the yard.

"Earl Fraizer paid Nick Gallus a thousand dollars to sabotage your hay crop. He paid him to tear down your fences, as well. The plan was to ruin your harvest and generally cause you so many headaches you'd be ready to sell when Earl made his offer."

Although incredible, this much of the story at least started to explain a few of the questions whirling through Sarah's mind. "But if Earl was so interested in buying this place, why didn't he just come to me and make me an offer?''

''Who knows?'' Logan replied. ''From what I've been able to gather, he did the same thing to Stan Bailey. He pushed the man to the brink of ruin and then moved in and picked up the property at a fire-sale price.'' He spoke evenly and without emotion, and Sarah couldn't explain the distinctly angry tone that seemed more directed at her than Earl Fraizer.

''Nick has been Earl's minion for the last two years. And now he's going to help put his boss behind bars.''

Sarah felt shaken, realizing the men she'd trusted were, for all intents and purposes, ruthless criminals. ''When Nick was confessing to his crimes, did he say what connection he has to my mother? Why his name appeared in Will's notes?''

Logan shook his head. ''He claims he has no idea.''

''Do you think he was telling the truth?''

''Strange as it may seem, yes. The man confessed to arson…''

Her eyes posed the question.

''He was responsible for the fire that destroyed Stan Bailey's barn,'' he explained. ''That's an offense that will mean jail time, especially in light of his record.'' He went on to explain what Cole had told him about Nick's crimes in Amarillo and the subsequent conviction. ''By the time he finished talking to Glenn, he was ready to confess to anything in order to go on record as cooperative and hopefully reduce his jail time. At that point it's hard to believe, if he knew anything about your mother or why his name showed up in Will's notes, he would have lied.''

''What about Earl? Do you really think his lawyers can get him off?''

Logan shrugged. "It's hard to say. Glenn will be able to tell us more in the morning."

Sarah sighed, feeling suddenly drained, but relieved to have at least this portion of the mystery behind them. Now it was time to find out why Logan had been so strangely insistent she follow him out into the yard.

"Why did you drag me out here, Logan? There's nothing you've told me so far that couldn't have been discussed in the house."

He sat looking at her a long quiet moment, then he rose and paced a few steps across the lawn. Sensing he was a man engaged in some terrible inner struggle, Sarah merely sat, waiting for him to find the words to say what was driving him in this inexplicable way.

The moon was only half full, but it shone with a startling white light. When Logan finally walked back to the table and stood staring down at her, it cast a shadow over his face that made him seem strangely ominous.

Sarah swallowed hard and searched his face for some flicker of the man who'd held her last night, who'd whispered tender assurances and promised her everything would be all right.

"Logan?" She despised the raspy trepidation in her voice, but the intensity of his gaze frightened her.

"Why, Sarah?" There was such a mix of anguish and rage in his simple question that she flinched and found herself unable to respond. "Why did you do this to me? To her? To us?" he demanded, his voice barely above a whisper.

Her stomach lurched and her heart hammered against her rib cage.

"How? How could you do this to me? Did you think I wouldn't love her?" He grabbed her hands and yanked her to her feet. "Tell me, Sarah," he demanded, his eyes moist and glistening and his voice ragged. "Damn it, tell me why I shouldn't hate you?"

"Logan, please—"

"No!" he shouted. "Talk, Sarah. Tell me."

Suddenly all the shock and the fear fused into anger, and she jerked free of his grasp. "All right!" she said. "You want to know, I'll tell you. I left for her. You didn't want her."

"I didn't know!" he reminded her scathingly.

"But what if I had told you I was pregnant?" she demanded. "What if I had told you? What then, Logan? Can you tell me you'd have been happy? That you'd have changed your life to be the kind of father she deserved?"

"And so you chose Will." The bitterness in his accusation scalded her.

"Yes," she declared defiantly. "I chose Will. Will Breedan, a man who wanted the same things I did. A home. A family. A man driven by his love for his family, not by some twisted need to prove himself to his dead father!"

One look at his face, and she knew he'd felt slapped by her accusation.

"Is that what you thought?"

"It's true, isn't it? All those hours working to be supercop, putting in the extra shifts, risking your life, fighting for the promotions and the commendations. It was all for him. Not me. Not us. Not our future, but to prove to him that you were worthy. That he hadn't made a mistake, after all. That the child who ruined his life had finally amounted to more than he ever could." Her chest heaved with emotion and her eyes stung. "I didn't want that for her. I didn't want her to ever feel she owes her father anything, that she has to prove she's worthy or that she belongs." Suddenly she couldn't look at him, and she turned her back and stood looking unseeingly into the moonlit night.

"I chose Will," she said softly. "I wanted a better life for Jessica than I'd had. Will wanted the same thing. He said he loved me. He wanted me. He put us first. He was a good father."

Her words echoed between them, and for a moment neither of them spoke or moved. It was as though time hung suspended, as though this moment of startling pain would never end.

"I loved you," he said quietly. "I would have married you."

"I know," she said without turning around. "You're an honorable man. But I didn't want your honor, Logan. I wanted you. I wanted you to love me enough to make changes in your life for us. You didn't love me enough to help me find my dream."

"Nor you me," he said.

She did turn to face him then. "You're right. We were both wrong. Both selfish. I knew you would have done the right thing. Out of honor. Out of duty."

"Out of love," he said so softly she almost didn't hear.

His quiet admission tore at her heart and bright tears filled her eyes as the grief of losing him a second time engulfed her.

"I was wrong," she admitted to him and herself. "I'm sorry."

His laugh was joyless. "Sorry," he scoffed. And when he turned and walked away, she felt her heart shatter beyond repair.

Chapter Seventeen

All at once she was consumed with the need to go after him. "Logan," she cried as she ran. "Please. Stop. Wait. You can't just…"

She caught up to him and he spun around to face her, his eyes glistening with tears. "I never held my baby," he said, his voice cracking with sorrow. "I didn't hear her first word or see her first smile. What was it like, Sarah? What did it feel like to hold our angel in your arms?" The tears slipped from the corners of his eyes, and Sarah felt gutted.

"I quit the force for you," he said. "I've been working for the FBI, strictly freelance, for some time. And I was ready to give that up, as well. For you. I thought if I left law enforcement I could win you back. I came back to find Will's killer, but from the beginning all I wanted was another chance for us." His hands were clenched at his sides and his voice shook.

"Oh, Logan." She reached for him, but he pulled away. "I—I was wrong. I know that now. I see how you are with her, what a good and kind father you would have been."

His expression changed in a heartbeat from abject sorrow to steely anger. "Not would have been, Sarah. Am. What kind of father I am. I am her father. And I always will be."

The force of his declaration rocked her, stole her breath and left her trembling.

She had no idea how long they stood there, locked in that heart-wrenching impasse, searching for some way out of the awful nightmarish moment, some way to heal their wounded lives.

But then the screen door banged open, and Jessica ran out onto the porch and down the steps. Dressed in her nightgown, her feet bare and her blue eyes wide, she raced toward them. Her small face had a look of stark terror.

"Jessica!" Sarah exclaimed when her daughter reached her. "Honey, what is it? What's the matter?"

"Oh, Mommy!" Jessica's face crumpled and she began to sob. "Come quick! Something's wrong with Terri!"

Sarah bent to scoop the frightened child up into her arms as Logan ran to the house. Clutching Jessica, Sarah raced after him, her heart pounding.

When she burst through the front door, she found Logan bending over Terri, who was curled into a ball on the floor.

"It...it's the baby," Terri gasped. "I...I think it's time."

Just then a beam from a pair of headlights swept through the room, and Sarah turned to see a pickup careering toward the house.

The truck wasn't slowing, and she screamed when it crashed into the fence. Then she watched in stunned disbelief as Johnny shoved open the door and staggered out from behind the wheel.

Everything happened quickly, in a mass of confused activity. Logan helped Terri to her feet and guided her to the couch. "Sit tight. I'll bring my pickup around."

Johnny staggered up the steps. "Sarah," he sputtered. "I d-didn't mean to... I mean, I th-think I hit your f-f-fence."

"Sarah, call the hospital," Logan shouted. "Tell them we're on our way."

When Johnny stumbled through the door, Jessica started to cry. While trying to soothe her, Sarah grabbed her father's arm and guided him into the room, where he promptly collapsed on the floor. "Dad!"

"Sarah, please. Call the hospital!" Logan shouted again as he ran through the kitchen and out the back door.

If she had ever felt so torn, Sarah couldn't remember when. The world was spinning in a dozen directions at once, and she didn't know which way to turn.

When Terri shrieked, the sound propelled Sarah to act.

With a glance over her shoulder at the old man crumpled on the floor, she moved quickly to the couch, still holding Jessica in her arms.

"Terri," she said, forcing her voice to be steady in a way that belied her shattered nerves. "It's going to be all right. Just calm down. We're going to get you to the hospital."

She set Jessica down on the couch beside Terri. "Jess, I want you to stay here with Terri and talk to her while I call the hospital. Can you do that, honey? Can you help Terri? She's going to be all right. She's not sick. She's going to have her baby and we have to help her."

Jessica sniffed and nodded, and Sarah ran to the phone.

When she came back, Terri was talking quietly to Jessica. "It...it's all right, pumpkin. I'm going to have my baby. Won't that be great?"

Just then, another contraction hit her, and she grabbed Sarah's hand and squeezed for all she was worth. Jessica whimpered.

"It's all right," Sarah told both the terrified teenager and her own child, putting an arm around each of them. "This is natural. This is what happens when a baby comes. It'll be all right." She stroked Terri's hair and gave Jessica another hug. "Honey, do you want to help some more?"

Jessica gave a tentative nod. She'd stopped crying and now seemed mesmerized by all the excitement.

"Good. What Terri needs right now is a pillow. Do you think you can go get one and bring it to her?"

"Sure," Jessica said, and raced into the bedroom. By the time she came back with the pillow, Terri's contraction had subsided, and she smiled as Jessica slid the pillow under her head. "Thanks, pumpkin," she said. "You're such a big girl."

Jessica beamed. "I'm going to help you, Terri. I'm going to help you get your baby."

Sarah and Terri exchanged nervous smiles.

"Terri," Sarah said gently, "your contractions seem to be coming pretty close together. I want you to listen to me and do what I say."

Terri nodded uncertainly as Sarah reminded her of the breathing techniques she'd been taught in childbirth classes.

"But what about Grandpa Johnny?" Jessica asked.

Sarah glanced past her daughter's shoulder to where her father still lay. "He'll be all right, sweetheart. Listen—do you hear that? He's snoring. Maybe you could get him a pillow, too? He just needs to sleep a bit, and when he wakes up he'll be just fi—"

Terri screamed when another contraction hit and once again the momentary calm was shattered. When the contraction ended, Terri assured Jessica she was going to be okay. Just saying the words and having to find a way to comfort the child seemed to give the young woman strength.

Sarah listened to Terri and couldn't have felt prouder if the young woman had been her own daughter.

She leaned over to hug the brave teenager, and when she did she whispered in her ear, "You're going to be a wonderful mother, Terri. Don't worry. Everything's going to be all right."

Terri nodded and managed a smile, but in her eyes Sarah saw the doubt. "But what about Hank?" she asked, her voice shaking. "Should I... I mean, do you think we should call him?"

"Yes," Sarah said. "We'll call him now. He can meet you at the hospital."

"But what if..." Terri's eyes filled with tears. "I mean, what if he doesn't want to come? What if he doesn't want me, doesn't want the ba—"

"We can't second-guess the future, Terri. We just have to trust. You have to give Hank a chance. He has the right to make his own decisions. This is his child, too, you know?" She smiled for Terri's sake. "It's the right thing to do. None of us knows what the future holds, but you owe it to yourself and to your baby to give Hank a second chance. You're a family now. You, the baby and Hank. People make mistakes. But people can change. He loves you, right? Didn't he tell you he loved you?"

Terri nodded.

"Give him a chance to prove it. Don't do anything to push him away. There's so much at stake, and the choice you make now will affect all of you forever. Love is a powerful force, Terri. Give it a chance."

She heard a noise behind her and thought for a moment it was her father coming around, but when she looked up she saw Logan was standing right behind her. His eyes moved over her face, his expression unreadable.

"I had to move Johnny's pickup to get mine close to the yard. Is she ready?"

Sarah stood up. "Jessica," she said, "would you stay with Terri a minute?"

Jessica nodded emphatically. "We're going to have a baby," she told Logan. "And I have to take care of Terri."

When he smiled, pure love shone from his eyes.

Sarah placed a hand on his arm. "Come into the kitchen a minute," she said in a low voice.

Once alone with him, Sarah fought to ignore the myriad emotions she now saw reflected in his eyes. "Her contractions are very close together," she said. "Not more than two or three minutes apart. I'm not sure we have time to get her to the hospital."

Logan frowned. "I'd like to try. There's no way of knowing if there will be complications, and with a first baby, we need all the help we can get."

Having this strong capable man to lean on calmed Sarah. "You're right. But what about Johnny? We can't just leave him here like this."

Logan shook his head. "No. And I don't think Jessica needs to be involved in any more trauma tonight. I'll take Terri to the hospital. You stay here with Jessica and your father."

Sarah's heart sank. "But I've gone to all the birthing classes with her, I always thought I'd be with her when the time came."

"Which might happen sooner than we think. Do you really want Jessica in the front seat of a pickup if that baby decides to make his appearance somewhere along the highway?"

The thought of the intensity of that situation and the effect it might have on her child made Sarah shudder. "No, of course, you're right."

"Did you call the hospital?" he asked as he strode back into the living room to help Terri off the couch.

Sarah nodded. "They're expecting you. And I'll call Hank and let him know you're on your way."

Terri smiled her appreciation over Logan's shoulder as he assisted her out onto the porch. "I just hope we make it that far," she said in a small voice.

"It's going to be all right," Logan told her. "When I was a cop, I delivered a baby in the back of a pizza delivery van and another in the dressing room of a department store."

Sarah and Jessica followed them across the yard and watched while Logan eased Terri into the passenger seat of his pickup and closed the door.

"Don't worry," he told Sarah, "or you, either, kiddo. I'll take good care of Terri." He bent down and kissed Jessica on the cheek, and Sarah's heart overflowed.

When he straightened he managed a smile.

"But what if—" Jessica began, only to be stopped by Logan's gentle touch.

"Shh. No what-if's tonight, little one." His gaze captured Sarah's and held it. "We can't second-guess the future. We just have to trust."

And as he backed his truck out of the drive and steered it down the ranch road, Sarah clung to his words. The words she'd used to give Terri hope he'd given back to her, and she clung to his gift and wrapped her arms around his child and pressed them both to her heart.

AFTER A BUBBLE BATH and a story about a lucky little cowgirl who had been blessed with two very special daddies, Sarah sat beside Jessica's bed until the child fell asleep. When she heard her father moving around in the other room, she quietly slipped out of Jessica's room and closed the door.

Johnny was sitting on the couch with his arms resting on his knees and his head in his hands. Outside, the sound of a storm blowing in rattled the shutters. The wind whistled through the branches of the trees, and the smell of rain accompanied the distant roll of thunder.

"Dad?" she asked tentatively. "Are you all right?"

He raised his head. "Yeah, but I think I'm going to feel like hell in the morning," he said morosely.

Sarah was sure of it. "You can stay here tonight. There's a storm moving in. I'll go put some coffee on."

He nodded, but didn't seem able to meet her eyes.

A few minutes later she came back into the living room and noticed that he'd washed his face and combed his hair. He was standing near the window, gazing at the rain splattering against the pane.

His shoulders were hunched and he seemed suddenly very old and spiritless. "I guess I did a pretty good job of ruining your gate," he said without turning around.

She released a weary sigh and sat down in the rocking chair beside the couch. "Yes. I guess you did."

"Sorry."

"Yes, well, I expect you to repair it."

He nodded.

"I'm a no-good drunk, Sarah. You deserve better. Always have."

"Don't start," she told him. There was an edge in her voice she hoped would warn him that he'd pushed her far enough for one night. "I've heard it all before." *Too many times to count.*

He moved to the couch and sank onto it as if the weight of the world were on his shoulders. "I want to tell you something. It's something I should have told you before, but…well, I just couldn't."

She sighed, out of patience. "Please, Dad—" A crash of thunder shook the house.

He ran a hand over his face and his two-day stubble, then rubbed the back of his neck. "I'm sorry, Sarah, about…everything. You've got every right to be mad, but you've got to hear me out. This won't wait.''

She rose and paced across the room. ''I said I don't want to hear it! I know all your excuses by heart. If you want to talk to someone, go check yourself into a treatment facility and get some help. I can't do it for you, Dad. No one can. It's something you're going to have to do for yourself.'' She was tired and angry, worn-out from the emotional confrontation with Logan and the startling situation of Terri's going into labor two weeks early.

He nodded. ''I know you're right. I should have done something a long time ago. I guess I was just…too big a coward.''

Here it comes, Sarah thought, the remorse and slobbering self-pity that invariably followed Johnny's tumble off the wagon. ''I'll go check on the coffee,'' she grumbled.

He surprised her when he followed her into the kitchen. He stood in the doorway while she poured them each a cup of the brew she'd made strong enough to sustain her through what would probably be a long night. ''Come on,'' she said. ''Sit down and drink your coffee.''

Despite her irritation, she couldn't help feeling sorry for him. He looked terrible. His eyes were red-rimmed and his face seemed to have lost all color. But strangely he seemed amazingly coherent and almost sober.

When the phone rang, Sarah crossed the room in two bounds and grabbed it. It had to be Logan calling from the hospital to tell her they'd made it and that Terri and the baby were fine.

But it wasn't Logan. It wasn't anyone—or at least it wasn't anyone who would talk. ''Hello,'' Sarah said a second time. ''Hello. Is anyone there?''

There was a click and then the dial tone. Sarah stood with the phone in her hand and glanced at the clock. It was after midnight. No one but Logan would be calling. A uneasiness slid over her. She tried to tell herself the storm had disconnected the call, but for some reason couldn't believe that.

"Who was it?" Johnny asked from the doorway.

"I wish I knew," Sarah said as she replaced the receiver. The vague feeling of concern wouldn't be dismissed. Her hands shook as she lifted her cup and sipped her coffee. "I wonder…" she said almost to herself.

"What?" Johnny asked.

She shook her head. "I'm sure it was nothing. It's just, well, Logan has been getting some strange calls, and I thought…" She chased the possibility from her mind. "Never mind. It couldn't be him. He would have called the trailer."

"You're talking about the anonymous calls, aren't you?"

Sarah's head shot up. "Yes. How did you know?"

In a voice so low she almost couldn't hear it above the sound of the storm, he said, "Because it was me. I made those calls."

She stared at him, utterly confused. "What? You? I don't understand."

He moved farther into the room, but didn't sit down. "I made those calls, Sarah. It was me."

He wasn't making sense. "Dad. What are you saying?"

"It's what I want to talk to you about. It's about your mother," he said. "About Daisy."

Chapter Eighteen

Sarah dropped into her chair, trying to remember, but failing, the last time Johnny had spoken her mother's name aloud. "What about her?" she asked. "What's she got to do with the calls? And why did you make them? For heaven's sake, Dad, tell me what's going on!" A feeling of unnamed dread lodged in her chest.

"I—I should have…that is…" His face had changed from colorless to gray. "I should have told you sooner. I thought Logan would uncover the truth, that it wouldn't come to this."

She rose quickly and walked over to him to stand squarely in front of him, demanding answers. "Dad, talk straight. Tell me what this is all about. What do you know about Will's death?" She held her breath, waiting for his answer.

"Sit down, honey," he said quietly, and when she didn't move, he said, "Please, just sit down, Sarah."

She pulled her chair up next to his and sat down woodenly. The ominous note in his voice and the grave look on his tired face frightened her.

"I never meant to hurt her," he began.

"Oh, come on, Dad," she broke in angrily. "You couldn't very well expect her not to be hurt by the things you did, always drinking, never holding down a job.'' Although she couldn't imagine any reason for a mother abandoning her child, Sarah could well understand why her mother had decided to walk out on Johnny Allen. ''I was just a kid, but I knew what was going on.''

For the first time he looked her directly in the eye. ''No, you didn't, honey. Not really. You didn't know what she was really like.''

His words tore at the scars in her heart, ripping them open and exposing them like fresh wounds. ''No. And thanks to the two of you, I guess I never will.'' She stalked out of the room to check on Jessica, afraid their voices and the sound of the storm might have awakened her. But when she stole into the room to stand beside her daughter's bed, she saw that the child was sleeping soundly. The excitement had obviously worn her out.

When Sarah rejoined Johnny, he seemed stronger, as if he'd drawn himself up and tapped into some inner strength. ''She loved you, Sarah,'' he said softly.

When she made a disgusted sound, he raised his hand to silence her. ''She wanted to come back for you, Sarah. I...I know she did.''

''When was she coming back, Dad?'' she asked. ''In five years? Ten? When she finally got around to remembering she had a child?''

Sadness and a look of resignation stole over his face. ''I don't know when, but she wanted you, Sarah. She did. I know because she told me the night she left.''

''What are you talking about? What would you know about it?'' Her voice quivered with emotion. ''You were so drunk you couldn't see straight.''

''I know because I saw her that night after she left the cabin. She told me.''

Sarah's heartbeat kicked up another notch, and without

realizing it she held her breath. "What do you mean you saw her? When? Where?"

He lowered himself onto the chair as if his legs could no longer support him. "I saw her at the Round-up, where she'd gone to meet her lover. She was planning to run off with him, and they were planning to come back for you." His voice was bitter. "I know because she threatened me. She said she was going to get herself settled, come back and take you away from me forever."

Sarah felt shaken. Was this possible? Was he telling her the truth? "But she didn't," she said quietly. "Why not?"

He lowered his gaze and balled his hands in front of him on the table. "That night, I followed her into town. She didn't know, 'cause I hung back. I swore this time I would catch them together, and when I did, I would..." His voice broke. "But when I got there she was just leaving. I saw her in that pickup between the two of them."

"Two? She left with two men? Dad, you're not making sense."

But he went on as if he hadn't heard. "I pulled in behind them and followed... Lord, I was so damn drunk I don't know how I kept my truck on the road. They went way up on the ridge, where the old logging road crosses the creek."

Sarah sat transfixed, unable to take her eyes off him, spellbound by what he was saying. This was a part of her family's history she knew nothing about.

"When they stopped I kept going. I parked a little ways off, you know...so they wouldn't see me."

There was a faraway look in his eyes, as though time and space had disappeared and he was there again on that old logging road all those years ago. "I parked the truck and started off through the timber. Lord, it was cold, and so dark. I didn't know where I was going—I was so drunk, so dizzy. It was a full moon, so I could see pretty good.

And then I saw her, standing there in the trees, all dressed up in that tight black skirt and those shiny black heels. She saw me right off, too, and, oh, wasn't she surprised! The others, the ones who brought her, were gone, or at least I thought they were gone. Anyway, if they were close by, I didn't see them. All I saw was Daisy.''

His voice had risen and he seemed to have all but forgotten Sarah was even in the room. "Anyway, she took one look at me and acted like she was glad to see me. She ran toward me, begging me to take her home." His face curled into an ugly sneer. "Caught you, didn't I? I say. You little tramp! You slut! Where is he? Where's that son of a bitch?" Johnny's voice was deep, growling and filled with a rage Sarah had never heard before.

The rain and wind slashing against the house had nothing on the storm raging in Sarah's own heart. Her hands were shaking when she reached across the table and touched his arm. "Dad! Please. You're scaring me."

He blinked and pulled his hand away from hers. "She started toward me like she wanted to make up, you know? Like she was going to fool old Johnny again. Like she could just sweet-talk her way back home—that's what she figured, I guess." His face went blank, devoid of all expression. He gazed past Sarah as if he could see Daisy standing there close enough to touch.

"I told her she wasn't ever coming home. That she was no kind of wife and not fit to be your mother."

Sarah winced.

"Then she starts walking past me. Walking real fast. I try to stop her, but I can't. I—I can't seem to get turned around." His eyes blazed. "Tell them other bastards I'm going back to town, she says, and I look around, but I still don't see anybody. I can't seem to focus my eyes. The whiskey is playing tricks on me. I'm drunk. So drunk. And now I'm feeling sick.''

He shifted his gaze to Sarah's face to stare at her with unseeing eyes. "Not so fast, I say. But she just says, get the hell out of my way. Your truck down there? she wants to know. Are your keys in it? Give me the keys, she says. I'm going to get my kid. Don't try to stop me, Johnny. You can't. He's rich. He's young. He'll fix you good if you get in our way. We're leaving, Orrin and me, and there isn't one damn thing you can do to stop us.''

Sarah gasped. *Orrin? Orrin Fraizer had been her mother's lover?*

Johnny's face contorted in pain. "And then I hit her," he gasped. "God help me, I hit her with everything I had. Then I go all numb, you know, like it was her who hit me, instead of the other way around. I see her face go all pale and surprised, and I watch her fall back, and I think, she's faking it, she's trying to trick me. She's nimble and young and she'll spring right back up on those shiny black heels. But she doesn't. She just lies there, not moving, not talking. Not even crying. I try to go to her. I start moving, but something's wrong with my legs, and my eyes, too. I'm sick as death.''

His voice trailed off and tears rose slowly in his eyes. "I turn around and walk. I can't even see where I'm going, but I know I have to get out of there, I have to get back to my truck.''

He hung his head as if all the strength was drained out of him. "I was going to just leave her, like the coward I've always been. I couldn't face what I'd done.''

Sarah's heart felt caught in the grip of tightening steel bands, and when she spoke, her voice was choked. "What are you telling me? That you left her there?" She fought for breath as the unthinkable question hung suspended between them. "Dad, please, tell me! Did you kill her?"

"I blacked out," he said miserably. "And when I came to, th-they told me sh-she was gone."

Sarah was on her feet, standing over him, fighting the urge to shake the life out of him. "Who? Who else was there? What happened to my mother?"

"They said they would help me," he explained. "That no one would ever have to know. They said they would take care of everything." He covered his face with his hands. "Then they buried her. They buried her up there on the ridge."

Sarah felt frozen, too horrified to even speak.

When Johnny's hands fell away from his face, he released a shuddering sigh. "When you and Will started trying to find her, I got scared. I knew the truth would come out, and in a way I guess I hoped it would. I didn't mean to hurt her. I knew Will was a good man and he'd find a way to help me. But they said if I ever told anyone what happened, they would hurt you." He lifted his tortured gaze to hers. "I couldn't let them do that. I'd already hurt you enough. But the truth had to come out. You had the right to know. I figured if Will could just find her, find her body—"

"You!" she gasped, rocking back a step. "You're the one who wrote him that note. You made him go up to the ridge. You...you killed Will! You killed my husband!" The words tore her throat and drove pain deep into her heart.

"No!" He jumped to his feet and grabbed her shoulders. "I didn't kill Will. I loved him like a son. I wouldn't...I didn't...it was them. They followed him. They—"

"You damned fool!" The sound of the deep voice coming from the doorway slammed into Sarah's brain, and she spun around to see Earl Fraizer standing in the doorway.

His face was crimson and his eyes blazed with a lethal fury that matched the threat of the gun he held in his hand. "I should have killed you that night, done away with both of you when I had the chance."

Johnny's hands fell away from Sarah's shoulders, and he took a step back.

"You just couldn't leave well enough alone, could you? Well, now it's over and you're going to die, old man. You and the rest of your family. None of you will be causing me any more trouble."

Sarah thought her heart would explode as all her thoughts, every ounce of her being, focused on one thing: protecting the innocent child sleeping in the next room. She drew a sharp breath and lunged for the door, but Earl was too quick. His fingers closed around her arm and jerked her back. His grip dug into the tender flesh of her upper arm, and she wanted to scream. It was only the thought of waking Jessica that stopped her.

Her mind scrambled for an escape. There had to be some way to save her child from this nightmare. "Why, Earl? Why did you do it?" Maybe she could stall him or try to talk him out of his murderous plan. "I have to know."

His voice was as hard as the steel barrel of the pistol he aimed at her. "She was a tramp," he said flatly. "She seduced my boy—just a kid, barely out of college. She would have ruined his life." He drew in a breath. "I couldn't let that happen, don't you see? He was on his way to the top. There was nothing that could stop him. Not that boy, no sir! Earl and Gaylene's boy. Good old Earl and Gaylene," he scoffed. "Not good enough to join their fancy clubs or talk to after church, but good enough to serve them their whiskey and keep their dirty little Saturday-night secrets.

"But our boy was good enough. Smart. Handsome. He was going to show them all. He was going to be somebody, don't you see?" Earl's voice was agonized, almost pleading. "I didn't mean to hurt her," he told Sarah, his eyes moving over her face. "All we meant to do was scare her off. We caught her outside the bar, where she was going to meet Orrin. We didn't want anyone to get hurt." His hand shook. "I thought taking her up there and scaring her would fix things, maybe just rough her up a little and then leave her there alone for a night to think about what she was doing."

He scowled and turned his glare on Johnny. "But then you came along," he hissed, "and everything got all mixed up. You hit her and then you passed out. Riley wanted to leave. And at first I thought I would just do that. But then she started coming around. Her head was bleeding and she started to cry. I told her to be quiet, that she was going to be all right, that she'd learned her lesson. And now she knew I would stop at nothing to save my boy." His voice was ragged. "But she wouldn't listen. She said she would call the police and have me arrested. I told her to shut up, but she wouldn't. I hit her and she started screaming. And then I…hit her again." His voice dropped another notch. "After that, she never woke up."

He looked at Sarah. "I couldn't let her ruin my boy's life. But I've tried to make it up to you, Sarah. Orrin and me. He paid your college bills, did you know that? And he fixed up that phony insurance policy so you could take care of things after Will died. Orrin is a good man. He never once thought of hurting you. He felt…well, you know, kind of responsible."

Sarah's heart seemed to convulse. Her sense of betrayal was overwhelming.

Earl went on, his voice hard as he finished his gruesome story. "When Johnny came around, he was all ready to take the blame—and it *was* his fault, damn it! All of it! If he'd been man enough to keep his wife away from my boy, if he hadn't come after her..." His voice drifted off and he swung his gaze to Johnny. "And then you had to go and drag Will into it. And then Spencer. And now I'm going to have to kill you, Johnny, just like I should've done all those years ago."

Sarah saw him shift the gun to take aim at her father.

"Please," she shrieked. "Earl! No!"

She saw him pull back the hammer as if in slow motion, and all at once, raw instinct took over. She brought her arm down to knock the gun out of his hand, and she saw a blur as her father rushed him.

The gun went off at the same time a crack of thunder rattled the heavens. Without warning, the world exploded before her eyes. Johnny fell back with a gasp, and blood turned his shirtfront red.

She raced out of the room, blindly down the hall and into Jessica's room. Earl's footsteps thundered after her, but the sound was lost to the frantic pounding of her own heart and the storm raging outside.

Mind reeling, she closed the door behind her and locked it, a split second before she heard Earl cursing the knob that would not turn.

Behind her, Jessica stirred and let out a sleepy moan. "It's all right," Sarah murmured, her voice trembling with fear. She gathered the blanket around the child and hugged her. "Go back to sleep, sweetheart. It's just the storm."

Lightning forked across the sky, illuminating the bedroom for an instant. The sound of the front door slamming coincided with thunder rumbling across the valley.

Sarah held her breath and listened, but she couldn't hear anything but the battering storm.

Logan! her heart cried. What would he think when he returned to the ranch and found the gruesome remnants of Earl's night of madness?

Where had Earl gone? Maybe he'd panicked, realizing he could never get away with the mayhem he'd planned. A glimmer of hope sprang to life inside her, and suddenly all she could think about was getting to the phone.

In her mind she visualized the wall phone in the kitchen, with Johnny lying beneath it on the floor, bleeding. If not already dead, close to it.

Slowly she lowered Jessica back down onto her pillow and planted a gentle kiss on her forehead. The child murmured something Sarah couldn't understand and nestled down into the covers, still sleeping.

Without making a sound Sarah edged over to the window and peered into the stormy night. The rain sheeted against the pane, and when the lightning traced the sky, she could see that Earl's pickup was not in the driveway.

Slowly, cautiously, with breath held and heart quivering, she crept to the door and stood listening. If he was still out there, she couldn't hear him. But what did that mean? His pickup could be parked on the other side of the house. He could have slammed the door to coax her out into the open. Was he standing there waiting for her? Would he level his gun on her and then… Oh, God, he wouldn't kill Jessica, would he? Her mind shunned the unthinkable.

She turned the knob silently and inched the door open. She could see no one. Nothing moved. She pulled the door farther open with agonizing slowness, then turned the lock and closed the door behind her, stepping out into the darkened hallway.

If Earl was lying in wait for her, the locked door would give her precious child at least a small measure of safety. On legs weak with fear, she moved along the wall toward the kitchen and the phone.

She heard a groan and realized it had come from her father. Johnny was still alive! Driven by love and desperation, she ran the last few feet down the hall and into the kitchen to see her father's eyes flicker open.

"Dad," she gasped, and dropped down beside him.

His face was pale and his eyes were glassy with pain. "Sarah," he whispered. "I'm sorry. I—I'm no good. A no-good drunken coward."

The tears scorched her cheeks and she pressed her face to his. "No, Daddy," she whispered. "You're just a man. And tonight you acted brave and good. You told the truth and you tried to save my life. Mine and Jessica's."

His body trembled in the grip of some unseen and unrelenting pain.

"It'll be all right," she told him in a rush of emotion. "Hang on." She jumped to her feet and reached for the phone just as she heard the front door bang open and footsteps race down the hallway.

Her fingers punched out 911, and without waiting for an answer, she dropped the phone and left it swinging by the cord as she raced out into the hall. At the sight of Earl standing outside Jessica's door, she rushed headlong down the hallway toward him.

He turned, startled, and it registered somewhere at the back of her frantic mind that she'd surprised him. He'd assumed she was still locked in Jessica's room.

His gun was in his hand and he raised it. But even the

thought of dying didn't make her turn back. Losing her own life meant nothing. Nothing mattered but saving Jessica.

She saw his hand on the trigger and, eyes closed, she launched herself at him. *Goodbye, Jess,* her heart cried. *Goodbye, Logan. I'm sorry. I love you both.*

She braced herself for the pain. For the bullet that would shred her flesh and pierce her heart.

Somewhere outside her she heard screams—her own and Jessica's. She heard the shot. It echoed endlessly. But there was no pain. And she did not fall. She opened her eyes, but Earl wasn't standing there. He was on the floor, his mouth open, his eyes glazed. Motionless. Dead. And Logan was standing behind him with a gun in his hand.

Through her shock came the sounds of Jessica sobbing, rattling the doorknob, fumbling with the lock. "Mommy! The thunder. The thunder woke me up and I can't get out of my room."

Relief flooded her, but her mouth had gone too dry to speak.

Logan's arms wrapped around her as he moved her with him past Earl's body to Jessica's door. "I tried to call, but the phone... It must have been the storm. Oh, Sarah!" His voice was choked with emotion as he hugged her to him.

"Earl attacked Glenn and his deputy when they stopped him on the road. He shot him, Sarah. Glenn is dead. The deputy was wounded, as well, but managed to drive the cruiser to the hospital. He arrived just as Terri and I pulled up to the entrance. When I realized what had happened, that Earl had escaped, I drove back here as fast as I could."

Sarah couldn't comprehend the horror.

"Mommy!" Jessica wailed from the other side of the door. "I can't get out!"

"It's all right, kiddo. I'm here," Logan said. "We'll get you out of there. Just calm down. Everything's all right. Mommy's right here, and so am I."

Chapter Nineteen

At ten o'clock the next morning, Johnny was still in surgery. Earl's bullet had wreaked havoc, but the doctors said
Sarah's father had a fighting chance.

The waiting had been grueling for Sarah. Logan noted
the shadows under her eyes and wished he could say or do
something to make them go away.

Visits to the nursery to see Terri's baby—a bouncing
nine-pound boy—took some of the strain off everyone's
nerves, as did the hot chocolate and doughnuts Bess
brought with her when she came.

Of all of them, Jessica seemed the least affected by the
events of the harrowing night. Sarah had been amazing,
comforting her child and distracting her while the para-
medics had done their job last night at the ranch.

This morning she'd found a way to keep her daughter
busy during the long wait. She'd suggested that Grandpa
Johnny would need lots of artwork to cheer him while he
recuperated, and so, to that end, Jessica sat intently coloring
pictures of Barney to decorate his hospital room.

At last the word came: Johnny had come through surgery
and was expected to recover fully. The look of utter relief
on Sarah's face reflected everyone's feelings—even

Hank's, although the young man seemed oblivious to anything but his son and his soon-to-be wife.

"Bess," Logan said, taking his aunt into the hallway outside the waiting room where Sarah, Terri, Hank and Jessica were gathered. "I know Sarah will want to wait until Johnny's out of the recovery room before she leaves. Would you take Jessica home with you for a while? She's had a long morning." On the heels of a long and traumatic night. "I think a visit to the Spencer ranch and a quiet afternoon with you would be the best thing for her right now."

Bess smiled. "I'd love nothing more. The child is a delight."

"She's more than that," Logan told her, as he walked with her down the corridor. "She's your great-niece, Bess." And when his aunt's eyes widened, he said, "I know. It came as quite a surprise to me, as well."

"Does that mean you and Sarah…" Her voice trailed off wistfully. "Are you going to stay here with them?"

"I don't know. We have a lot to work out."

Bess looked up at him and frowned. "I don't understand."

"She was pregnant when she left me." Just saying the words brought fresh pain. "She never told me. She thought if she stayed, I'd resent her and Jessica for the rest of my life."

"But you wouldn't have!"

He shook his head. "To be truthful I don't really know. I know I love them now. That I want them, want to prove to them how much they both mean to me."

"Then what's the problem?" Bess said in her usual pragmatic way.

"I don't know. What if Sarah doesn't feel the same way?"

Bess waved her hand dismissively. "Why, anyone with eyes can see she loves you."

"If she loved me, she would have told me about Jessica in the beginning."

"If she didn't love you, she wouldn't have allowed you to stay this long. She would have found a way to keep you and Jessica apart."

Logan searched his aunt's face, wanting to believe her.

"Remember what I said about your father's pride? How he never learned to conquer it? Well, that Spencer pride cost Josh a relationship with his son. Are you going to lose your daughter and the woman you love for the same reason? It's up to you, Logan. Give her a reason to believe. Give yourselves and your daughter a second chance."

If only it could be that easy.

"Tell her you love her," Bess urged.

Surely Sarah already knew he loved her desperately. Surely she could see that all he wanted was a life with her and Jessica.

"Let her know that your dreams can work, that you both want the same things now. That what you want, the dreams you've both been chasing, are not so different, after all."

Could Bess be right? Sarah's dream of coming back to the valley and of building a home and family had to do with what she'd been seeking all her life. Home. Family. Love. And hadn't his own dreams been based on the same need? To be loved, to be respected?

Had the answer to making both their dreams come true been as near as each other's arms?

As they walked back to the waiting room, Logan thought about the chance he'd been asking Sarah to give him. Was she ready to do it? And could he really take the risk?

In asking Sarah to build her future with him, he'd be putting his pride squarely on the line. She'd left him once without a backward glance. In opening his heart to her, he'd be giving her the chance to hurt him. Again.

He looked inside himself and knew the answer. Sarah and Jessica were worth any risk. And if Sarah turned him down, at least he'd have Jessica. Even though he would be only a part-time father, he would do everything in his power to make every moment with his daughter count. And yet, even as he considered that alternative, he knew life without Sarah would be hopelessly empty.

Sarah seemed relieved when Bess asked if Jessica could go with her for a little while. As his daughter and his aunt said goodbye and prepared to leave, Logan looked into his child's eyes and felt his heart overflow with love.

Could they really do it? he wondered. Could they build the kind of family this wonderful child deserved? Would Sarah believe him when he told her theirs was now a shared dream and, if she'd only believe, their shared reality?

When Bess and Jessica had gone and Terri and Hank went back to the nursery with their baby, Logan sat down beside Sarah.

"We need to talk," he said without hesitation.

"About Jessica."

He nodded. "Yes." And so much more, if he could find the words.

She sighed. "We'll work it out," she said wearily. "I promise you'll have time with her, and when she's older, I'll make sure she understands that it was my doing that kept the two of you apart for so long."

He nodded. What a brave woman she was. What an honorable and selfless soul. "Now I want to talk about us," he said.

"Us?" she said wistfully. "There is no us." The light of her inimitable spirit seemed to dim.

"There *was* no us," he corrected her. "Because you ran

away from me when we needed each other most.'' She'd needed him, yes. With a child on the way and no home. But his need for her had been just as great. Without her he'd lost his perspective, and his anchor.

"Please, Logan," she said as she rose and walked out into the hall, "there's nothing more to say. Let's not hurt each other anymore."

He followed her and put his hand at her elbow, then led her out of the hospital and into the sunshine. "Sarah, listen to me. We've both had enough regret to last a lifetime." He turned and put his hands on her shoulders. "When you left, I lost my way. For days, I couldn't think straight. I couldn't eat. Hell, I couldn't even work." He offered her a thin smile. "I kept thinking you'd come back, that sooner or later you'd realize you needed me as much as I needed you."

Her hair glistened in the morning sun, and her blue eyes had never seemed softer. "I needed you," she admitted. "More than you knew. But I didn't want to force you to marry me to give our child a name. I couldn't do to you what your father believed had been done to him. I couldn't stay and run the risk that someday you'd grow to resent me and resent our child. I didn't want our love to be a burden to you." She sighed. "But I never meant to hurt you, Logan." Her voice was husky with emotion. "I've always loved you and I know now that I always will."

Her words were like a balm, healing every wound. She loved him. She always had. She always would.

"I'm sorry, Sarah. Sorry that I gave you every reason to leave me." He sighed. "I told you before that I had changed. And I have. I've made peace with my past, and in my heart I've forgiven my father. It may take a little work, but I think eventually I can forgive myself. And now I want to make my peace with you, Sarah. Will you forgive me? I didn't let you know how much you meant to me five years ago, but I'm telling you now. If you'll let me stay, give me another chance, I'll show you every day for the rest of our lives just how much I care.''

"Every day?''

He smiled. ''Yes. Every day. Right here, in the valley. In our home, the place where we both belong. Where our child belongs.''

He wrapped his arms around her and hugged her close to his heart. She tilted her head back and looked up at him. Her eyes were shining with emotion. ''I love you, Logan.''

He bent his head and kissed her. ''Will you marry me, Sarah? Will you give us the chance to build our dreams together?''

"My dream,'' she whispered against his lips, ''has already come true.''

Lost & Found

All new...and filled with the mystery and romance you love!

SOMEBODY'S BABY
by Amanda Stevens in November 1998

A FATHER FOR HER BABY
by B. J. Daniels in December 1998

A FATHER'S LOVE
by Carla Cassidy in January 1999

It all begins one night when three women go into labor in the same Galveston, Texas, hospital. Shortly after the babies are born, fire erupts, and though each child and mother make it to safety, there's more than just the mystery of birth to solve now....

Don't miss this *all new* LOST & FOUND trilogy!

Available at your favorite retail outlet.

HARLEQUIN®
Makes any time special ™

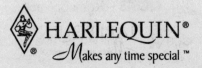